LORD OF LIGHT

A MEDIEVAL ROMANCE NOVEL

BY KATHRYN LE VEQUE

Printed by Dragonblade Publishing in the United States of America

Text copyright 2013, 2014 by Kathryn Le Veque
Cover copyright 2013, 2014 by Kathryn Le Veque

Library of Congress Control Number 2014-015
ISBN 1494782510

KATHRYN LE VEQUE NOVELS

Medieval Romance:

The de Russe Legacy:
The White Lord of Wellesbourne
The Dark One: Dark Knight
Beast
Lord of War: Black Angel
The Falls of Erith

The de Lohr Dynasty:
While Angels Slept (Lords of East
Anglia)
Rise of the Defender
Steelheart
Spectre of the Sword
Archangel
Unending Love
Shadowmoor
Silversword

Great Lords of le Bec:
Great Protector
To the Lady Born (House of de Royans)

Lords of Eire:
The Darkland (Master Knights of
Connaught)
Black Sword
Echoes of Ancient Dreams (time travel)

De Wolfe Pack Series:
The Wolfe
Serpent
Scorpion (Saxon Lords of Hage – Also
related to The Questing)
Walls of Babylon
The Lion of the North
Dark Destroyer

Ancient Kings of Anglecynn:
The Whispering Night
Netherworld

Battle Lords of de Velt:
The Dark Lord
Devil's Dominion

Reign of the House of de Winter:
Lespada
Swords and Shields (also related to The
Questing, While Angels Slept)

De Reyne Domination:
Guardian of Darkness
The Fallen One (part of Dragonblade
Series)

Unrelated characters or family groups:
The Gorgon (Also related to Lords of
Thunder)
The Warrior Poet (St. John and de Gare)
Tender is the Knight (House of d'Vant)
Lord of Light
The Questing (related to The Dark Lord,
Scorpion)
The Legend (House of Summerlin)

The Dragonblade Series: (Great Marcher Lords of de Lara)
Dragonblade
Island of Glass (House of St. Hever)
The Savage Curtain (Lords of Pembury)
The Fallen One (De Reyne Domination)
Fragments of Grace (House of St. Hever)
Lord of the Shadows
Queen of Lost Stars (House of St. Hever)

Lords of Thunder: The de Shera Brotherhood Trilogy
The Thunder Lord
The Thunder Warrior
The Thunder Knight

Time Travel Romance: (Saxon Lords of Hage)
The Crusader
Kingdom Come

<u>**Contemporary Romance:**</u>

Kathlyn Trent/Marcus Burton Series:
Valley of the Shadow
The Eden Factor
Canyon of the Sphinx

The American Heroes Series:
The Lucius Robe
Fires of Autumn
Evenshade
Sea of Dreams
Purgatory

Other Contemporary Romance:
Lady of Heaven
Darkling, I Listen

<u>**Multi-author Collections/Anthologies:**</u>
With Dreams Only of You (USA Today bestseller)
Sirens of the Northern Seas (Viking romance)
Ever My Love (sequel to With Dreams Only Of You) July 2016

<u>Note:</u> All Kathryn's novels are designed to be read as stand-alones, although many have cross-over characters or cross-over family groups. Novels that are grouped together have related characters or family groups.

Series are clearly marked. All series contain the same characters or family groups except the American Heroes Series, which is an anthology with unrelated characters.

There is NO particular chronological order for any of the novels because they can all be read as stand-alones, even the series.

For more information, find it in **A Reader's Guide to the Medieval World of Le Veque**.

TABLE OF CONTENTS

AUTHOR'S NOTE

This novel utilizes some supernatural elements as part of the storyline. Is it paranormal? Or is it divine intervention? That is left to the reader's interpretation.

PROLOGUE

1189 A.D.
The Holy Land

Gᴏᴅ'ꜱ Bᴏɴᴇꜱ, ʙᴜᴛ *the thunderstorms in this, the most holy of lands, could be exceedingly violent.*

They seemed to appear out of nowhere and suddenly you were fleeing for your life, searching out any bit of shelter that might protect you from the stinging rain. Lightning would streak across the sky and God's shout could be heard in the thunderous roar. And then the rain would pound mercilessly, as if the Holy Father was whipping his insolent children for the battles they were creating in his beloved land.

Two knights struggled through the downpour. They were separated from their comrades, wandering the rocky hills surrounding Jerusalem searching in vain for their army. It was deadly to be lost out here.

"Let's hide in the Holy Sepulcher," cried one knight, "for it should be dry in there."

Having few options and ignoring the possible sacrilege of invading holy ground, they reined their chargers, great muscular beasts, through the olive trees and up the rocky slope until they came to what they had been told had been the burial cavern of our Lord Jesus Christ. The holy men of Jerusalem had pointed it out to the Crusaders of the Third Quest and everyone declared what a magnificent thing it was when in fact it was only a small cave, rough and hardly worthy of the Son of God. But it was enough at the moment to shelter them from the rain and they hoped God wouldn't mind their intrusion.

The chargers had to remain outside, sheltered beneath the barren olive grove, but inside the cool musty cavern, two knights of Richard's great crusade milled about and tried to not leap like frightened animals every time the wind howled and the lightning flashed. One of the knights noticed the slab on the floor and pointed to it.

"Look, that's where Christ lay in his shroud and where the Angel resurrected him. Can't you see the scorch marks?"

The other knight looked at the crude slab of limestone and disputed that there were indeed marks of the resurrection. It was an eerie feeling as he stared at the stone, not a reverent one, and the larger knight of the two wished the rain would soon stop so they could leave this place. He removed his helm, wiping the water from his sea green eyes and slicking his cropped golden hair away from his face as he gazed out at the stormy sky.

He, unlike the other, wasn't impressed by holy relics as he once had been. In fact, he was becoming disillusioned with this entire quest. They were healers, the Order of Hospitallers of St. John the Baptist, but so far they had done little healing and much killing. When they were supposed to be elite healers of a Holy Order, they were grouped with the common fighting men and expected to slaughter.

"Roane, come and look at the slab," called his companion.

The big blond knight turned away from the stormy visions outside and focused on the chalky, pitted limestone.

"What's to see?" he asked cynically and his companion laughed, running his hands over the stone.

"Can't you feel the goodness of this?" his companion asked, but Roane refused to give into the man's reverence. He was simply caressing an old stone as far as Roane was concerned. He didn't see God or Glory or the images of angels on it as the other apparently did.

"How can you see it at all, John Adam?" Roane asked. "With your one bad eye, vision in this dark light is nearly impossible."

But the knight laughed at him. "I don't need to see it, for I can feel it far better," he said.

Roane smirked at him. "As you wish, John Adam. So tell me what it is you feel."

The knight with one glazed-over eye continued to smile. "I feel God," he said softly. Then he backed away from the slab. "Come touch it, Roane," he said again, "and mayhap you will feel better about our mission here."

Roane gazed at his companion, who seemed to be so perceptive even with his one bad eye. Sometimes he could see things that others could not, like strengths and weaknesses and faults of character. John Adam knew how Roane was feeling about their quest, or lack thereof. King Richard hadn't even reached the Holy Land yet and the English were taking their orders from Philip Augustus or Barbarossa because the English commanders were not strong or intelligent enough to lead their men. Roane was certainly intelligent enough, but he was a mere knight against those who easily outranked him.

"Come touch the slab," John Adam said yet again, "mayhap it will renew your glory in our task."

Roane simply stared at him and shook his head. "Nay, I do not wish to renew my glory," he said.

But John Adam was insistent. "Come touch the slab," he demanded.

Roane resisted again and again until finally he could stand no more and simply to quiet his friend he put both of his hands on the slab in a defiant gesture.

"There," he said snappishly, "are you satisfied now? I feel nothing holy or extraordinary about it!"

John Adam had not the time to reply when suddenly a shriek of lightning lit up the sky so brightly that those who saw the blast were instantly blinded. The massive bolt struck an old olive tree atop the mount of the Holy Sepulcher and the tree shattered, scattering pieces of wood across the rocky terrain. But the lightning did not stop there; it traveled down through the rock, piercing the walls of the cave and traveling with blazing speed through the nickel ore that was heavy in the rock.

When it reached the dirt floor of the cave there was nowhere for the lightning to go except to the slab that lay upon the ground, the holy slab that Roane's hands were still upon. The slab lit full of fire and Roane felt the lightning cut through his fingers, his great muscular arms, and finally his body as it tossed him across the cavern and slammed him into the wall on the other side.

For a moment, the world was dim and spinning and Roane could smell burnt flesh. He could hear John Adam beside him, asking if he was well. Of course he wasn't well. He had just been cooked by a bolt of lightning and he wasn't feeling well in the least. Blindly, he reached up and came into contact with a bushy brown head. He could hear John Adam babble, then moan about the heat from Roane's hands, until finally he gasped and fell silent. When the worlds stopped moving and his senses returned, Roane opened his eyes to find John Adam weeping pitifully at his feet.

"What's wrong, John Adam, are you hurt?" Roane asked, but John Adam continued to weep.

Roane was disoriented and snappish. "John Adam, what's wrong, are you hurt?" he demanded again, but John Adam suddenly grabbed his hands and kissed his fingers until Roane had to shove him away. "What's the matter with you?" he wanted to know. "Why do you kiss my hands and weep like a woman? Have you gone mad?"

John Adam's head came up and the one milky eye wasn't milky any more. It was brown like the other one.

"You touched me and now I can see, Roane," he cried softly. "Through the slab you touched God has given you a great gift, can you not see that?"

Roane was appalled at such blasphemy. "You are a fool, John Adam; I've done nothing of the kind."

But John Adam grabbed him and forced him to look in his now perfect eyes. "Look at me, Roane, this only happened after the lightning struck you and you touched me. You are the lord of light! You give miracles now!"

But Roane refused to believe him. John Adam continued to weep and worship him as if he was God, and Roane ran off into the wild storm, still *smelling his burnt flesh and wondering what curse had been brought upon him in the dank confines of Christ's supposed grave.*

He had yet to imagine.

CHAPTER ONE

1192 A.D.
Shropshire, England

THE BANGING WAS as incessant as the rain. At first, he wasn't sure he had heard correctly, but soon there was no doubt that someone was pounding on the old door of the abandoned abbey he called home. The storm outside had been so deafening that he was surprised he could hear anything at all. But someone was seeking entrance, obviously shelter from the weather.

His first reaction was to ignore the rapping. But the lightning blared and the thunder rolled, and he thought that mayhap he should consider being charitable since the weather outside was so terrible. After all, it was extremely rare that he had visitors He ran off most of them, but some he allowed to stay on the premises as long as they didn't stay more than a day. He couldn't stand being around people any longer than that. Two and a half years of virtual solitude gave him the amiability of a nasty old bear.

The knocking continued. Hunched over an old table that was barely standing, quill in hand and parchment before him, he glanced up from his writing as if he could see through the massive double doors at the end of the long, shabby room. A soft fire crackled near him in a firepit that was more a hazard than a comfort. In fact, the entire abbey was crumbling around him and water leaked down the old stone walls, but he continued to stay because it was remote and he didn't have to worry about being found. But there were, on occasion, travelers seeking shelter.

Which was the immediate case. Annoyed, he tossed his quill aside and marched on his muscular legs across the dirt floor. The pounding wouldn't stop until he told whomever it was to go away. It was dark near the old dusty door and he almost stepped on his dog; the large black animal scattered and he muttered a curse at the near miss. Reaching the door, he was in no mood for foolery as he yanked it open.

Rain and water poured in, dousing his worn black boots and thick woolen hose. A small figure stood before him, swathed from head to toe in a drenched cloak. The swiftness by which the door had opened startled the figure, and as it took a stumbling step back, the face beneath the hood came into focus.

A most beautiful woman was gazing back at him. "Forgive my intrusion, my lord," she said through chattering teeth. "I am looking for Sir Roane de Garr. I was told I could find him here."

Now it was his turn to be startled. But his shock gave way to apprehension and anger, and he reached out and grabbed the woman roughly by the arms. "Who are you?" he growled.

Her brilliant green eyes filled with fear. "I am the Lady Alisanne de Soulant," she gasped. "I was told…."

"Told *what*?" he roared.

He was hurting her. Alisanne did not struggle for she knew that he would only hold her tighter. He was a large man, as large as she had ever seen, with piercing sea green eyes and a granite jaw that implied utter strength. The hands that gripped her arms were the size of trenchers, fingers as large as small branches, and she could feel them biting into her flesh. But for all of the power he exuded, she wasn't truly afraid; in fact, she sensed more fear from him than she herself felt.

"I was told that Sir Roane could help me," she said with forced calm. "If I've not come to the right place, then I will beg your forgiveness and leave."

He stared at her a moment, his harsh gaze studying her. Then he glanced around. "Who has accompanied you?"

"No one, my lord," she said. "I am alone."

Disbelief mingled with his rage. "Don't lie to me."

"I speak the truth, I swear it," she insisted. "My... my father is too ill to come and I could not find a suitable escort, so I came alone. I must speak with Sir Roane. Are you he?"

He stared at her. Through his fury and anxiety, he reaffirmed his opinion that she was a strikingly beautiful woman and he could hardly imagine that she had traveled alone to his desolate mountaintop abbey. More than likely, she indeed had escorts and he suspected she was some sort of decoy. A cunning wench meant to destroy him, but he was not about to make an easy target. They had finally found him, he realized, and he shoved her away as he bolted back inside.

"Be gone!" he bellowed. "My sword knows no boundaries, man or woman."

Alisanne struggled to recover her balance; the road was wet and extremely steep. A wrong step would see her plunged several hundred feet down the precipitous slope. Water dripped down her face as she stared at the closed abbey door and it was difficult not to feel a tremendous sense of despair. But she could not give up; she'd come much too far over dangerous ground and it would take more than the demands of a surly knight to turn her away.

"Please!" she rushed to the door and began pounding on it again. "Please, I must speak with Sir Roane!"

There was no answer and she continued to pound. She pounded all night.

C3

DAWN CAME AFTER a very long night of turmoil. He hadn't slept a wink, positive that an intrusion of armed men was imminent. And the woman had kept him on edge a good deal of that time with her constant pounding. But just before first light, the pounding had stopped and an eerie quiet settled. Roane didn't know which disturbed him worse; the constant rapping or the tense still. He rose from his pallet in the corner of the great room, sword still in hand as he stealthily made his way to the barred entrance.

He couldn't see or hear anything, but a pungent smell certainly had his attention. The abbey was old and there were many gaps in the walls, and he prowled around, peering from between the slats to see if there was someone lingering outside to ambush him. Cold air poured from the open rifts, kissing his stubbled face. Carefully, he unbolted the great door and saw that the day was dawning bright and beautiful after the horrific night. His breath hung in the air as he took a step or two into the narrow courtyard, cluttered with debris and puddles of dirty water.

His weapon was in his hand but he made no move to raise it and would not unless set upon; he was confident his reflexes were fast enough. He noticed almost immediately that there was a fire in the center of the ward and something lay roasting upon it; it was a crude spit and the animal impaled upon it, he suspected, was a rabbit or pigeon. They were always plentiful after a good rain. His worn boots tread carefully across the mud, his ears and eyes alert, but all appeared to be deserted. Yet he knew instinctively he was not alone, and he made his way back to the great doors of the old abbey. Closing the door behind him carefully, he sighed and sheathed his sword; something was going on and he wasn't yet sure what it was.

"My lord," came a honeyed voice. "I *must* speak with you."

Roane stiffened, wishing he hadn't put his weapon back in its scabbard. The dog hadn't made a sound at the intruder, which was unusual since it normally howled at the rats in the corner and the owls in the rafters. That damnable dog croaked at *everything.*

"Your presence is considered a threat, and I will destroy any threat to my wellbeing," he growled as he turned to face her. Her luminescent green eyes were hauntingly visible in the shadows. "Be gone or I shall not hesitate."

Alisanne didn't move. "You don't really consider me a threat."

"You presume to know this?"

She nodded bravely. "If you did so, you would have killed me last night. Instead, you let me pound on the door until the sun rose."

"That was your choice. I told you to leave, and I meant it."

Alisanne took a deep breath, indicative of her frustration and desperation. "My lord, I am only seeking Sir Roane de Garr. If you are not he, then please tell me and I shall indeed be on my way." She took a step forward so he could see her better and realize she was unarmed and clearly no threat. "But if you are he, then I must tell you that I am in desperate need of your aid. I am told you are the only one who can help me."

Roane didn't trust her in the least, but he wasn't on edge as much as he had been. In truth, she had a very calm, soothing voice, something he knew he could grow pleasingly accustomed to. And she didn't radiate even a hint of devilry or mischief, but sincerity and honesty. But her ploy to draw him outside so she could enter had been clever; foolish for a seasoned knight to fall for it, but clever for her nonetheless. He was surprised a woman possessed such slyness.

His jaw ticked as he studied her more closely. "The fire outside," he jerked his head in the direction of the door so she would understand his meaning. "You?"

Alisanne nodded as if embarrassed. "Aye," she said. "Well, you would not let me in. So the logical thing was to draw you out."

Roane grunted, chagrined that a woman had so easily duped him. But if she had accomplices, as he suspected, then she had had help. "What did you do with Samson?"

"Who, my lord?"

"My dog."

Alisanne pointed to a corner of the great dusty room where the black hound chewed happily on a hunk of the meat that had been roasting outside. She lifted her shoulders. "He was… hungry."

"The meat isn't poisoned, is it?"

She looked shocked. "No, my lord."

Roane lifted an eyebrow at the dog, happily wolfing down his meal. The lady had been quite thorough in her plan. Turning away from her, he moved to an ancient chair that sat near a fire pit Roane had dug in the old floor. The abbey had no hearth, so he had to make due with lighting a fire in a hazardous hole and hoping the smoke would stay up near the ceiling and find its way out. Sometimes, if the wind blew, he found himself smoked out. But today was a clear, still day and he stirred the embers, all the while keeping very alert of Alisanne's presence. She remained in the shadows, carefully observing every move he made.

"Where is the rest of your party?" he asked her.

"I told you I came alone, my lord."

"That is a lie. No woman travels alone."

"She does if she has no choice."

He shook his head in disbelief, but also a measure of confusion. If she were indeed a decoy for a party of assassins, they should have struck by now. He knew the minds of imbeciles well enough to know that, and the mystery of her presence grew.

"Are you Sir Roane?" she asked again.

Not only was she cunning, she was persistent as hell. His face took on a strange expression, one he made sure she did not see. He stoked the fire, stirring embers up into the air. "What is the matter with your father?"

Alisanne blinked at the shift in subject. "He… he has a weak heart."

"And cannot travel?"

"No."

"Yet he would let you come alone to seek help for him."

"The help is not for him, my lord."

"Then who is it for?"

He was asking questions, yet supplying her with no answers at all. She countered him. "I will only tell Sir Roane. If you are not him, then I shall be on my way."

Roane hid a smile. She was indeed a clever little thing. Taking a long, hard glance at her, his opinion was reaffirmed that she was also a lovely little thing. Prettier now that she was drying out. The cloak of her hood draped her shoulders, revealing silky brown hair to frame her brilliant, if not slightly bloodshot, green eyes. In fact, he didn't ever think he'd seen a woman so lovely, not in all of his travels. Though she was small, which implied delicacy, she radiated a great strength. Certainly if her story was true and she had indeed traveled alone, then she was brave as well. Very admirable qualities which made him soften toward her ever so slightly, though he knew his reaction could cost him his life.

"We will eat your roast first and talk later," he said, rising from his fire pit on legs as thick as tree trunks.

He marched past Alisanne and out into the ward beyond. In truth, she wasn't feeling nearly as strong and confident as she was projecting. Days of traveling plus a night in the driving rain had rendered her weak and exhausted. But this man was harsh and cold and his manner gave her the strength she needed to convince him of her purpose. It was a distinct surprise that she had actually reached this place alive, and she was not going to let him discourage her from her intent.

As he went into the ward and removed her rabbit from the fire, the smell of the meat suddenly hit her and Alisanne realized how terribly hungry she was. Her legs, inexplicably, became very unsteady. Mayhap she was more exhausted than she thought, as it had easily been a couple of days since she last ate. She simply hadn't had the time to stop and rest or eat, knowing the sooner she reached her destination, the better. She tried to ignore the dizziness, but after a few steps her knees gave way.

Roane heard the thud and looked up in time to see Alisanne picking herself up from the doorway. He turned back to the meat in his hand when he heard another dull crash and saw that the woman was lying on the wet ground. This time, she did not get up.

Roane watched her from the corner of his eye, waiting for her to move. He thought it was some sort of plot to play on his sympathies. But Alisanne remained motionless and he finally sighed irritably, retracing his steps to where she now lay. As he came close, he realized that she was indeed moving; she appeared to be gasping and he reached down, rather roughly, and grabbed her by the arm.

Alisanne's reaction was to pull harshly from his grasp. She was conscious, though barely. "I am perfectly capable of getting up," she panted. "Just… allow me to catch my breath."

He instantly complied and went back to his meat. *Stubborn wench*, he thought. Alisanne pushed herself up, first to her hands and finally to her knees. Roane pretended not to notice or care, but in truth, he was very aware of her slow progress. He suspected the night in the rain had sufficiently weakened her and now she was ill, and he didn't want a dying woman on his conscience. With another grunt, he went back to her.

"Come," he grasped her arm and pulled her to her feet; she was terribly light. "Since you caught and killed this beast, you should eat some of it."

Alisanne was pale, her porcelain skin unnaturally white against her glimmering brown hair. She tried to pull away from him but hadn't the strength. "I don't need to eat," she insisted petulantly, though they both knew it was a lie. "I must speak with Sir Roane. That is the only matter of importance right now."

She wasn't walking very well. Roane swept her into his arms, immediately aware of how sweet and soft she was. Her hair brushed him, her small hands gripping his neck in surprise, and he found himself fighting urges he hadn't felt in years. The remembrance of a woman in his arms, the sweetness of her voice softening his hardness, all mingled into a heat that began in his chest and spread to his limbs. By the time they reached the small pit fire, he wasn't sure he wanted to put her down at all. He rather liked her against him. But for sanity, and safety's sake, he did.

"Eat," he thrust a succulent piece of rabbit into her hand.

Alisanne eyed him stubbornly before chewing on the meat. Her hands were shaking as she shoved it into her mouth and Roane watched her, feeling himself weaken. She wasn't any more of a threat to him than his dog was, assassins in the shadows be damned. He didn't eat any more of the rabbit; he sat back and watched her delicate little mouth devour the entire thing. She needed it.

The sun was bright as the morning deepened. The color returned to Alisanne's cheeks, a beautiful blush of pink against her skin, and Roane found himself more enchanted by the moment. And he was also intensely curious as to how so delicate and frail a lady apparently faced such great danger to find him. *Why?* As she licked the grease from her fingers, his need to know grew overwhelming.

"Now, mayhap you will tell me why you seek Sir Roane," he said.

Alisanne looked up from her dirty hands. "I will only tell Sir Roane. You have not made it clear if you are him or not."

"Is your business so personal?"

"It is."

"Yet you do not know him."

"If I did, then I would know if you were him, would I not?"

He cocked an eyebrow at her insolence. But he secretly liked that she was not afraid of him. Most people were terrified. But it was clear that they were at a stalemate; she would not tell him her business unless he revealed himself, and he was not inclined to do so at the moment. At least not yet.

So he sat back, feeling the warmth of the dying fire through his worn soles as he gazed up at the crystal blue sky. "Let me see if I understand, then," he said. Samson wandered out of the open abbey doors, a fat hairy thing, and he eyed the dog fondly before continuing. "You come seeking a man named Sir Roane de Garr on personal business, traveling alone in a land of bandits and murderers to reach him, yet you do not know him."

"Aye, my lord."

"Is it news you come bearing that would affect him somehow?"

"No, my lord."

"Are you an assassin?"

She looked indignant. "No!"

He had slipped that question in simply to gauge her reaction and he was not disappointed. Her denial, in his opinion, was sincere. As a man who had stayed alive the past three years depending on his suspicions, he trusted his senses.

He lazed back on one arm, studying her without a hint of warmth. "Where are you from, Lady Alisanne?"

"Near Kidderminster."

"That is a considerable distance," he said. "All by yourself, you say?"

"Aye, my lord."

"Then your business must be very important to risk your life in such a manner."

Her brilliant green eyes grew intense. "It 'tis a matter of my life."

He lifted an eyebrow and sat forward, stirring the last of the fire. "It is a matter of your life, yet you risk it just the same traveling many miles to have it saved?" he shook his head. "That does not make sense."

Alisanne had had enough. She was exhausted and sick, and quite frankly she was irritated by the man's evasiveness. If he wasn't Sir Roane, then he should have told her a long time ago and not have wasted both their time. True enough, it would not have been difficult to sit and stare at his handsome face day and night until she grew old and died, but time was of the essence at the moment and she could not waste it playing games.

"It makes sense when you consider what is at stake," she countered. "I will ask you again and I will politely ask for a simple answer. Are you Sir Roane de Garr, yea or nay?"

Her tone was sharp, but he didn't flinch. He found he rather enjoyed her fire. "Who told you he was here?"

She gazed at him, her delicate jaw ticking with the force of her frustration. "I was told I could find Sir Roane de Garr in the town of Church Stretton, at the abandoned abbey on the hill. I traveled a great while and risked my life asking many people where I might find this town. This is the only abbey for miles as far as I have been told. Am I incorrect, then, to presume that you must logically be Sir Roane?"

Her voice was quaking with emotion and there wasn't any reason not to tell her what she already knew.

"No," he said slowly.

Alisanne almost collapsed with the surprise of his answer. She had expected more bartering, more evasive answers, not a simple word of acknowledgement. She suddenly didn't know what to say and much to her chagrin, her eyes welled with fat tears that treacherously splashed onto her cheeks. She wiped them away quickly, but Roane could not help but see them.

"What's the matter now? Don't you believe me?"

She shook her head and looked away, trying to recover her composure. Roane watched her struggle. "Lady Alisanne," he said. "Tell me why you weep."

She swiped her eyes with the back of her hand. "I… I am not sure," she whispered. "I suppose it is simply relief. Now that I've found you, I am not even sure where to begin."

As much as he found himself softening to her, still, he did not trust her and tears somehow made his skepticism return, as if she was trying to lull him somehow and play on his sympathies. He wasn't sure what to think.

"You can start by telling me who sent you here."

Alisanne opened her mouth to reply when the heavy pounding of hooves echoed up the narrow path that led to the abbey. She and Roane turned in time to see a great silver charger roar up the muddy trail, resplendent in full armor and draped with banners in yellow and green. The man was armed to the teeth with weapons, a shocking sight in the peace of the ruined abbey.

"Ah *ha!*" the knight aboard the charger bellowed. "There you are!"

Alisanne was so startled that she toppled back onto her arse before she even gained her footing. Roane, however, was much more agile. Even as he moved past her, his eyes glared daggers into her.

"Liar!" he roared.

Alisanne had no idea what he was talking about. "Sir Roane, I don't…!"

He paused long enough to shove his flushed face into hers, his angry breath hot on her face. "He was lurking here all the time, wasn't he?

Christ, and I almost believed you!"

He dashed past her so quickly that she could not argue with him. But the other knight, in his clanking, arrogant armor, was nearly on top of her and she struggled to get away from him.

"You'll not escape me so easily, wench!" he cried. But his shields and weaponry were so bulky that he was having trouble getting an arm out to her. "I've followed you from Hereford to Shropshire and I intend to have you!"

Alisanne shrieked, dodging an outstretched gauntlet. "Stay away from me!"

He reined his changer around the fire, chasing her. "You belong to me, you little chicken. How dare you run from me!"

Alisanne dashed through a crumbling outbuilding, hoping to lose him in the clutter of stone and wood. "I don't belong to you! Go away from here!"

The knight boldly plowed his charger through the stone. "I've come a very long way, Alisanne, and I am in no mood for games. You are mine as surely as the sun rises and I demand you cease this foolishness at once."

"Never!"

"Stop running, you silly wench!"

Alisanne slid down the slope near the trail that led up the mountain to the abbey. She knew it was too steep for the destrier to follow. She came to a stop several feet down, turning to see where the knight was. "My father never consented to you, Dodge," she said, struggling to catch her breath. "He has never given you any indication that he would pledge me to you."

Dodge stood at the top of the trail, gazing angrily down at her. "He has no choice," he snarled. "My lands surround yours. He is a weak old man, feeble and dying, and it is only logical that you and I should wed." He pounded his thigh dramatically. "Why must you be so difficult about this?"

Alisanne's pretty face was dark. "Because I don't want to marry you,

Dodge de Vere. You are an arrogant buffoon and I despise you."

He raised his visor, revealing a less than attractive face, rather bland in appearance. "That is of no concern to me," he said crisply. "It is only reasonable that you and I marry, Alisanne. I want your land and you, in turn, need to be taken care of. A rather fair arrangement, wouldn't you say?"

"I don't need your care. I don't want it. How many times must I tell you this? Go away and leave me alone."

Dodge leaned forward to rest on his saddle. "You were always stubborn, Alisanne. If you make me chase you down this hill, then I can guarantee I'll beat every stubborn bone out of your body. Do you comprehend me?"

She stood firm. "I'll not marry you, Dodge, and you cannot force me."

"Is that a challenge?"

"A promise."

"And I say that I can indeed marry you. All I have to do is take you to the church in the village and pay the priest. 'Twill be over and done with before you can utter a word of protest and your foolish behavior, lady, will have been for naught."

"I *am* protesting. And I say leave before…"

He sneered. "Before *what?*"

"Before I run you through."

Roane reappeared in the center of the ward, near the fire where the rabbit had cooked. He wore no armor, only a heavy linen tunic with a leather vest and thick, worn hose, but he was the most intimidating man Alisanne had ever seen, for in his hand lodged a sword of such massive proportions that she swore it was nearly as long as her entire body. Roane handled the sword as if it was a featherweight, left handed he was, as his eyes fixed on Dodge as a cat beholds a mouse.

"This is my property," he growled. "You will remove yourself immediately."

Dodge gazed at the massive man with the equally massive sword.

He was more irritated than alarmed. "Who are you?"

Roane assessed the knight; in truth, he had been doing precisely that for the past several minutes. He had heard the majority of the warrior's conversation with Alisanne and it was blatantly obvious, even to a suspicious man like himself, that the knight was not interested in the hermit named Roane de Garr, but in a young lady named Alisanne de Soulant.

"Who I am is of no concern to you," Roane said. "You will do as I say and leave immediately."

Dodge looked at Alisanne. "Did you hire a protector?" he asked mockingly. "You should have found someone a little more worthy, my dear. Why, he does not even have any armor."

"He is not my protector," Alisanne said, though she was both surprised and pleased Roane was taking it upon himself to defend her. "But you should do as he says and leave. I do not want your death on my conscience, as much as it would relieve me."

Dodge couldn't decide whether to laugh or become angry. But the immediate need was to rid himself of the intrusive protector and he unsheathed his sword.

"You have invited more trouble than you can handle, little man," he said to Roane.

Roane cocked an eyebrow; he had been called many things before, but never a little man. As Dodge charged at him, he didn't flinch nor did he lift his sword until the very last possible moment. Fending off a crushing blow, he spun around and used the flat side of his weapon to whack Dodge across the back and unbalance him. The knight wobbled dangerously before righting himself. Turning his horse about, he glared angrily at Roane.

"Don't use your childish tactics on me," he snorted. "Fight like a man and I will be merciful."

Roane couldn't help it; he smiled with genuine humor, probably for the first time in months. He shrugged his big shoulders as if the thought of clean fighting had actually just occurred to him. "As you wish."

Dodge charged at him again. This time, Roane reached out and neatly yanked the knight from his horse, unseating him so quickly that Dodge had no time to react. Face down in the mud and seeing bright bits of stars dance across his vision, Dodge grunted as he struggled to roll over.

"Bastard!" he roared. "Now I shall kill you as painfully as possible, wheedling away your innards so that not even the buzzards will find a good meal!"

Roane stood over him. Suddenly, the tip of the massive weapon was pointed at Dodge's throat and the armored knight saw the need to mayhap amend his hasty insults. Gazing up into the eyes of his opponent, he could read the cold resolve in the depths and a chill of fear ran through him.

"If you kill me, you will bring the House of de Vere down upon you," he said, his pompous nature deflated. "I warn you to consider what you are about to do."

Roane appeared thoughtful. "You were about to kill me. Have I not the right to defend myself?"

"I am no threat at the moment."

"You never were."

Dodge's face reddened. Out of the corner of his eye he caught sight of Alisanne, watching the battle with wide-eyes, and his humiliation deepened.

"Why would you defend this woman?" he demanded. "She cannot pay you. I know she has no money."

"I do not defend her. I simply want you off my land."

"And suppose I leave. Then what will you do with her?"

"That is my affair."

Dodge grew furious as he realized the knight's true motive. "Her purity belongs to me."

"From what I heard, nothing belongs to you. Be gone before I change my mind and string you up amongst the oaks."

He moved away from the mud-covered knight. Dodge pushed himself up heavily, grunting and growling like an old bear. He stumbled to where his horse stood nibbling on wet grass and roughly grabbed the animal's reins. He was too heavy and too slovenly to mount the horse without a good deal of help, so he had to walk from this place in humiliation. Alisanne watched him go, making sure to stay well clear of him. She avoided his gaze, but Dodge stared her down harshly.

"I will wait for you at the bottom of the hill, Alisanne," he grumbled. "You cannot stay up here forever."

She didn't answer. The soft, wet noises of his footfalls faded and Alisanne dared to turn to watch him as he trailed off down the slope. She almost couldn't bring herself to look at Roane, unsure of how he was feeling at the moment. Just when she had established some sort of rapport, Dodge appeared and ruined everything. It was a horrible coincidence and she was positive that Roane's wrath would turn on her next.

But she forced herself to look at him. In spite of everything, he had just done her a great service and she needed to acknowledge him. "Thank you," she said softly. "I don't know how I would have gotten rid of him."

Roane gazed at her, so lovely and sweet in the morning light. But she was also infinitely terrifying for reasons he couldn't even begin to understand and his sense of self-preservation was overwhelming.

"You are trouble I do not need," he said quietly and turned back for the abbey. "I would suggest taking the lesser used trail over to the right, between those trees. If he's waiting for you at the base of the main trail, he'll miss you if you exit off the southern side."

He was helping her and vanquishing her at the same time. Alisanne felt a terrible sense of desperation. "But, Sir Roane, I still need your help!"

He walked away from her, shaking his head. "I have given you all the help I intend to."

The abbey door closed behind him with the loud reverberation of finality.

CHAPTER TWO

I T WAS GLOOMY, wet and drippy. Alisanne sat upon a rotted stump, staring at the crumbling old abbey and wondering if Roane was ever going to show his face again. It was increasingly difficult to wait him out, for her instinct was to pound on the door again until he opened it. But the marginal trust she had been able to establish two days ago had been dashed by Dodge's appearance, and she knew it would be difficult to regain it. But regain it she must. Beating the door down wasn't going to help.

She put her head in her hands for a moment; Dear God, it had taken so much simply to come here. She simply couldn't turn away now. Everything in her life depended upon Sir Roane de Garr's generosity. It was so cold and wet upon this hill and the ruins of the outbuildings were hardly any shelter at all. The dry wood she had found to make a fire the past two days had dwindled down to nothing, and her throat was beginning to ache. She knew that shortly she would become sick and she dreaded the thought. She couldn't become ill, not now when there was so much to accomplish.

Behind her in the trees she had constructed a makeshift shelter that at least had kept her dry. Heavy branches formed a sort of dome and a small, dwindling cooking fire smoldered in front of it. A small satchel spilled open beneath the shelter, having held nothing more than a few bits of dried meat, stale bread, a small iron cooking pot and an old woolen blanket. Alisanne had traveled light and swift, carrying only what she needed.

The meat and bread were gone and the pot sat atop the smoking fire, gently bubbling a thin soup of ingredients Alisanne had been able to gather; the remainder of the cooked rabbit, turnips and wild brown beans she had found locally, and then half of a wilted cabbage and a few carrots she had scavenged from the town. In truth, it was a good soup and the smell had been tantalizing her all morning. Having hardly eaten yesterday, she was understandably famished, but the soup needed to simmer a good while before it would be consumable. The fire was weak, making cooking difficult.

Finally she could stand it no longer and slurped down nearly half the pot, burning her tongue in the process. From the dark-stoned abbey, she could suddenly see movement and she watched closely as something, an animal apparently, wandered through the stones of the ruined outer buildings. A sleek black tail came into view, followed by the rest of Sir Roane's big black dog, who plopped himself down several feet from Alisanne and wagged his tail. She threw the dog a precious piece of cooked meat.

"You needn't starve, even if your master intends to," she said to the dog. "And your name is Samson."

The dog wagged his tail happily in response. Alisanne thought it might be a very good idea for the big dog to keep her warm and she called to it softly, encouraging it to come and lie down beside her. Samson did just that, excited to be near the food. Between the two of them, they finished off the soup and lay back against each other in gluttonous contentment.

"Your master, Samson," she said as she reclined against the hairy back, "how am I going to speak with him if he stays like a hermit inside his abbey?"

The dog wagged its tail in reply, thumping against the wet ground. Alisanne scratched the dog's fur, surprisingly clean for the conditions he apparently lived in. Soon, she fell asleep and when she awoke, the sky had cleared and the late afternoon sun shone brightly. Feeling refreshed, Alisanne rose and, with the dog in pursuit, began to walk among the outer buildings, trying to think of a way to coerce Roane from his cave.

Samson trotted past her and skimmed the length of the abbey. As

Alisanne watched, he slipped into a hole in the side of the building half-hidden by crumbling debris. Alisanne gazed at the hole a moment; why should she lure him out when she could just as easily enter? Swiftly, she followed the dog.

The interior of the abbey wasn't much of an improvement over the exterior. Green moss coated the damp walls in some places, giving the air a moldy smell. The ground was uneven and worn, and she could see the evidence of pews and an altar. Cautiously, she crept her way along the old wall, heading toward the area at the back of the abbey where Roane lived. Samson kept running up to her, happily, as if to show her the way, and she tried to shoo the dog away as discreetly as she could.

Finally, she reached the area that Roane had carved out for himself, a rough pallet to sleep upon and a crude firepit for cooking. As her eyes struggled to acclimate themselves to the darkness of the abbey, her gaze fell on a worn table and chair, both of which were cluttered with expensive parchment and other writing materials. She thought it rather curious that such an obviously destitute man should have parchment and other scribing items usually reserved for the rich or the important. All of it simply added to his air of mystery.

Samson wouldn't leave her alone. He kept sniffing and licking, and Alisanne was positive the dog would give her away. She had wanted to approach Roane carefully, but with the element of surprise so he couldn't run her off. In truth, she really didn't know why she had sneaked her way into the abbey. He was only going to chase her away again. But something inside her simply wouldn't give up.

"Did anyone ever tell you that you have the persistence of a gnat?"

Alisanne jumped at the sound of Roane's voice. He stood behind her, in the cavernous shadows of the dark abbey, as Samson ran excitedly between the two of them. Heart thumping in her throat, she faced him.

"I would not have to be so bothersome if you would simply give me the opportunity to speak with you," she said.

He stepped into the light and she was surprised to notice that he did not appear angry. He looked rather nonchalant, in fact.

"You did speak to me, if you recall," he said. "I cannot help you."

She looked puzzled. "How do you know that you cannot help me when I haven't even told you what it is I need?"

"You don't need to tell me," he walked past her, his great lumbering presence comforting and frightening at the same time. "What you need is quite obvious, and I have no idea who told you I could help you."

She was more confused than before. "Obvious? What is obvious?"

He moved to the firepit and stirred it. It seemed to Alisanne she had seen him do this before and it was apparently a nervous habit. "I cannot protect you from the man who seeks to marry you, no matter how much you will pay me. Is that clear?"

She followed him timidly, finding herself lingering by the dying fire. "That is not what I came to ask."

He looked up at her, struck by her beauty in the soft light of the fire. She had the most magnificent eyes he had ever seen, and there was a sensual curve to her face that invited exploration. But he shook off those thoughts.

"Then what did you come to ask?"

Alisanne suddenly forgot how to speak, realizing the moment of truth was finally upon her. All of the pre-rehearsed things she had planned to say flew out of her head and she struggled to say something, anything, to him that would make some sense.

"Father Joseph Ari sent me to you," she said softly.

"I don't know Father Joseph Ari."

She swallowed nervously, nodding her head. "I know that you do not recognize the name. But you indeed know the person. You see, he is my uncle, my mother's brother."

"What is he to me?"

"You knew him as John Adam. He took the name Joseph Ari when he returned from the great quest."

Roane felt as if he had been hit in the pit of his stomach. The room suddenly grew unsteady but in spite of that, he rose to his feet. The expression on his face was one of extreme suspicion and extreme disbelief.

"John Adam," he breathed. "He is your uncle?"

Alisanne nodded. From the look on his face, she wasn't sure if she was helping her cause or hurting it. "When he returned from the Crusade, he devoted his life to the priesthood," she could sense she was losing ground with Roane and struggled to bring forth everything. "Sir Roane, I know about your gift. I know that when the Hospitallers found out, they accused you of witchcraft and punished you unspeakably. I know that you have been hiding from them for the past three years because if they find you, they will surely kill you. My uncle helped you escape, and it is he who has sent me here."

It was almost too much for Roane to absorb. He sought out his chair and sat slowly, listening to the wood pop and groan. His chest was constricted with conflicting emotion, made worse when he gazed into Alisanne's magnificent eyes.

"Your uncle and I made a pact when I fled the Holy Land," he said after a moment, his voice hoarse. "We would never again see or speak of one another because of our association… it would be deadly should those who seek to persecute me find out. To send you to me is seriously dangerous at best. I simply cannot believe he would break our pact."

Alisanne's face was solemn. "He had a very good reason, Sir Roane, if you would just…."

"On your trip here, how many people did you ask directions from? And, Christ, how many times did you mention my name?"

She shook her head. "I never mentioned your name. I was simply looking for the deserted abbey near Church Stretton."

He stared at her a moment before sighing heavily, running his fingers through his cropped blond hair. "It does not matter," he rumbled. "If there are brothers out there, they will hear of this."

"How could they hear of anything if I never mentioned your name, nor my reason for coming?"

He still wasn't comforted. Samson meandered by, rubbing his big hairy body on Roane's leg; the knight reached down to absently stroke the dog. His eyes were distant, staring off into the darkness until the silence became heavy and uncomfortable. Alisanne wasn't sure what else she could say or do to ease him.

"Please, Sir Roane," she finally said, rounding the firepit and coming to kneel beside him. "I am not here to lead you to doom, nor coerce you into defending me against an imbecile. I am here for a far more serious reason."

He looked down at her, like an angel at his feet. Before he could stop himself, his eyes greedily drank in every contour of her face, every glittering strand of her buttock-length hair. He had to turn away lest he reach out to touch the magic.

"Tell me what that reason is and be done with it."

Alisanne gazed up at his strong profile, his impossibly powerful and handsome features. She realized she was shaking again; it seemed that all she ever did was shake around him. He had the ability to elicit the most potent, yet odd, response from her, so much so that it was difficult to maintain her focus.

"It is a complicated story, but I shall be brief," she said quietly. "My father is a baron with a good deal of land. It is excellent land, to which I am heiress. Dodge de Vere is the bastard of Sir Aubrey de Vere, the man who built Rochester Castle in Kent, and also a member of the widely powerful de Vere family. Dodge's lands surround our own and has demanded that my father pledge me to him."

Roane looked at her again; somehow she was closer to him than he originally thought and a peculiar warmth began to blossom in his chest. "Surely you've had other suitors."

Alisanne nodded. "Many. But Dodge has chased them away."

Roane cocked an eyebrow. "I cannot imagine, lady, that any man would be easily chased from you. They must have all been weaklings, and undeserving of you."

She blushed furiously and Roane held back a smile; Christ, she was such a lovely creature. "No one wants an invalid wife, my lord. They were understandably swayed," she said.

His urge to smile vanished. "Invalid? What do you mean?"

Her blush deepened and much to her embarrassment, tears filled her eyes. Swiftly, she turned away from him. But before she could move completely out of range, Roane reached out and grabbed her. She pulled, he pulled, and she ended up stumbling backwards onto his lap. The more she struggled, the tighter he held her.

"Cease your struggles," he said in her ear.

"Let me go!"

"Shhh," he whispered. "Tell me why you weep."

She grunted with frustration, still fighting him. "Let... me...!"

"Shhh," he said again. "Stop struggling, Alisanne, and tell me why you weep."

Her sweet body relaxed, but not entirely. She was usually in control of her composure, unusual for a woman, but Roane's powerful arms around her completely unnerved her. She'd never been held by anyone but her father, and his frail old arms simply could not compare to Roane's magnificent embrace. She thought foolishly, at that moment, that she wouldn't have been entirely unhappy to stay in his arms forever.

"I... I...." she stammered and sniffed.

He realized he was squeezing her gently, knowing he should very well let her up but being unwilling, or unable, to do so. "Slow down and take a deep breath. That's a good girl. Now, tell me why you weep."

She was quiet, gaining control of her sobs. When all was still and she simply sat, on his massive thigh, her sweet voice was faint in the dank abbey air.

"Uncle John Adam told me that you have the gift of miracles," she whispered. "I came seeking a miracle."

His curse. Roane sighed imperceptibly, leaning forward so that his forehead was resting on her back. He had suspected that was the reason she was here from the very beginning. "I don't perform miracles, Alisanne."

Her tears threatened again, but she held them back. "You healed my uncle."

"I didn't mean to. I didn't know what I had done."

She took a deep breath, unaware that she was leaning back into him and he was holding her closer. "I have the same affliction as my uncle," she said miserably. "My eyes hurt constantly and my vision dims. One time, I had blisters on my eyes and Dodge sent his physic to take care of me. It was his physic who discovered that I shall very shortly be blind, and he told Dodge. That is how Dodge chased away any suitor I ever had. No one wants an invalid wife, no matter how prized her dowry."

Roane held her tightly, more tightly than he realized, as his eyes stared off into the darkness. "So he marries you, takes your lands, and then casts you off."

"My father is afraid he will kill me."

Roane took a deep, long breath. Although he had only been acquainted with this woman for three days, already he knew he could not let that happen. Before he could say anything, Alisanne shifted in his embrace and he found himself face to face with her. They were inches from one another, the thrill of their closeness casting palpable sparks. But the seriousness of the situation overwhelmed any blossoming excitement.

"I cannot pay you for this miracle," her lips were quivering as she spoke. "But my father has told me to tell you that if you restore my sight, our payment to you will be my hand in marriage, which includes Kinlet Castle and the Craven barony."

He'd never had a more attractive offer. But it was too overwhelming at the moment and he was unsure how to react. He gazed into her magnificent eyes, seeing the irritation that lent credence to her tale.

"On my oath as a knight, I would like nothing better," he said softly. "But there is something your uncle did not tell you about my... gift."

"What is that?"

"That I swore never to use it."

She blinked, as if uncomprehending. "But..."

"Never, Alisanne."

She could feel her panic rising once again. "But... why would he send me here if he did not think you would help me?"

Roane shrugged faintly. "Mayhap he thought I had changed my mind over the years. I don't really know. But I have not changed my mind; if anything, I am more resolute than ever."

She didn't know what to say. With a strangled cry, she pitched herself off his lap and threw herself at his feet. "Please," she gasped. "Please, you must help me. If you don't, surely… it is the end of my family!"

"I will not let that happen," he said, pulling her up so that they were mere inches from each other, gazing headily into each other's eyes. "Nothing will happen to you, Alisanne, I swear it."

She was sobbing again. "I care not for me," she wept. "But my father… he is old and feeble, and if I can no longer take care of him when my sight leaves me, then he will be at the mercy of Dodge."

As Roane gazed at her, he realized that the woman had no self-pity that she was losing her sight, but rather her concern was the fact that losing it meant hardship and even death to her father and family line. Her sense of self-sacrifice impressed him tremendously.

"Don't worry about him," he lifted her to her feet, brushing off her already-dirty dress where her knees had skimmed the floor. "I promise you that you will not have to worry about him any longer."

She wiped her nose with the back of her hand. "How?"

He smiled at her, the very first time since they had met. If his mere presence caused her to shake inexplicably, then his smile was enough to make her feel faint.

"You will let me worry about that," he said. "Right now, I fear I have been inhospitable to John Adam's niece."

She watched him quit the abbey with Samson on his heels. When he returned, it was with Alisanne's small satchel in his hand. He sat it next to his own pallet.

"You may sleep here," he said. Bending down, he scooped up an old wooden bucket. "And I would imagine fresh water is in order, for one reason or another."

Alisanne quickly took the pail from his hand. "I'll get it," she said. "'Tis the least I can do if I am stealing your bed."

He smiled again, deep dimples in both cheeks. She returned his smile, rather bashfully, and strolled from the abbey feeling more terrible than she ever had. She turned around once to see that he had followed her into the bailey. As she walked down the narrow path, she told herself that all that mattered was her father's safety and she had to do what was necessary. He trusted her now, which had been her goal. But terrible things were going to happen now, things for which she was consummately guilty.

There was a small brook that ran at the base of the hill, shielded by some heavy oaks. Dodge was waiting for her when she reached the bottom.

"Well?" he demanded.

Alisanne looked up at him, her eyes heavy with burden and sorrow. "He is alone."

"And trusting?"

"He followed me out into the ward. He should still be there."

Dodge gazed up at the slope, seeing the tops of the ruined abbey from where he stood. "Excellent, Alisanne," he said. He motioned with his arm and suddenly the trees came alive around him; men in armor with weapons. He grinned down at her. "Your father thanks you."

Alisanne could not look at the men, wishing with all her heart that there had been another way to go about this. "Just… please don't hurt him," she murmured.

"Who? De Garr or your father?"

She looked up at him, shielding her eyes from the weak sun. "Both of them. Please."

Dodge didn't reply except for a smirking expression. Alisanne grabbed his leg imploringly. "Please," she repeated. "Don't hurt him."

There was something in her tone he didn't like. She spoke far too fondly of de Garr, and it inflamed him. Spurring his horse forward, he and his men charged up the hill.

CHAPTER THREE

IT WAS RAINING again, a heavy deluge that soaked man and beast. South of Church Stretton by several miles, night was falling and Dodge and his men made camp in a saturated meadow that had small rivers of mud running through it. Alisanne disembarked from the old wagon, standing aside in the rain as the men made her a haphazard shelter against the elements. It was better than nothing and she huddled beneath it, cold and hungry, as Dodge dealt with his trophy in the back of the rig.

It had taken nine men to subdue Roane, but they had managed to do so by overwhelming him. Still, all but one of the men had come away with some sort of broken limb, or teeth, or a split skull. Roane had been like a bull, charging and bashing everyone in sight as he tried to make it back into the abbey to claim his sword. But he never got close, and after nearly a half hour of fighting, Dodge's men had brought him down from the hill slung across the back of a charger like a prize deer. At first, Roane had thought Dodge had captured Alisanne, too, as part of his campaign against her, but he realized soon enough that his instincts had been right. She had been a charming decoy, and he had fallen for it like an idiot.

Huddled in the tent, Alisanne watched Dodge and his men gleefully harass Roane. They seemed particularly fond of thumping him on the head. When they grew tired of the sport, they made for Dodge's lean-to where they drank and ate well into the night. A few of them eyed Alisanne leeringly, but she kept her attention well away from them, ignoring the food one of them had brought her. She prayed they would soon fall asleep which, thanks to the alcohol, they did fairly quickly. As their snoring mingled with the thunder, she made her way silently to the wagon where Roane lay.

She could barely see him in the darkness. He lay on his side, trussed up like a pig to roast, and Alisanne's heart sank at the sight of him. She felt so horrible, knowing she had betrayed him when she had worked so hard to gain his trust, but she also knew that she had had no choice. Not that it would matter to him, but she hoped he would at least allow her to explain. She couldn't stomach the thought of him thinking she was a deceitful scamp.

The thunder rolled and lightning flashed across the weeping sky. Afraid that Dodge might see her standing beside the wagon, she climbed up into it and lay down beside Roane. The darkness made it difficult to see him and when she thought she was lying against his back, she realized too late that she was pressed very firmly against his front. Roane's wide-open eyes startled her.

"Sir Roane," she gasped. "I... I...."

He was gagged, the cloth saturated with saliva. Quickly, she removed it, if only to make him more comfortable and also to prove that she wasn't entirely the enemy. "I am so sorry for what has happened," she whispered. "But... you must understand that I had no choice. Dodge forced me to...."

"Cease your insincere apologies. I have nothing to say to you."

"Please... if you will only...."

"Listen? I've done that. Now see what my compassion has gotten me."

He tried to turn away from her, ignoring her. Alisanne lay beside him, the rain soaking her, wondering how she could make amends to him. She had never felt more awful for something she had done. Mayhap her actions had saved some, but they could very well mean the death of another. He had done quite well evading the Hospitallers until she, and her horrible deceit, had lured him out of hiding.

"I am so sorry," she repeated, her throat tight with emotion. "He forced me to, Sir Roane. I had no choice."

She sat up and Roane felt her scoot to the edge of the wagon bed.

There was something in her voice that, as it had before, broke down his resistance. As angry as he was at the moment, she was fortunate he didn't break his bonds and wring her pretty neck. But instead he felt himself softening.

"Who in the hell is he?" Roane's voice was hoarse.

Alisanne turned to him. He was staring at her openly. "A bounty hunter," she whispered.

Roane didn't say anything for a moment. Odd that he felt a strange peace now that he knew who the man was; he'd dealt with bounty hunters before and had always managed to elude them. They were a stupid, greedy lot. But this time, the hunter had been clever and had used the right bait to trap him. He gazed at Alisanne, so pale and remorseful, and resisted the urge to comfort her.

"I think you had better tell me everything," he said quietly.

She slowly moved back to him, lying down carefully beside him. When she spoke, it was slow and halting. "Dodge came to my uncle because he had been told by the Hospitallers that my uncle had once been your friend," she murmured. "He and his men came to our home and tortured my uncle, but he would not tell them anything. Finally, he broke and confessed all. Dodge knew that if he simply charged to Church Stretton that you would fight him, so he told me that if I didn't help him capture you, he would kill my uncle and father."

"So there really is a father?" Roane asked. "And your uncle really is John Adam?"

She nodded, daring to look at him. He cocked an eyebrow. "And that story about your sight leaving you, was that true?"

She nodded again. "It is. Which is why Dodge thought it would be a perfect way to earn your trust."

"You did not travel alone as you said you did."

"No."

Roane sighed, licking his lips as the rain ran down them. "Where are they holding your father and John Adam?"

"At my father's seat, Kinlet Castle, to the north and east of

Kiddminster."

"There really is a barony, too?"

"My father is Baron Craven, a title that Dodge will claim when he marries me."

"So your father has indeed pledged you to him?"

She smiled ironically. "Just as I wasn't given a choice, neither was he. Dodge saw a prime situation and bullied my father until he agreed."

"And do his lands truly surround your own?"

"No. It was a story Dodge had concocted to make everything sound more believable." She paused a moment, feeling as if she was confessing her most grievous sins to him. "His appearance in the abbey ward was merely to confirm that you were there, and to make a show of it. He thought you might feel more chivalrous toward me if you thought someone was out to do me harm."

Well, the man had that right. Roane didn't think he could feel any more of a fool than he already did. "Is his name really Dodge de Vere?"

"That is what he has told me."

It was a convoluted, ugly mess. Alisanne could sense his turmoil and it matched her own. "Sir Roane, everything that I have told you is true with the exceptions I have already mentioned. I did not do this for any reason other than I was told if I didn't help Dodge capture you, he would kill both my father and Uncle John. I harbor no ill-will against you. In fact, you will never know how sorry I truly am for all I've done to you."

Roane was silent. He wasn't surprised by the story and he didn't blame her in the least. But the fact remained that he was now in a good deal of trouble. "So the sect has hired Dodge de Vere to bring me to ecclesiastical justice," he snorted softly. "They hired many before. Seems no one had Dodge's initiative to find John Adam, my oldest friend, and use him accordingly. No doubt the sect told Dodge exactly where to find John Adam."

Alisanne nodded guiltily. "They would have found him at his monastery, but he was visiting us at the time and the priests told Dodge where he was. He followed him.”

A displeasing series of events that led Dodge directly to Alisanne's doorstep. Roane could see that she was as much a victim in all of this as he was.

“Christ,” he hissed. “Will those bastards stop at nothing to condemn me? Now you and your family have been hurt by all of this, and God only knows who or what else.”

Alisanne could feel his anger. Not knowing what else to do, she put a small hand on his wet, bare arm. “'Twill be all right, Sir Roane. If I can think of a way to free you without risking my father and uncle, I surely will. But... at the time, in Church Stretton... I simply did not know what else to do.”

He turned to look at her, their faces very close on the bed of the flooded wagon. Though it was chilly, there was a warmth between them that erased the discomfort from the elements. He was stupid to have believed her, but God help him, he did. She was so sincere, so genuine, that he couldn't help himself.

“You needn't worry about me,” he said huskily; she was far too close and he was feeling quivery inside. “I can take care of myself. I've been evading these idiots for three years and I can get out of this. But the problem is not risking your father and uncle's life in the meantime.”

She could sense by his words that he was not angry with her and the relief she felt was overwhelming. Impulsively, she kissed him on the cheek and fled the wagon. Had Roane's hand not been tied, he would have done far more than kiss her.

CB

THE MORNING DAWNED foggy and wet. Dodge and his men were up at sunrise, folding their makeshift camp and tormenting their prisoner. Last night, Alisanne had been terrified to show any measure of compassion to Roane while the men were beating on him, but after a restless night where visions of his strong face danced through her head, she had awoken to realize she felt extremely protective of him. This was all her fault, after all, and she could not stand by while those ruffians who held her father pounded on a defenseless man. She had to help him.

She also woke feeling rather poor. Her sore throat had developed into a cough and her clothes were wet and musty. She stank, and she was miserable, but it didn't dampen her sense of determination. Snatching a hunk of bread that one of Dodge's men had offered her, she stomped across the wet grass to the wagon. Two men were standing in the bed of the wagon, telling Roane all of the terrible things they were going to do to him as she walked up. They kicked him once, twice, before she screeched and put a halt to it.

"Get away from him," she said, her voice gravelly from her developing illness. When they stared at her as if she had two heads, she exploded. "Get away I say. Get away before I beat you myself!"

One leapt off. The other one stayed. Alisanne glared at him as she climbed up on the bed of the wagon, like two dogs challenging each other for the kill. Alisanne's bright green eyes were blood shot and unnaturally bright as she waved her hand at Dodge's man. "Go," she hissed. "Go!"

He snarled at her and slid off the wagon. Alisanne watched him and his partner slink away, like two scolded wolves. She knew they were going straight to Dodge and she hurried to remove Roane's gag, which they had apparently replaced.

"Here," she held the bread to his mouth. "You must be famished."

His handsome face was bruised from the beating he had taken. But the eyes that gazed up at her were bright and alert. "Have you eaten this morning?" he asked.

Her brows furrowed. "No," she said, "but that is of no matter. You haven't either, and you must have your strength."

He smiled at her, his dimples deep. "I am strong enough. You, however, are becoming ill. I heard you coughing all night."

She looked surprised. "You did?" she said. Then, she blushed, flattered that he would be thinking of her. "I am well enough. Please, eat this and hurry. Dodge will be here any moment."

He rolled onto his back, gazing up at her warmly. "I cannot protect you from these idiots, nor can I dry your wet clothing or shield you from these elements. But I can refuse your breakfast so you can maintain your strength. Will you not allow me that privilege?"

Alisanne blushed madly. Having very little experience with men, she wasn't as practiced as she should have been in controlling her reaction. "After all I've caused, you would still show me kindness?"

"It is my pleasure."

"But why?"

He lifted his eyebrows carelessly. "Would you rather I curse the ground you walk on?"

She grinned and looked down at the bread in her hand. She held it up timidly, like an offering. "I would feel better if you ate it."

He laughed softly, his teeth straight and white against his smooth lips. "Very well," he said. "I shall divide it with you, if that makes you happy."

She tore it in half and put a piece in his mouth. "Here, let me help you sit up," she said, grabbing hold of his leather vest and pulling him up. He was heavy and it took a good deal of effort; she had no way of knowing that he had done all the work. "There. Is that better?"

He nodded and swallowed. She popped the second and last piece into his mouth, squealing when he pretended to bite her fingers. Giggling like a little girl, she ate her own portion happily. Roane tried not to stare at her, for she grew more lovely and enchanting by the moment. Had he not been concerned with his present situation, he would have realized he was completely smitten with her. Maybe it was because he had been so out of touch for the past three years, but maybe not; she would have enchanted him in a room full of enchantresses.

"I've been thinking," he said as he chewed, "that we are in a precarious situation."

She swung her legs in rhythm with her jaw munching the bread. "We?"

He cast her a sidelong glance. "Of course. You have gotten me into this mess and now I must get us out."

She stopped chewing and looked at him with big, sad eyes. "But you just said…."

He gave her such an exaggerated expression that she knew instantly he was jesting with her. "I know what I said, you little troublemaker. I can see that this situation, and you, will be the supreme test of my cunning abilities."

She finished her bread and brushed off her hands. "I've always been a troublemaker. You may as well know that."

He eyed her with overstated wariness. "Since when?"

"Since my mother died giving birth to me."

He sobered dramatically. "My mother died in childbirth as well."

"With you?

"Giving birth to my younger sister, who also perished," he said. "I vowed at that moment that if I ever married, my wife would never have children. I would not want to burden her with my child only to see her die an agonizing death."

Alisanne was silent a moment, listening to the cold wind blow through the thick trees. "But one is married to perpetuate the family."

He lifted his big shoulders, gazing off across the white cloaked land. "I joined the sect of the Hospitallers of St. John the Baptist when I was twenty-one years of age, a sect that practices celibacy, so that is something I've not had to worry about in fourteen years."

Alisanne didn't know why she felt a strange sense of disappointment in his statement. "So you will never marry?"

He didn't reply. He was so still that Alisanne wondered if he had even heard the question. She was beginning to regret asking it.

"Since my sect is trying to kill me, I don't suppose I need to be loyal to my vows," he said thoughtfully. "Marriage would be considered under the right circumstances, I suppose."

"What circumstances would that be?"

He turned to look at her. "Why? Do you want to marry me?"

She blushed so brightly that he thought her face might explode and he laughed at her. "Alisanne, if there was one woman in the world I might consider marrying, it would be you. But since you are already betrothed...."

"My father only said what he did because Dodge forced him to," she insisted. "But if you were to mayhap vanquish Dodge somehow, then I would be free to marry whomever I choose."

He was still grinning, lifting an eyebrow as he spoke. "Like me?"

She mirrored his jesting expression. "Are you asking?"

He looked away. "Never."

Her smile faded. "I don't blame you, of course. No one wants an invalid wife."

Roane turned sharply to look at her, noting that she was staring out into the veil of fog. Her brilliant green eyes were bloodshot and swollen this morn, reminding him of what she had told him. *I am losing my sight,* she had said. He'd never once in three years reconsidered his vow never to use the curse God had given him. But as he stared at Alisanne, he found himself doing precisely that.

"Are you really losing your sight, Alisanne?" he asked softly. "Tell me the truth."

She didn't say anything for a moment. Then, when she spoke, it was soft and distant.

"A year ago I began having trouble with my eyes," she murmured. "They were very red and everything seemed blurred, so my father engaged a physic from Worcester to examine my eyes. He said that I had a disease that would eventually blind me. Since then, my eyes have grown steadily worse. It is much better in bright light, and fog like this is... well, everything simply looks gray."

"It *is* gray," he murmured. "It's fog."

She looked at him and saw his gentle smile. He was teasing her again. "Be that as it may," she lifted an eyebrow at him, "when Dodge first came to my father's castle, my eyes were blistered over with an infection. I get them from time to time. Afraid I had something contagious that would spread to him and his men, Dodge brought the same physic from Worcester to examine my eyes, and the man told him everything about me, including my eventual loss of sight. So Dodge was able to invent the story to lure you into his trap, and also coerce my father into pledging my hand to him. It was all very convenient for him."

Roane's gaze on her was steady. He knew, exactly, what he had to do. "If I could touch you right now, I would heal your eyes."

She looked at him, astonished. "What... what do you mean?"

"Exactly that."

"But... your vow!"

"I made it. I can break it."

She stared back at him, feeling his sincerity, experiencing a deeper sense of emotion than she had ever known. "No," she shook her head slowly. "I would not let you. It would only give your persecutors more evidence against you. If you perform miracles as they say you do, then they would surely burn you at the stake for performing another one."

"You let me worry about that."

"But I could not let you jeopardize yourself so."

They were so involved in each other that neither one of them saw Dodge and his men approach the wagon. Suddenly, a fist pounded into Roane's face and sent him falling back against the wagon. Alisanne shrieked as Dodge leapt up on to the bed for another blow, but she regained her wits in an instant and threw herself between the bounty hunter and his victim.

"No!" she bellowed. "You'll not touch him!"

Dodge paused, but only momentarily. The look on his face was pure malevolence. "Get out of the way. He'll not philander with my intended and get away with it."

Alisanne threw out her arms to block Dodge's advance. "Leave him alone or the next opportunity I have, I'll run away and you'll never have the chance to marry me. No titles, no land, no castle. Do you comprehend me?"

Dodge's brown eyes flickered with indecision. "I'll tie you up alongside your friend if your threat is serious."

Her voice grew cold. "Tie me up and I'll hang myself with the same rope. Then you'll surely never have anything."

Dodge was a professional man. His ability to earn a living depended on his cunning, his choices, and how well his men respected him. He could not have a woman shaming him in any way. Reaching out, he grabbed her by the hair and slung her roughly off the wagon.

"Take her to my horse," he instructed his men. "Tie her hands and make sure she does not escape."

"Leave her alone, de Vere," Roane said steadily. "Your anger is with me."

Dodge cast him a baleful glare. "I shall deal with you, have no fear." He flicked a gloved hand at the men holding Alisanne. "Take her."

"De Vere!" Roane boomed; somehow, in the blink of an eye he had leapt onto his feet and now stood towering over Dodge. "Harm her and know that these powers I have, this devil-given curse, shall be fully turned against you and your men. Do you understand me?"

The men holding Alisanne paused, looking at Dodge for guidance. They certainly didn't want to be cursed. But Dodge could not risk losing face; therefore, at the expense of possibly dooming himself, he stood firm against Roane's threat.

"Go ahead," he growled. "Curse me. But my men are still going to take the lady to my horse, and once you are delivered to London, I am going to take her back to Kinlet Castle and marry her. Curse or no curse, there is nothing you can do about it."

Roane wasn't about to back down. "You are mistaken. There is a great deal I can do about it. Are you willing to take that chance?"

Dodge turned away from him. But suddenly he swung around and landed a heavy blow into Roane's abdomen. The man grunted but didn't go down. Angered, Dodge shoved him in the jaw and toppled him to the wagon bed.

"You'll not curse me, you bastard," Dodge growled as he leapt off the wagon. He looked at Alisanne, gasping at the sight of Roane's supine body. "He's already bewitched you, hasn't he? Have no doubt I'll erase him from that pretty head."

Alisanne snarled at him. "You couldn't if you tried."

Roane heard a sharp sound, like a slap to a soft, white cheek. Anger such as he had never known filled him. With incredible agility, he threw himself up to his feet again, only to be met by a violent blow to the head as one of Dodge's men came within range.

In a burst of stars, everything went black.

CHAPTER FOUR

THEY STOPPED SOUTH of Leominster for the night at an inn with no name, but a wooden plaque over the doorway with a badly carved dragon on it. It was a small, dirty place with two rooms over the main hall. Dodge had confiscated one room, placing Alisanne in it with two guards at her door. Of course, he planned on joining her when he had his fill of ale and wenches.

Alisanne knew this and the thought terrified her. She couldn't imagine how she was going to fight off Dodge were he seriously determined to have her. The room itself was in horrible condition; every time she sat on the bed, tiny white bugs leapt onto her. Keeping clear of the lop-sided mattress, there was nowhere to sit other than the floor, and that had urine covering it in all corners and dirt everywhere else. She didn't plan to stay here any longer than she had to and since the moment of her arrival had been thinking of a way to escape.

As far as she knew, Roane was still down in the wagon. She didn't even know where the wagon was, only that it was probably somewhere outside. Dodge had whisked her into the tavern before she saw where his men had deposited themselves for the night and she didn't relish the thought of wandering around in the dark looking for him; the longer she looked, the more likely she was to be caught. But her trepidation was of no matter; the trip to Leominster had been filled with the sounds of Dodge's men abusing Roane and she, riding behind Dodge at the head of the group, had been helpless to stop them. Now she had to make her move.

The plan was obvious. The tiny chamber had a window, but there was a good two story drop to the wet ground below. It was the only way out, save the door, and Alisanne forced herself to touch the lice-ridden bed to gain the sheets from it. The old, stained linen tore easily and she ripped it into strips, tying the strips together to form a rope.

As she tied, she kept glancing out the window to make sure no one was guarding her room from below. Two of Dodge's dogs were in the hallway; she could hear them pawing and scratching and laughing at her door. Her sense of urgency grew as she finally finished the rope and prayed to God that she would be able to descend without breaking her neck. With a final glance out the window to make sure all was clear, she secured one end of the rope to the heavy bead and tossed the other end out.

Her descent was a nightmare. Halfway down, the bed shifted under her weight and dropped her several feet as it slid across the floor. The sudden stop when it rammed into the wall by the window was enough to snap her off the rope, and she landed heavily in the mud below. Her wrist was killing her and her hip was sore, but at least she hadn't broken anything vital. She was rather happy that she was in one intact piece. Scrambling up from the mud, she went in search of Roane.

The night air was cold and heavy with moisture. In early spring, the scent of new foliage was pervasive as she moved through the trees surrounding the inn, glancing at the two or three encampments in the area until she finally realized that the one she sought was the closest to her. It stood among several birch trees with a weak fire offering soft illumination into the night. She could see the wagon, plainly, but she could also see several men milling about. She would have to wait until they went to sleep, but that also meant the chance of Dodge discovering her missing greatened. The longer she delayed, the worse the trouble would be.

The minutes ticked by with painful slowness. Alisanne was aching and wet and stinky, smelling herself and wishing fervently she could take a bath and wash her clothes. So much travel and filth was a terrible thing to a young lady. Dodge's men finally settled down by the campfire, several feet away from the wagon, and Alisanne couldn't wait any longer. The scattered birch trees would offer some hiding places and she crawled, trotted and rolled from tree to tree until she was fairly close to the wagon. The men around the fire were laughing and drinking and she lay down on her stomach, like a snake, and slithered to the tired old rig. She lay there underneath it for several moments, making sure she had not been sighted, before pulling herself onto the bed.

The flat bed was shielded from view by the wooden sidings. It also made it rather dark and, with her bad eyes, difficult to see. But she could clearly see a figure on the slats and she crept forward, sick to her stomach that Dodge's men had thrashed him so soundly. Alisanne could make out the outline of his head and she reached out to touch him, only to find his hair wet and sticky.

"Alisanne," he suddenly hissed. "Christ, I didn't know it was you."

His voice startled her and she clamped a hand over his mouth. "I've come to rescue you," she whispered. "Are you well enough to travel?"

His face was gradually coming into focus as her eyes grew accustomed to the darkness. "Well enough. But are you all right? Did Dodge hurt you?"

A warmth spread over her; he was worrying about her when he was in far more trouble than she could imagine. "I am fine," she said softly. "But we must get out of here."

"Where is Dodge?"

"He's at the inn," she said. "Please, there is no time for talk. We must leave!"

He couldn't argue that, though the circumstances were fuzzy to him. He wouldn't know how feasible their escape was unless he had some facts. "Where are the men who are watching over me?"

"Sitting around a fire several feet away."

"How many?"

"Six, I think."

"Drinking, no doubt."

She nodded. "They're all well on their way to becoming drunk. We can slip away, but we must hurry."

Roane wouldn't argue. He'd already been beaten soundly; if he were to escape and be captured again, he couldn't imagine the punishment would be much worse and suspected he had nothing to lose in an attempt. But Alisanne… the consequences would be severe for her were she to be found a traitor. She had risked so much to come to him, to "rescue" him, as she had put it. He had to get her out of here.

"Untie me, love," he said.

She hastily complied, but with some difficulty. The fact that he had addressed her fondly made her heart feel strange and fluttery, and her fingers were having a hard time picking at the knots. But eventually the rope fell away and for several moments Roane's hands were useless because the ropes had cut off his circulation. He feebly rubbed at them, but Alisanne took charged and massaged them vigorously until some feeling returned. He watched her as she kneaded his palms, emotions sweeping him that he had never thought to feel.

"You have a magical touch," he said softly. "Thank you."

She blushed furiously; he could see it even in the dark. Before she could respond, laughter sounded from the campfire and they instantly stilled. In the warmth of the moment they had almost forgotten about their perilous situation. Roane peered out from a hole in the side of the wagon, studying the men in the distance.

"Come on," he turned away and grabbed her hand.

Roane was stiff and dizzy from the position he had been kept in for more than a day, but he didn't make a sound nor falter as he lifted Alisanne from the wagon and swept her off into the trees. They were clear of the camp and putting more and more distance between them and Dodge's men. But they were also on foot, a considerable disadvantage, and Roane knew they would have to find a horse at some point very soon. They couldn't run all the way back to Kinlet Castle.

… *Kinlet Castle?*

"Alisanne," he said as they ran through a cluster of trees and into a wet clearing, "how many of Dodge's men hold your father?"

"At least four," she panted.

"How many men does your father have?"

"No men," she replied. "We have three servants, though. We provide them with a place to sleep and food to eat, and they do the domestic work."

They slowed their pace as they came to a stream. Roane dropped to his knees and drank deeply. Washing the blood off his face, he glanced at Alisanne. "We must get to your father and John Adam before Dodge does," he said. "In order to do that, we must travel swiftly. We must find a horse somewhere."

She looked puzzled. "But… but you are free now. Why would you go with me to Kinlet Castle?"

His expression was a cross between amusement and annoyance. "Because you risked your family to help me. I cannot let anything happen to them."

She thought on that a moment, torn between him being recaptured and the fate of her father and uncle. But she was very glad he had offered to help her. "What will you do?"

He shook the water off his hands and stood up. "I am not sure yet," he said. "But we must get to Kinlet immediately."

He took her by the hand, his great wet paw closing over her warm fingers. She skipped after him as they headed once again for the shelter of the trees. "Roane," she tried one last time; if something happened to him because of her, she would never forgive herself. "You have more pressing problems of your own. If Dodge catches you again…."

"He won't."

"How can you say that?"

Roane turned and winked at her. "I stole his bait."

α

"YOU *IDIOTS*!" DODGE screamed. He was kicking anything that moved. "Where are they?"

Dodge's men cowered like frightened children. It was the middle of the night and they were all terribly drunk, including Dodge. But he wasn't so drunk that he didn't realize that both of his quarries were missing. He stomped through the embers of the campfire his men had made, scattering sparks everywhere. As the warmth of the inn blazed in the distance, Dodge danced around the muddy ground of the encampment like a madman.

"Where are they?"

"Dodge," one of his men tried to calm him. "They couldn't have gotten far. We shall find 'em!"

"Argh!" Dodge shouted in frustration, swinging his fist at someone who was too slow to move. "Find them and bring them to me so I can cut de Garr's heart out and eat it for breakfast!"

His men were already mounting their horses. The wagon that Roane had been kept in was being hitched to the team of big heavy oxen that pulled it. They didn't move fast, but the man harnessing them would have done anything to redeem himself to Dodge. He was supposed to have been watching over Roane, but he had fallen asleep. Stupidly enough, he hadn't even been drunk.

Dodge would not be comforted by any amount of apologies or reassurance. He ranted and raved, kicking and hitting. His men began to scatter and he screamed at them, furious most of all that he had been denied a night with Alisanne. He had quite been looking forward to exploring her sweet virginal body, but she had had other ideas. She was cleverer than he gave her credit for, slipping out of the window by tying sheets together. He blamed himself for that; he should have kept a closer eye on her. But he fully blamed his men for allowing her to free de Garr; the man was ruthless and cunning, and Dodge knew, even in his drunken stupor, that recapturing him would not be easy.

He grabbed a man on horseback as he raced past him; it was the same man who had assured him that de Garr and the lady hadn't gotten far. He was an older man named Peale who had been with Dodge several years. Dodge knew he was trustworthy and loyal.

"Pick up their tracks," he said, struggling to think clearly through the alcohol. "Hunt them down like animals, but don't hurt them. Leave that to me."

Peale nodded his red head. "Where do ye think they'll go? Back to Church Stretton?"

Dodge shook his head. "Imbecile. They'll not go back there. If it were me, I'd go straight to Kinlet Castle." He scratched his sweaty cheek and seemed to calm dramatically. In fact, he even smiled after a moment as if everything was suddenly right in the world. "As a matter of fact, I think I'll go there and wait for them. Don't bother picking up their tracks, Peale. I know exactly where they're going."

"Are ye sure?"

"Of course," he said with drunken confidence. "Think on it; Lady de Soulant knows we hold her father and uncle. We have threatened to harm them if she did not help us. Wouldn't your first instinct be to go and help your relatives? Of course it would. And now she has de Garr, the big idiot, to help her. We shall capture them both without any additional effort." He suddenly swung about. "Hook!"

A man standing nearby turned at the sound of his name. "My lord?"

"Ride to Birmingham immediately, to the Hospitallers' stronghold of Clavell Hill on the outskirts of the city. Tell His Grace Father Bordeleaux that Roane de Garr is at Kinlet Castle. Tell him to send men immediately to collect him."

Hook appeared confused. "De Garr is at…?"

"Don't argue with me, you fool! Just do it! And tell the good priest to send my reward as well; I'll only turn over de Garr if I have my money."

Hook nodded and fled. Dodge, full of himself, turned to Peale and shook his fist in the air. "I am brilliant!"

Peale wasn't sure how brilliant he was. But by morning, they were all riding like the devil toward Kinlet Castle.

ෆ

ROANE TOOK THEM well off the main road north. Alisanne was exhaust-

ed from walking for hours but he couldn't spare the time to stop and
rest. He finally collected her in his arms and told her to lay her head
against his shoulder and sleep. She was unsure, mayhap even a little
timid at being held so close, but he insisted, so she finally complied.
Wandering through clusters of trees and farmer's clearings, it was close
to dawn when Roane came across a small town with a marketplace that
was already bustling.

Farmers were coming from their fields to sell wagons of turnips,
beets, carrots, peas and lentils. One farmer had huge baskets full of
dried sunflower seeds. Roane came out of the trees and onto the road,
making a strange sight holding a limp lady as he wandered into the
town of small mud-brick buildings and several scattered thatch houses.
A few of the folks gave him a second glance, but most went about their
business.

The sunrise was weak through a heavy bank of morning clouds.
Roane's worn boots were soaked and falling apart as he walked upon
the muddy ground, but his attention was focused not on his poor attire
but on a small building near the edge of the village. It was a single story
structure made of thatch and mud, but already he had seen a couple of
men wander in and out. It could only be a tavern or hostel of some sort,
and he made his way toward it. Even at this time of the morning, the
place was busy.

He tried not to think on the fact that he didn't have any money.
Alisanne needed a place to sleep for a few hours, and he needed the
opportunity to beg, buy or borrow a horse. His mind wandered to the
days when he had a fine charger and armor and never wanted for
anything. Even as a youth, his family had been wealthy landowners and
his father, a powerful warlord. Roane and his older brother had been
pampered with the best of everything money could buy, but to Roane, it
had never been enough. He had always felt he lacked something. When
he found that "something" in the Hospitallers, his father had disowned
him and his brother had inherited everything. He never wished he'd
had his share of the money until now.

The tavern was unbelievably small and smelly. The floor was littered with broken-down chairs and dog feces. With Alisanne slumbering heavily in his arms, Roane walked up to the slovenly barkeep.

"My lady requires a room and a bath," he said. "Though I carry no money, I will be happy to work off the price."

Roane couldn't believe he had swallowed his pride so easily. The barkeep, however, looked at him as if he was lower than dirt. "Get out of here," he snarled. "I've got enough poor customers. I am not runnin' a charity here."

It was a brave thing to say to a man who stood head and shoulders above all the rest. Roane could have spent all day begging and negotiating, but he had not the time nor the patience. Freeing a hand, he snatched the barkeep around the neck and the man gasped in terror.

"Then listen well," Roane growled. "My brother is Baron Coniston and controls all the land from Kendal to Skipton, a massive expanse near the Pennines. He has hundreds of men at his disposal, which I suggest you consider very carefully before refusing me again. Now, you will give me a room and food and send him the bill. Is that clear?"

The man was rightfully fearful in the face of the great blond knight. "But… but you said…!"

"I said I didn't have any money with me. I did not say I was poor. I offered to work in exchange for trade but you, in your ignorance, insulted my honor and now I will tell you exactly what is going to transpire at this time, whether or not it suits you. Is this in any way unclear?"

The man started into Roane's eyes with terror. "No," he gasped.

"Excellent," Roane let him go so that the man almost fell back against the wall in his haste. "Now show me a room. Immediately."

There were only two rooms; one where the barkeep and his wife slept, and the other one, a larger one, for paying guests. While Roane deposited Alisanne on the sagging bed, which was surprisingly clean, the barkeep shouted for his wife to bring hot water and the tub. Roane sat down beside Alisanne as the barkeep started a fire in the small hearth and his fat, wild-eyed wife brought a large, dusty copper tub into the room and began filling it with buckets of hot water from a big pot over the fireplace in the main room.

Roane saw bits of straw floating in the water and was told the tub was used to feed the livestock when not in use as anything else. It took some time to fill it half-full and Roane thought that was good enough, but it took quite a while before the barkeep located a bar of soap. Made from fats and tallow with bits of rose petals and calendula, it was the barkeep's wife's personal soap. From the looks of her, she hardly ever used it. Roane chased them both away and closed the door.

"Are you really Baron Coniston's brother?" Alisanne, who had presumably been asleep during the entire commotion, opened her blood-shot eyes and grinned at him. "Or were you just making that up so he would give us this room?"

Roane tried to look serious but it was difficult when she was smiling so openly at him. "Of course I didn't make it up. I was born and raised at Gargrave Castle in Yorkshire, seat of Baron Coniston."

"But that does not make you the baron's brother. You could have been the lowly son of house servants."

He cocked an eyebrow. "Do I *look* lowly?"

She giggled. "You know better than to ask me that."

He pretended to frown; a foot was sticking out from beneath her gown and he grabbed it, pretending to tear off her shoe and tickle her small foot. "Insolent wench, I'll teach you some respect."

She squealed in delighted terror. He grinned and let go of her foot. "Your bath awaits you, my lady. I thought you might enjoy one."

She sat up on the bed, her shimmering brown hair askew. "You noticed my smell, did you?"

"Everybody smells."

"Not this bad."

"Aye, I'll agree you are hard to miss."

"You should be on my end."

His smile broadened and he put his hand on the door latch. "I would like to be."

He quit the room chivalrously. Alisanne sat on the bed, smiling like an idiot for the longest time. When the giddy warmth passed over her, she shook herself free of her thoughts and tore her mucky, stinky clothes off with eager abandon. It was cold in the room but warm in the tub, even though there was barely enough water to cover her. Still, a bath was a bath. Lathering herself up with the barwife's soap, she scrubbed vigorously with the cheesecloth that had been left for her.

She had soap on her face and in her eyes when she heard the door open. "Who's there?" she demanded.

Roane laughed softly. "Forgive me, my lady, I swear I am not looking. The barwife offered to clean your clothing."

She put the cheesecloth on her face, wiping the suds off. "But I'll have nothing to wear for hours!"

"You would rather put dirty clothing back on?"

She peeped one red eye open. True to his word, he wasn't looking at her. "Well, I suppose not," she said. "But what am I going to wear in the mean time?"

"Trust me."

He closed the door again and was gone. Alisanne doused her whole head in the water to wash off the soap, wondering if she was going to spend the rest of the day wrapped in bed linens to keep from catching her death. She felt rather vulnerable without her clothing.

She sat in the tub until the water was tepid and still no Roane. Climbing out of the tub, she tore the coverlet off the bed and wrapped herself in it, and went to sit by the fire. Running her fingers through her hair, she felt it slowly dry in the warmth of the blaze. Still, no Roane. The morning advanced and the barwife came and brought her bread and tart, white cheese to eat, but said nothing about Roane when Alisanne inquired. She was beginning to think she may have been abandoned.

Finally, her hair was dry in shiny brown waves. The barwife had left her a fishbone comb and she stroked her hair absently. More than perturbed and just the slightest bit fearful, Alisanne nearly jumped from her skin when the door popped open and Roane entered. He moved so quickly that she didn't see what he had in his hands until he thrust it in her face.

"Well?" he demanded. "What do you think?

It was a wonderful garment of yellow linen, very well made and lined with several layers of a soft cotton fabric so the skirt was thick and full. The bodice was laced with a fashionable crisscross corset, the bust line daringly low cut, and the sleeves long and flowing. Holding it up in one hand for her to see, he tossed something on to the bed with his other hand. Alisanne saw a pair of matching slippers.

"Well?" he repeated.

She was stunned. "I… it's lovely," she fingered the linen. "But… where did you get it?"

"From a woman in town who makes gowns and other garments," he said, somewhat quietly. "She is a friend of the barwife's. We determined your dress to be unsalvageable, so I thought mayhap a new one was in order. Do you like it?"

She nodded her head, too surprised to speak for a moment. "Where did you get the money?"

"I traded your gown, and a few other things, for it."

She looked at him suspiciously. "What else did you trade, Roane? You had nothing of value."

He shrugged and laid the dress across the mattress. It was then she noticed that he was not wearing his heavy leather tunic and she pointed at him accusingly. "Your vest. Did you trade it as well?"

He avoided her question. "Try the gown on. I wish to see how it looks. It's been a long time since I've seen a lady in finery."

She reached out and grabbed him before he could leave the room. Her grip was minimal but it was enough to stop him. "Roane," she said softly. "Why did you trade your vest? It must have cost you a small fortune!"

He gave her a lop-sided smile. "It does not matter. It is more important that you be clothed in something suitable."

"But I could have made do with my other gown."

"How old was it?"

She faltered. "A few years, I suppose."

He lifted an eyebrow. "A few years?" he disputed her. "There were worn spots and mended areas all over it. If it wasn't the only gown you had, then it was close to it."

She shrugged and lowered her gaze. "I make due."

He picked up the linen dress and tossed it on her lap. "No more making due," he said with gentle gruffness. "Put it on."

She picked it up, the light of gratitude in her eyes, and he didn't mind losing his leather vest one bit. It had been the one bit of protection he had since he no longer possessed his armor, but he didn't care. It was more important that Alisanne be properly clothed and he held no regrets.

"I am really not your responsibility," she said softly. "I am not sure I can accept this in good conscience. I cannot pay you for it."

"You paid for it when you helped me escape."

He left the room. After a moment's hesitation, she put the gown on, feeling Roane's concern and warmth embracing every inch of her.

CHAPTER FIVE

"**Y**OUR DAUGHTER IS a traitor," Dodge said. "You know, of course, how traitors are dealt with."

He was directing his venom to a small, older man seated near the hearth in the great hall of Kinlet Castle. Kinlet was comprised of a stout pele tower, several out buildings, and a great hall, relatively new compared to some of the castles in the country, having been built by Edward de Soulant's father a mere fifty years before. Unfortunately, the years had seen the de Soulant fortune deteriorate and the once-fine castle looked twice its age without the care and money devoted to its upkeep. There had never been a great deal of soldiers or servants populating the place, but now it was almost deserted. Every time Dodge looked at the place, he could see what his ill-gotten gains could improve.

Edward still could not stomach the thought of his daughter married to a bounty hunter, no matter what it would mean for the good of Kinlet. "Is that what you plan to do, kill her?" he asked, his voice soft. "You'll never gain what you want that way."

Dodge laughed bitterly. "I don't plan to kill her, at least not before the wedding," he said. "But I will punish her. Mayhap not directly, but I will punish her, rest assured."

"What does that mean?'

Dodge leaned forward, his lip curled in an unattractive snarl. "It means that I have sent word to Birmingham. I've told the Hospitallers to come to Kinlet and collect their criminal. It means that your daughter will see her lover taken away in chains and her father thrown in the vault permanently and that, my dear Baron, should be punishment enough."

"You have no heart, de Vere. You are an animal."

Dodge only laughed again and turned away. Beside Edward sat a man with shaggy brown hair, his hazel eyes clear and bright. He watched Dodge pace around the barren great hall, grumbling to the hoodlums that had accompanied him. Father Joseph Ari leaned over to his brother-in-law.

"They're going throw us all in the vault and destroy the key," he whispered.

"Mayhap," Edward said steadily. He dared to glance at the priest. "Tell me of this friend of yours, de Garr. What kind of man is he that my daughter has risked her life for him?"

Father Joseph Ari kept his eyes on the men holding them captive. "A finer man I have never known. Brave, wise, strong. Surely Alisanne saw that in him. And if I know Roane, and I did very well once, he is not running to save his own hide. He is thinking of a way to help us."

"What makes you so sure?" Edward hissed. "My daughter helped the bounty hunters capture him."

"But then she helped him escape," Joseph Ari reminded him. "Nay, Edward, it is my suspicion that Roane is coming to our rescue. For certain, our captors think so."

Edward's brilliant green eyes trailed to the men milling about his beloved hall, spitting on the floor and cursing so that the very walls were tainted. He wished to God that he was stronger, that he possessed a few soldiers, for he would run the ruffians out and hex them should they ever return. But his health was gone, his men gone, and there was nothing to do but wait.

"If that is true," he said, "then de Garr and my daughter are walking into a trap."

Joseph Ari's eyes twinkled. "Roane isn't that stupid. You must have faith, brother. He has outwitted the Hospitallers before, and bounty hunters are mere toys for his intellect. He shall prevail, have no fear."

Edward was silent a moment as he watched one man urinate in the corner of the room near the vestibule that contained a makeshift altar.

He turned away, unable to watch any longer. "I pray that you are correct."

Joseph Ari nodded confidently. "Have faith," he repeated.

℃

ROANE'S LEATHER VEST hadn't merely purchased Alisanne a gown; it had also purchased a rather worn-looking mare that turned out to be swifter than it appeared. Bathed and dressed and re-clad in the old worn cloak that the barwife had actually managed to clean adequately, Alisanne was mounted behind Roane as they cantered gently along the road leading north.

Evening was setting in, not a particularly ideal time to travel, but Roane knew he could waste no more time. There had been no sign of Dodge's men, though they had managed to stay out of site, and it was his suspicion that Dodge, being a logical man, assumed where they were heading. In fact, he suspected that Dodge was already at Kinlet waiting for them. Dodge knew Alisanne would not leave her father to the wolves, and he further knew that Roane more than likely had offered to help her. Thus, Dodge was doing the smart thing by letting his prey come to him, and Roane was planning to do just that.

"Are you warm enough?" he asked Alisanne; she was seated in front of him, wedged up against his broad chest.

She nodded her head, tickling his chin with her silky brown hair. "For the first time in a great while, I am. Mostly because you generate more heat than a roaring blaze."

He grinned. "It is a rare day when I am cold."

"Good," she said. "You stay right there and keep me warm. I am always cold."

To prove her point, she put her arm up and lay her hand against his stubbled cheek. He clapped a big hand over it as if she had shocked him with her touch.

"Christ, woman, you are freezing," he snorted.

She giggled but she did not move her hand. He gradually wound his fingers into her own and brought her hand down, holding it, and her, against him. Alisanne's stomach twisted wildly and it was a struggle to maintain her steady breathing; everything about his touch seemed to ignite her beyond reason. Never in her life had she felt more safe or protected, in strange competition with the dread she felt for her father and for Roane.

It was a peculiar dilemma, compounded by the always-present physical discomfort of her eyes. They were very irritated and the cold air seemed to aggravate them even more. With her free hand, she began to rub them vigorously.

He watched her poke and scratch. "Are your eyes troubling you?"

"They ache."

"How is your sight?"

She shrugged. "Blurred. But that is usual."

She sounded so resigned. But in truth, he'd never once sensed any self-pity from her and refrained from asking again if she would allow him to touch her eyes. Mayhap the truth was that she was afraid of him; many people were. The Hospitallers were, which is why they were intent on persecuting him. It wasn't as if lightning flew out of his fingers or anything; in fact, John Adam was the only person he had ever healed, but it had been enough to convince his sect that he was a grave danger. He knew he was viewed as nothing short of a witch by some.

He pushed those thoughts aside as they rode into the steadily deepening night. He didn't want to think of old wounds right now. Roane knew their traveling in the dark wasn't safe and he wished he had his sword with him. But he wouldn't dwell on the negative; all that mattered was getting to Kinlet Castle, which, he estimated, was still a day's ride away. With the wide berth they had taken to stay off the main road and away from Dodge, they had to make up lost ground.

The dead of night came and went, with Alisanne sleeping dreamlessly in his arms. He watched her, the fragile curves of her face, the long dark lashes that fluttered every so often, thinking that God must have brought her to him for a reason. Thoughts of his curse came back to him once again and he thought mayhap that God had given him this curse, or gift as some called it, for just such a reason. Mayhap the reason was lying in his arms right now and he was too blind to realize it. In spite of her protests or fear or whatever reasons she held to refuse him, he felt at that moment that he needed to heal her more strongly than he had ever felt about anything in his life. It was ridiculous, even sacrilege, for him to possess this talent and not use it for the only valuable reason he'd ever come across.

When the horse slowed to a walk and all was still and quiet around them, Roane timidly put his hand across her eyes, unsure of what he was doing but determined to do it just the same. He found himself praying so hard that tears sprang to his eyes. He hadn't prayed in three years, not since he had denounced God for giving him this horrible curse. But the more he prayed, the easier it became, and he found himself begging for Alisanne's sight. *God, if you've never heard me before, then hear me now. Help me heal her!*

Over the battered road they traveled and Roane had no idea how long he had been praying. He prayed and prayed as if he had been doing it all of his life, the words flowing freely in his mind and his body enveloped by a holy warmth. But the warmth eventually faded, like a dying fire, and suddenly Roane awoke as if from a deep sleep, looking around to notice unfamiliar ground, strange trees and fields. He didn't even recognize the road behind him. His head hurt and his hands were shaking, and he was baffled that he had lost so much time.

Against him, Alisanne continued to sleep peacefully and as he gazed at her, the oddest sense of contentment swept him, as if he had finally done something good and right with his life. He suddenly wasn't sorry in the least that he had been cursed. Still a bit dazed but nonetheless confident, he kissed her on the forehead and prayed again, this time that his attempt had worked.

Pink and gold ribbons of dawn began to fill the eastern horizon. It was freezing at this time in the morning, but Alisanne and Roane were warm and content wrapped in each other. Roane hadn't slept all night and he looked worse for the wear; his face was pale and sporting a two-day's growth of beard. His sea green eyes were dark circled, but they were nonetheless alert. He wished they could stop and rest, but Kinlet wasn't far in the distance and they needed to make it there in quick time.

He was lost to his thoughts when Alisanne stirred in his arms, mewling like a newborn kitten. Her nose wrinkled and she sneezed, and then she immediately began rubbing her eyes. He smiled at her even though she couldn't see him, helping her to sit somewhat upright. She rubbed and rubbed, picking at the morning crust around her lashes.

"Good morning," he said softly. "Did you sleep well?"

She stopped rubbing her eyes long enough to blink them several times. Then she rubbed them again, more furiously. Her eyes were red and tearing when she stopped rubbing, and she suddenly looked around wildly, blinking and blinking.

"My God," she gasped.

Roane's heart leapt into his throat. He was excited and terrified, afraid to ask if his attempt had been successful. He couldn't tell from the look on her face and the suspense was maddening. *Please, God, give us a miracle!*

"What's wrong?" he asked as evenly as he could manage.

She didn't say anything for a moment. Then, her expression crumbled and she began rubbing her eyes again. "Dear God, no," she wept.

Roane was seized with horror. He drew the horse to a rough halt. "Alisanne," he said. "What's wrong? What's happened?"

She pulled her fists from her eyes, looking at her gown, turning her hand over in front of her face, as tears poured down her cheeks. "I can't..." she gasped. "It's worse, Roane, so much worse!"

He felt as if he had been struck. Everything horrible and odious that could befall him suddenly had, and for a moment he could hardly breathe. *It couldn't be...!* He thought desperately. Grasping her face between his hands, he forced her to look at him.

"Look at me, love," he whispered urgently. "Look at me; what do you see?"

She was looking at him, but her red-rimmed eyes were unfocused. "I…," she was struggling against her sobs. "I can see you but you are terribly blurry…." She put her hand out and touched his head. Then she burst into renewed tears. "But it's so foggy. I can barely *see* anything!"

He didn't know what to say. But it was clear to him that his curse was indeed a curse, for the one good thing he had tried to accomplish with it had gone awry. Instead of curing her, he had only made her worse. He'd done this to her as surely as if he had gouged out her eyes himself. Struggling with his guilt, he pulled Alisanne against him fiercely, feeling every sob to his very bones.

"Oh, God," he muttered. "I am so sorry, love. I am so very sorry."

She cried and cried, and he continued to hold her. "Don't worry, love," he murmured into her hair. "'Twill be all right, I promise. You… you needn't worry about anything. I'll take care of… everything, I swear it."

Alisanne didn't reply. She was imprisoned in a world of light and shadow where terror and uncertainty reigned. But she knew, distinctly, that Roane was her rock at this moment. Everything had gone horribly wrong and he remained a steady, comforting constant.

"My… my father," she wept softly. "I can't see enough to… I won't know where or how to…."

He squeezed her to silence her. "You needn't worry about your father," he insisted gently. "I shall make sure he and John Adam are well, and I shall dispatch Dodge and his band of nitwits. This I vow on my oath as a knight."

She rubbed at her eyes again and he gently pulled her hands away; she was only doing more damage. "I never thought it would happen like this," her voice was hoarse. "It had been so gradual that I hardly noticed it from day to day. I always thought I would have more… time."

His guilt was consuming him. He tried to hold her tighter, as if swallowing her into his big protective body. "Don't worry about anything," he didn't know what else to say. "I am with you now. I won't ever leave you."

She looked at him, her eyes red and unclear. "But… you cannot stay. If the Hospitallers find you, they'll kill you, and I cannot go with…."

"Why can't you go with me?"

Her tears were fading as another serious subject took hold. "Because… well, I just can't," she said. "Dodge is…."

He cut her off. "I'll kill Dodge before I'll let him have you. You once promised me your hand in marriage and the barony of Craven if I helped you. Well? Have you gone back on your word?"

Through her panic and pain, she could almost see his face. "No," she hiccuped. "But why should you want to marry me? Look at me, Roane; I can hardly *see*."

"And if I couldn't hear?" he fired back gently. "Would that make you… tolerate me any less?"

She thought on that, reluctant to admit he had a point. "Of course not," she murmured. "If you were deaf, it wouldn't matter at all. I would simply be your ears if you would let me."

He was touched beyond words. "And I shall be your eyes if you would let me.

She didn't know what else to say but the obvious. "I would let you, Roane. I would."

Roane's emotions had the better of him and he couldn't control himself. Pinching her chin gently between his thumb and index finger, he tilted her head as his lips slanted over hers. The kiss was tender at first, inquisitive, but just as quickly as a harsh north wind, it became eager and furious. Roane wound his arms around her and held her so tightly he thought he might crush her, but Alisanne responded to him without the distress of a compressed woman. It was heated and passionate and wonderful, and the world around them faded into oblivion as the embrace deepened.

He was lost. All he could taste, feel or see was Alisanne's sweetness.

It had been so long since he had kissed a woman and, in his opinion, the wait had been well worth the reward. But he couldn't ever remember feeling such fire and in a surge of passion, his tongue pressed into her mouth and he heard her groan but she didn't back down. She explored him as he explored her, and when he could stand it no longer, his mouth moved across her face, kissing and suckling everything in its heated path.

"You are going to be my wife, Alisanne," he breathed. "To the devil with Dodge. He is of no consequence to me."

She could hardly breathe, but it was the most wonderful suffocation she had known. "But… but what of the Hospitallers?"

"The bastards will not have me," he said with conviction. "My brother is Baron Coniston, one of the more powerful northern barons. 'Tis time we showed each other a measure of family loyalty."

He was still kissing her, though far less lustfully. Every taste was incredibly tender. "But I thought you were disowned," she said.

"By my father," he said. "But he is dead. My brother and I were always quite close."

"What are you going to do?"

He stopped kissing her long enough to look at her. Alisanne could see enough of his face to discern his determined expression.

"What I should have done years ago," he said softly. Before she could question him further, he kissed her on the nose and spurred the nag forward. "Come on. We have a date at Kinlet Castle, do we not?"

Alisanne's expression washed with trepidation. "I am frightened for you, Roane. What happens if…?"

He kissed her again, this time to silence her. "You will let me worry about that."

"I must worry about it too."

"Don't you trust me?"

"Of course, but…"

He put a large hand on her hand, pushing it down gently against his shoulder. "Rest, love. Ease your eyes."

He was effectively silencing her and Alisanne reluctantly complied. She lay back against him but did not close her eyes; the world was a blurry vision of shapes and lights and hazy features, and the urge for self-pity was very real. But it wasn't in her nature to sulk, especially when there were others in greater danger. Her mind wandered to her future with Roane, wondering if there would indeed be a future with him. Dodge was so determined to capture him. And her father; she could only pray that he and her uncle were still healthy and safe. There was no knowing how Dodge would treat them after her treachery.

CHAPTER SIX

THE ROAD TO Kinlet Castle came into view close to noon. The clouds had lifted somewhat, leaving the ground wet and green. When the manor itself was in sight, a great stone edifice on the hazy horizon, Roane reined the horse into the shield of a small glen. It was dark and cool, shielded by small hills and clusters of oak trees. He kept a sharp eye out to make sure none of Dodge's men were on patrol, but so far, he'd seen nothing. It only confirmed his suspicions that Dodge was waiting for him; he *wanted* Roane to approach Kinlet without hesitation.

Roane wandered about the glen, formulating his next move. He wasn't about to go strolling right into Dodge's hands, but he wasn't sure what else he could do. Glancing over his shoulder, he watched the pale form of Alisanne as she sat on a rotted stump, eating a piece of stale bread he had given her. His heart sank as he watched her; her eyes were not any better, even after a morning of rest, and his guilt was multiplying. He still couldn't believe what he had done, what God had allowed to happen. It made all of the conflicts with Dodge and his sect pale by comparison.

He walked over to her, kneeling beside her. "I wish it could be more," he said, referring to the bread. "It was all I could scavenge from the barwife. For some reason, she was eager to be rid of us."

Alisanne smiled, her brilliant green eyes bloodshot and strained. "Probably because we never paid her a cent," she quipped.

"My brother will."

She tried not to look doubtful. "You are certain of this?"

"Indeed," he said. "If I was smart, I'd send word to my brother of my current situation and ask his assistance. Dodge is no match for

Baron Coniston and his mighty army."

"What about the Hospitallers?"

He shrugged. "Neither are they."

Alisanne fell silent. "Then if your sect is no match for your brother, why haven't you asked for his help before now? Why haven't you gone home?"

Roane hung his head for a moment, thinking of all the reasons he'd never contacted his brother. They seemed so foolish right now. "I suppose because I was stubborn," he said quietly. "I was content on my own. No one bothered me and I had only myself to think of. And maybe I was punishing him in a sense for not having defended me more forcefully against our father, but I realize now it was because he had a powerful barony to consider. But now...."

"Now *what?*"

He looked at her, realizing as he gazed at her beautiful face that his priorities had changed drastically in the past few days. He was thinking differently, more wholly, than he ever had. "Now there are you and your father and uncle to contend with," he said. "There is no longer just me. I would be wise not to believe I can do this alone."

She smiled, a delicate pink shade creeping into her cheeks. He was declaring his intentions for her, though he'd danced around the subject for the better part of a day, more clearly than before. He was including her, wanting to be a part of her, and she of him. It was as if he was already planning their lives together.

"What are you going to do now?" she asked.

He was, in a sense, glad that she hadn't pressed him on that subject. The truth was, he wasn't even sure how to explain the bond he felt with her, or why in fact his priorities had changed so, only that they had. Standing up, he rested his fists on his hips as his gaze expertly scanned the area. "I think I shall have a look around and become familiar with the area. Then I shall approach the castle. Can you tell me about its defenses?"

She nodded. "We have curtain walls but no moat," she said. "The walls are very tall. You won't be able to get in unless the portcullis is raised. There's no secret entrance or additional gates."

He grunted unhappily. "One way in, one way out."

"Aye."

"And what structures does it have?"

"One main building that contains a great hall, three rooms for my father and I to live in, and a kitchen on the lowest level. There are also stables and soldiers' residences against the walls and incorporated into the gatehouse."

"Where is the vault?"

"In the lower level of the gatehouse."

He tried to picture it in his mind, but he needed to see the actual layout. "Thank you," he said, bending down to kiss her tenderly on the cheek. "Finish your bread. I shall return."

She looked up, trying so desperately to focus on him. "Please be careful, Roane. The country is open and you'll be easily seen."

He kissed her again, this time on the lips. He had only meant it to be quick and sweet, but she clung to him feverishly. Lacking any control of his own, Roane picked her up, holding her tight against him, hungrily devouring her lips, tongue, cheeks and neck. Alisanne gasped with delighted torment as he nibbled her shoulder, very aware that her new gown was deliciously low cut and the swell of her full white breasts were open and exposed. Roane was aware of it too; soon enough, his furious pace had slowed and his tongue began to move slowly and sensuously across the top of the rounded flesh.

The sensations were beyond her wildest imagination. Somehow his chin pushed her neckline down and his face was between her breasts, suckling and licking. In the heat of their passion, he had set her to stand on the stump and she could feel his hands pulling at her bodice, sliding it down over her arms and down her torso until she was naked from the waist up. Roane's hands were on her breasts, kneading and exploring as his mouth took in a tender nipple. Alisanne groaned softly and Roane merely grinned; he had never tasted anything so utterly wonderful in his entire life and his joy was without words.

Even so, there wasn't the luxury of time for this and he knew he should stop immediately. But he couldn't seem to muster the will. She was too fine, too wonderful, and his desire was overwhelming him. It wasn't so much that he hadn't had a woman in fourteen years; it was the mere fact that Alisanne was the perfect woman for *him*. The gown slithered off further and further, and his mouth worked its way down her torso until it came to the soft fluff of hair between her legs. Alisanne's grip on his hair tightened and he paused, looking up at her.

"I'll stop now if you wish," he said hoarsely.

She half-shook her head, half-shrugged. "I… we probably should, but…."

He suddenly took a look at their surroundings; here she was, standing naked on a tree stump in the middle of a glen. Not only had he cursed her sight, but now he was being an animal and ravaging her in the open for all to see. Guiltily, he pulled her dress up, modestly covering her.

"I am sorry, love," he whispered, kissing her and helping her dress. "I couldn't stop myself. It seemed the most natural of things to do."

She smiled, somewhat nervously. "To me, too, though I've never had a man touch me as you have."

He lifted her off the stump and helped her sit. "That is a good thing," he said. "I'd have to hunt him down and kill him."

She giggled, relieving the heat of the moment. "Have no fear, then."

He smiled, though she really couldn't see it. He did, however, kiss her again, this time on the cheek. "If I could have my way with you here and now, I most certainly would," he whispered against her ear. "But I should not like to explore your beauty for the first time without proper benefit of a bed and privacy, of which you deserve both."

She could only touch his cheek in response, thankful of his chivalry. "Hurry back to me, Roane," she said softly.

"I will," he said. He suddenly thought she looked rather wan. "What's the matter?"

She shook her head. "There is nothing," she said. Then she paused. "'Tis just that… well, I can't see very well and if a wild animal comes at me…."

"You don't want to be left alone."

"Not for long."

He understood completely, cursing himself that he wasn't more considerate of her fear. "I know you are frightened. But I promise I'll be back as soon as possible. You should be all right here, for a while."

He strolled off, his eyes scanning the ground, the trees as if searching for something. Alisanne could hear him and see his shape as he moved about. After several moments, she heard snapping and cracking, the distinct sounds of a tree breaking. When he returned, he placed a large stick in her hands.

"There," he said. "For protection. Just swing it at anything that moves."

She felt much better. "I will."

He kissed her again and was gone.

The day passed with tremendous slowness after that. Alisanne really had no sense of time, only knowing that Roane's absence seemed forever. It was actually a mild day, which was surprising for a volatile season like spring, so the conditions of her wait were not unpleasant. In fact, it gave her a good deal of time to think.

A week ago she had been in the throes of terror as her father and uncle were held hostage and she had been forced into aiding a band of bounty hunters to capture their quarry. Her only concern had been for her father and Uncle John Adam, not for a faceless knight named Roane de Garr. Now she was horribly concerned for all three, terrified that Roane would get himself captured, or worse. And the most terrible part was that she knew none of this would have happened if it hadn't been for her. Roane would still be safe on his mountain retreat, hidden from the world that wanted to torture him.

She did not regret going to Church Stretton, however. Had she not gone, she would have never known the most wonderful man, she was sure, in the world. He had been so standoffish and cruel at first, but he had had every right to be suspicious of her. Now he was so tender and warm that the very thought of him was enough to melt her. She thought of the children they would have, the strong sons that would continue the de Garr lineage. She hoped they would be comfortable with one another, that he wouldn't grow tired of her as the years passed, especially now that her sight was so terrible.

She thought about his reasons for marrying her. Truthfully, he'd never given her a logical one. His insistence to marry her even though her sight was gone seemed odd. But mayhap not so odd when one considered he had been disowned by his father. Alisanne had offered him the Craven barony once if he would only help her; he had accepted the offer even after everything that had happened. Mayhap he didn't want her at all; mayhap it was only the barony he was interested in now that his father had left him penniless and titleless.

They were dim, confusing thoughts in her suddenly dim, confusing world. She didn't know Roane at all, though she sensed he was genuine and true. Still, had she given him a golden opportunity he could not refuse? She truly didn't know. And if he was truly so fond of her as he seemed to profess, why hadn't he offered to heal her with his magnificent gift? Mayhap he wanted to keep her in the dark. Mayhap he, like Dodge, was only after one thing.

The sound of an approaching horse roused her from her thoughts. It was very faint at first but quickly grew in volume. Alisanne turned in the direction of the sound, seeing nothing but blurry trees. There was movement among them.

"Roane?" she called, relieved. "Where have you been?"

There was no reply. Alisanne's heart suddenly leapt into her throat. "Roane?"

The horse was nearly upon her. Blindly, she stumbled up from the stump, wielding the stick like a weapon. The person on the horse merely knocked it out of her hand.

"Well, well," came an unfamiliar voice. "What have we here?"

He sounded particularly pleased and Alisanne felt the blood rush from her head. *Oh, no, it can't be!* She thought wildly.

"Stay away from me!" she cried.

Peale couldn't believe his luck. He gazed at the wild-eyed lady and laughed bitterly. "Not bloody likely. Where's yer friend?"

She clenched her jaw. "I don't know."

"Don't lie to me."

"I am not," she practically shouted. "I don't know where he is. He went off and left me hours ago."

She could hear him dismount and move toward her. "He'll show himself soon enough now that we have ye. Damn bit of good fortune, I'd say, comin' across ye as pretty as a bird waitin' to be plucked."

She backed up, stumbling but catching herself in time. "How did you find me?"

"It wasn't difficult. Yer on Kinlet land, are ye not?"

She didn't know if she was or not. Not being able to see clearly denied her the ability to distinguish landmarks she had known since childhood. "Roane said he hadn't seen any patrols," she said, taking another uncertain step back. "Where did you come from?"

"Dodge thought de Garr would be stupid enough to come here. He's had us keep watch, but not outright search. Looks like he was right."

He stepped up his advance. Alisanne tried to run away, but she couldn't see her path very well and after a few steps, tripped and fell on her face. A rock cut her just above the right eye and her head buzzed strangely. Peale picked her up roughly.

"Ye've caused enough trouble," he growled. "Better come along peacefully now and not make it any worse."

Alisanne felt sick and dizzy. She wanted so badly to fight, but with her eyesight, it was extremely difficult. "My father," she breathed. "Is he well? You haven't hurt him, have you?"

Peale yanked her toward his horse but she stumbled again. He pulled her to her feet so harshly that her head snapped. "Your father is well enough, considerin',", he said. "What's the matter with ye, trippin' like a fool?"

"I can't see very well," she said quietly, the flush of embarrassment and terror flushing her cheeks. "My eyes... something has happened to them."

Peale looked closely at her. He waved his hand in front of her face; she followed the movement a bit, but seemed to be having trouble focusing. They were very red and irritated. He suddenly lashed out and squeezed her breast, roughly. Alisanne screamed.

"Then ye can't see when I do that?" he laughed.

She pulled back from him, struggling to cover herself against his attack. "Stop it!"

He lashed out another hand and pinched her buttocks. Alisanne yelped, trying to evade him. He laughed heartily and grabbed her by the arm again.

"Enough play, wench," he said. "As much as I'd like to roust ye, Dodge will be wantin' ye for himself. We'd better get along."

He didn't bother to seat her on his horse; tossing her across the saddle like a sack of grain, he mounted behind her and tore off in the direction of Kinlet.

CHAPTER SEVEN

ROANE RETURNED TO the glen much later than he had hoped. It was only mid-afternoon, but Alisanne had been alone a great while and in order to make peace with her, he had caught a rabbit for their meal. Still, his day of reconnaissance had been very productive. He had scouted all the roads in and out of Kinlet and memorized their lines, which would be very important in the event of their escape. He hadn't gotten very close to the castle itself because there seemed to be some activity going on and he did not want to tip his hand. Moreover, the factor of Alisanne's faded sight made him want to get back to her as quickly as possible. His guilt was as great as it had been, mayhap even more now that it had time to simmer.

The fat rabbit had been an easy kill. It was the only meat he had had since the hare Alisanne had used to lure him out of the abbey. He looked forward to sharing a meal and more time with her. In spite of all the terrible things that had happened over the past few days and hours, he was coming to feel very good about the relationship developing between them, looking eagerly towards their time together. The past few days had been heaven and hell, all in one fell swoop.

His horse was showing distinct signs of exhaustion as he made his way into the shady, secluded glen. Almost immediately, he spied the stump he had last seen Alisanne sitting upon. It was empty. Spurring the horse forward, he thought mayhap she has wandered away out of sheer boredom and he began calling her name, listening to his voice echo through the trees. After several minutes of shouting for her, his mind began to creep with foreboding suspicions.

He returned to the stump. Dismounting the horse, he tethered the animal and took off on foot to look for her. Calling and calling, she still did not answer him. He crossed a small stream and headed into a dense cluster of trees but still, he did not see or hear her. Frustration and concern mounted. Going back to his starting point, the stump, he suddenly noticed the hoof prints on the ground.

Roane dropped into a crouched position. He fingered the rather large hoof prints, his heart sinking and his mouth going dry. He could see the hooves move off toward the mouth of the glen, and presumably towards Kinlet. He closed his eyes tightly for a brief moment, as if to ward off what his eyes and senses were telling him. The signs were horrifyingly obvious. Somehow, while he had been out scouting, someone had happed across Alisanne and abducted her.

His hands were fists upon his thighs, pounding out his frustration and fear. How could he have been so stupid? He stood up, unsteadily, and wandered about like a confused man, his mind whirling with all of the possibilities at hand. He had thought himself so clever to leave her here, far from those who could harm her, but instead the joke had been on him. He had been the failure, the second strike against him where Alisanne was concerned. His curse seemed to be growing, touching other aspects of his life now, and he could feel his confidence wavering. Never in his life had he lacked faith in his abilities or decisions until now.

He had to get to her. He couldn't stand around here and lament what had happened, but it was difficult to think clearly through all of the physical agony he was experiencing. His stomach twisted and his heart churned painfully. Emotions he had never experienced were making him crazy with fear, but he knew a craze such at this could be deadly. He had to calm down and think like a rational man. He wouldn't do Alisanne, or himself, any good if he was dead.

He snatched the horse where it stood grazing several feet away. Mounting lithely, he spurred the tired old horse in the direction of Kinlet, all the while knowing he had no plan, but hoping one would come to him as he rode. Out of the glen and onto the muddy road, he was so focused on the castle in the distance that he failed to see a small party of incoming riders trailing behind him less than a quarter mile away. They, too, were heading for Kinlet, flying the black and white banners of St. John the Baptist. The Hospitallers.

Roane's horse tripped on a rut in the road and immediately came up lame. Roane dismounted and felt the animal's right front forelock, but not without a good deal of frustration. Not having a horse, even an old tired one, would make his life far more difficult. But the beast was exhausted and Roane knew there was no hope; the leg was already swollen. Now, on top of everything, he had to find another horse somehow. He was so lost to his own turbulent thoughts that by the time he spotted the incoming party of warrior-priests, it was already too late. Father Tertious Bordeleaux was at the head of the procession and knew Roane de Garr very well on sight; their gazes locked in an instant maelstrom of surprise and fury.

Roane wasn't sure how to react. He could hardly believe what he was seeing yet in truth, he shouldn't have been surprised. Several soldiers had their crossbows trained on him and he knew running would be futile. Oddly, a strange calm settled over him as he envisioned men he had once fought beside, arm to arm, men he had trusted with his life. So many memories flooded him all at once, good and bad. The men met his gaze, most of them recognizing him, their expressions torn between warmth and fear. It had been a long trek for them as well; chasing a man they had once admired, now had come to fear.

Roane simply stood there as the party closed around him in an ominous embrace. Bordeleaux reined his horse close, appraising Roane as carefully as he would appraise the devil himself. Bordeleaux was a thin man with long brown hair and dirty robes, resembling, in fact, every representation Roane had ever seen of Jesus Christ. Roane thought the man looked that way intentionally. In any case, though the Hospitallers practiced poverty and medicine, they rode fine horses in direct contradiction to their vows. And they also had enough money to pay bounty hunters to track down one of their own.

Strangely, Roane thought of his father as he stood gazing at the dirty, smelly warrior-priests astride expensive chargers; Darwich David de Garr, second Baron Coniston, had very nearly cried when his youngest son had told him of his choice in life. The older man had pleaded for hours with the strong-willed lad, begging him not to join a church sect. *They're all corrupt, Roane, can't you see?* He had pleaded. No, Roane couldn't see. Darwich was afraid the Hospitallers would take all of Roane's inheritance if they knew he had such a thing. It had been the most difficult thing of Darwich's life to disown his son. But it had been for his own good, and the good of Coniston. Roane saw all of that, very clearly, now for some reason.

They're all corrupt....

Had he really been that foolish? Of course he had. But his motives had been pure, to serve God and practice the arts of healing. This rag-tag band of hooligans didn't look like anyone he would want to associate with now. They looked like everything his father had ever warned him about.

"Let me guess," Roane said slowly, with contempt. "Someone told you that I would be at Kinlet."

Bordeleaux smiled humorlessly, his high-pitched voice full of venom. "What a striking coincidence to find you along this road."

Roane looked at him. "Not so coincidental considering that Dodge de Vere is waiting for me at yon distant castle. Trapping me between both enemies, as it were. So which rabid dog gets me first?"

Bordeleaux shrugged his thin shoulders. "We have unfinished business, Roane," he said frankly.

"Our business is quite finished. I am no longer a Hospitaller or subject to your laws."

"Not so. We never *did* finish our business."

Roane could feel his anger rising. "After three years, I should have thought you would grow bored of this foolish pursuit and focus your attention elsewhere. I am not dangerous, nor have I ever done anyone, save the enemy, harm. Why should you make it your life's goal to hunt me so?"

Bordeleaux's moderate expression of tolerance vanished. He motioned to the men behind him. "We have what we came for," he said. "Take him. And watch his hands; the devil works through those hands. Mind you don't find yourself a victim of his witchcraft!"

The men seemed awed; Bordeleaux fed upon their fear. "He's a minion of Satan. It is our duty, as brothers, to purge the earth of his malignancy. Take him and be quick about it!"

Roane instinctively stiffened; they were not going to take him without a fight. His comrades knew this; one man dismounted, an older man who had known Roane many years. He held out a quelling hand to the others, silently gesturing for them to wait. He then approached Roane carefully, his craggy features laced with remorse.

"Roane," he said softly in greeting.

Roane didn't dare let his guard down, but he could hardly refuse to acknowledge him. "Albert," he replied.

Albert stopped a few feet away, knowing that Roane would be wary of anyone coming too close. He put out his hand in a helpless gesture. "Bordeleaux will take you dead or alive," he pleaded softly. "Please come peacefully. 'Twill be better for you."

"Do you believe I am a devil, Albert?"

"You are my friend, Roane."

"That was not an answer."

Albert stared at him for a moment. "Please, Roane…."

"Answer me."

Albert's friendly warmth was now peppered with confusion. "All I know is that John Adam was going blind and you healed his eyes."

"Jesus healed the blind. Did that make him a devil?"

"But you are not Jesus, Roane."

"I am not the devil, either."

"He's a false prophet!" Bordeleaux roared, interrupting them. "Albert, subdue him, as is your duty!"

Albert looked to his liege and then back to Roane again. His indecision was blatantly evident. "Please, Roane. Don't make this hard on yourself."

Roane didn't say anything for a moment. He had no options left, except to fight, and that would only spell his demise. He'd be no good to Alisanne or her family if he was dead. Bordeleaux was looking for an excuse to kill him, to stamp out his evil, but Roane would not give him the opportunity. He was trapped. Without a word, he put his wrists together, held his hands out, and moved toward Albert in a gesture of submission.

"He's going to touch him!" Bordeleaux suddenly screamed. "Stop him, oh, *stop him!*"

The men panicked. A crossbow launched in the commotion; the long, wicked arrow struck Roane in the chest, sending him to the ground in a hard crash of flesh and bone. As he lay upon the muddy road staring up at the cloud-spattered sky, he could hardly believe he'd been hit.

His brain slowly fogged and his blood ran heavy into the dirt, and he knew he was going to die. His last cognizant thoughts were of Alisanne; he regretted so badly that he would never see her again. Now that he'd found what he'd waited his whole life for, he thought it a rather wicked trick of God to separate them so suddenly. They had so much potential as lovers and friends. Rather than pray for himself, he muttered a prayer that God would watch out for her. He didn't know why God should listen to a cursed man, but at least he had to try.

He could hear Albert's voice, growing more distant by the second. His ears seemed to be strangely muffled, his body lethargic and weightless at the same time. Gradually, the world faded away until there was nothing left but light and shadow, and then everything turned to black.

CB

ALISANNE SAT WITH her father and uncle on the floor of the great hall of Kinlet. The stone was cold and hard against her backside, but she would not show her discomfort. In fact, all of her energy was directed at comforting her father who, upon realizing his daughter's sight had grown worse, fell into a numbing mood of grief.

She tried to assure him everything would be fine. Roane would heal her when given the opportunity. No, she hadn't asked him yet, but she was positive he would. Father Joseph Ari heartily agreed. Edward felt better, but not entirely. To see his beautiful daughter blinded, lusted after by a bounty hunter and confined to a corner of his father's great hall made him ill with sorrow. He could hardly believe his life had come to such a crossroads. There seemed no other path to take.

Alisanne tried not to give in to her father's misery. Edward was a normally gloomy man as it was, but his self-pity was a cloaking, devouring mood. She sat next to him, feeling his heat, listening to the quiet conversation between him and Father Joseph Ari and wondering what had become of Roane. Surely he had returned to the glen by now. She could only suspect that he was formulating a brilliant plan of rescue.

The hope in her heart surged and crashed as her crazed thoughts returned. She thought of tall, immensely powerful Roane, so determined to marry a woman with poor sight. Certainly he wanted to rescue her so that Dodge could not marry her first and claim Kinlet for his own. It seemed nightmarish that she had become a trophy in a bizarre tug-of-war. And it was so terrible for her that she had feelings for Roane, emotions that she should very well forget. She told herself that she didn't need him, or anyone else, for that matter. She would rather be a blind spinster than an object of greed and indifference. But the thought of being without Roane nearly killed her.

"Where was Roane when you last saw him?" Her father was speaking to her.

Alisanne turned to him; all she could see was a shadowed outline. "He left me in the glen by the fork in the road," she said. "He left me to go and look around, to see if he could spy Dodge or his men."

"That was the last you saw of him?"

She nodded her head. "I don't know where he is."

Edward eyed the men milling casually about his great hall. "They haven't asked you?"

"No. Don't you find that strange?"

Edward sighed ominously. He wondered what the bounty hunters knew that he didn't. They had, after all, spent considerably more time around the pair. "Alisanne, did you and Roane… that is to say, what is your relationship with him?"

She blushed furiously and looked away. "His is… kindly towards me."

"*How* kindly?"

A bolt of anger shot through her. "He's never been anything but chivalrous, father. If you think…."

Edward put a hand on her. "I don't think anything, which is why I asked."

Joseph Ari was watching them both, analyzing the expression on Alisanne's face. "He warmed to you, did he not?"

She shrugged and Joseph Ari laughed softly. "Do you know I have never seen that man warm to anyone? All of the beautiful exotic birds in the Holy Land could not turn his head, but a sweet English pigeon certainly did."

He snorted with mirth and Alisanne's blush deepened. "It wasn't like that at all, uncle."

"The bounty hunters know he took a liking to you, do they not? That is why they haven't asked what you know of him. They hope to lure him here."

Her vacant eyes were wide, fearful with realization. "Lure?"

"Bait."

Her voice was a whisper. "I was the bait once before."

"Now, for a different reason, you are again."

Alisanne closed her eyes, squeezing off the tears. Since she had thrust herself into Roane's life, he had been abducted, beat, tormented and starved. She was a curse upon him, like a nasty vicious pox that would attack and attack until it ruined him.

"They'll kill him," she murmured. "If he comes here, they'll *kill* him!"

Edward had nothing to say to that, but Joseph Ari tried to be positive. "Roane is a bright man, Alisanne," he said quietly. "You must have faith that...."

He was cut off by a shout from the main entrance. Abruptly, the bounty hunters scattered, including Dodge, racing like mad toward the door. From where Alisanne and the others sat, it was difficult to see what was transpiring and even more difficult to hear. But it was obvious there was a great deal of activity taking place in the ward.

"What's happening?" Alisanne asked her father.

Edward shook his head, his brilliant green eyes focused on the carved doorway at the end of the room. "I don't know," he replied. Then, "Wait! They're carrying someone... they're dragging someone inside."

Alisanne was swept with terror. Who else could they be dragging but someone they had captured, someone reluctant to accompany them without a fight? There could only be one possible answer. Before she could utter her fears, Joseph Ari abruptly hissed.

"Roane!"

Alisanne was on her feet, stumbling blindly in the general direction of the door. Her heart was in her throat, the taste of panic in her mouth. Her father leapt up, grasping her, holding her back even as she fought valiantly against him.

"No, Father!" she grunted. "I must go to him, I must!"

Edward caught a glimpse of the massive blond man with an arrow hilt protruding out of his chest. His heart sank. "No, my dear, no," he said as gently as he could. "He's... he's injured and...."

Dodge was standing over Roane, watching Alisanne struggle against her father. His expression was smug. "He's not dead, not yet," he said loudly. He turned to Bordeleaux as the lanky man entered the hall. "I get paid whether he is dead or alive. I have delivered him to you as I said I would."

Bordeleaux held up a quelling hand. "And I have brought your reward. Excellent work, de Vere."

Dodge smiled triumphantly. Alisanne broke away from her father and staggered across the floor, following the shapes and sounds until she literally tripped over Roane's arm. Her father tried to stop her, but he was too late. Alisanne fell on Roane and nearly impaled herself on the arrow shaft in the process.

"My God," she gasped, her hands drifting over him protectively. "What have they done to you?"

Roane was ghostly pale, deeply unconscious. Alisanne didn't have to see him; she could feel him, already familiar with the lines of his strong arms and the texture of his hair. And she could smell him, the sweet musk that belonged only to him. Forgot were her crazy thoughts of Roane's greed and ambition; even if it was true, still, she couldn't help her own feelings for him.

"Roane," she whispered. "Don't worry, my darling. I'll take care of you. You'll be well again, I swear it."

He remained deathly still. Disoriented by her lack of sight yet determined to take charge of the situation, she began barking orders as if she were not a prisoner in her own home.

"Take him up to my room," she snapped to the men standing about. She could feel her father lingering behind her and she turned to him. "I'll need water and witch hazel and thread. And I'll also need a mustard and willow poultice. Hurry, father!"

Edward looked at Dodge and Father Bordeleaux. They seemed rather unemotional about the entire thing. "You didn't bring him here so that we could watch him die, did you?" he demanded softly. "You *will* let us help him."

Bordeleaux nodded his dirty head. "We brought him here because he would surely die before we got him back to Birmingham," he said coldly. "He must be of moderate health in order to face his trial."

"Trial?" Alisanne tried to fix on the outline of the man who was speaking; she didn't like the sound of his words at all. "What trial? He has done nothing."

Father Bordeleaux gazed distastefully at her. He thought on ignoring her but for some reason decided not to. Mayhap it was the lustful gleam in her eye as she gazed at Roane that inflamed him, prompting him to answer. "Tell the wench who this man is."

Dodge was already counting his money in his head, planning on the improvements he would be making to Kinlet. It didn't seem to bother him at all that his intended was fawning over a dying man. "Roane de Garr is a false prophet. He has powers wrought from hell, as you well know."

"That's not true!" Alisanne hissed. "He's no more a demon than you are, Dodge. What he has is a God-given gift, or are you all too ignorant to realize that?"

Dodge's good mood wavered in the face of her insult. "You are the one who is ignorant," he growled.

He stood there a moment, watching Alisanne's protective stance, like a lioness guarding her young. He should have felt jealousy to some extent, but more than anything, he felt anger. Roane de Garr was trying to take away what was rightfully his and he would allow no man to steal what he had worked so hard for. Alisanne was his, no matter what foolish emotions were involved otherwise.

Dodge was gripped with a surge of fury. All of his plans had come to fruition with the exception of one, and he intended to remedy that immediately. He could not risk delaying any longer. Like a snake striking prey, he reached out and grabbed Alisanne, yanking her away from Roane's supine form. As she gasped and struggled, he turned to Bordeleaux.

"You are a priest," he bellowed. "Marry us now!"

Bordeleaux expression didn't waver, but Alisanne, Edward and Joseph Ari crowed with horror.

"Dodge!" Edward breathed. "Not now, not with all of this madness going on. There will be...."

"Time enough later?" Dodge finished for him, snorting cruelly.

"Not a chance, old man. I am not going to wait for you or your foolish daughter to somehow elude me."

"I gave you my word," Edward said calmly. "We will not elude you, but this is hardly the circumstance for a wedding."

"It's the perfect circumstance," Dodge snapped, his calloused hand biting into the tender flesh of Alisanne's upper arm. He jabbed a finger at Bordeleaux, a sinister, demanding gesture.

"Marry us!"

CHAPTER EIGHT

"**S**HHH," HE HEARD soft voices in his dreams, sweet visions in his dark-hazed mind. "Don't move, Roane. You'll tear your stitches open."

He struggled with a groggy, sickening fog that seemed to cloak his body like a numbing vise. There was pain, though he wasn't sure where it was coming from. He only knew that it was everywhere, and even opening his crusty eyes proved to be a chore.

But open he did. The first thing that came into focus was Alisanne's beautiful face, her brilliant green eyes so red and irritated. "Alisanne," he breathed. "What... where...?"

She stroked his face tenderly. "It's all right, my dearest," she murmured. "You are going to be fine. Father and I have taken care of you."

Roane was completely confused. He blinked, perusing the sparsely furnished room until his gaze came to rest on a small, gray-haired man standing at the foot of his bed. The man smiled timidly.

"Sir Roane," he said. "My daughter has told me a good deal about you. Welcome to Kinlet."

Kinlet. The last conscious events flooded Roane's mind and he remembered the Hospitallers and the arrow penetrating his body with painful clarity. Anxiety surged through his lethargic limbs and in spite of his physical state, he struggled to sit up.

"Kinlet?" he repeated hoarsely. "Damnation, what's happened? Alisanne, where's...?"

She put one hand over his mouth, the other on his shoulder, trying to hold him down. "Please, Roane, you must be quiet," she begged softly. "I will explain everything, but you must calm down."

He didn't have the strength to fight her at the moment. In truth, the room was spinning and he forced himself to lie flat against the pillows. From the corner of his eye, he caught movement in the shadows and turned to see a familiar face emerge into his line of sight. Father Joseph Ari smiled warmly at his old friend and held out his hand. Immediately, it was as if they had never been apart.

"Roane," he said fondly. "I must say you were looking better the last time that I saw you."

Roane smiled weakly, glad to see his faithful old companion. "I was feeling better, too," he said. "Alisanne said that Dodge tortured you to find out where I was hiding. I am so sorry, my friend."

Joseph Ari waved him off. "Don't be. It should be I who am sorry for telling them what they wished to know. It was betrayal, Roane, and I must beg your forgiveness."

Roane patted his arm in a weak gesture. "There is nothing to forgive," he glanced at Alisanne. "Had you not been so cowardly, I would have never met the lady. For that, you have my eternal thanks."

Alisanne blushed furiously. Roane had never seen cheeks flush red so rapidly and her discomfort amused him. Joseph Ari grinned, watching the expression of adoration on Roane's face and amazed that the somewhat hard man he had known had the capacity for such emotion. But it would make what was to come that much more difficult.

"Roane," he said, not wanting to ruin the moment, yet knowing there were pressing matters at hand. "We are in a bit of a quandary, as you have probably suspected."

Roane reached out to take Alisanne's hand before replying. He seemed to draw strength from it. "I can guess," he said. "What is the situation?"

Joseph Ari stood back from the bed and began to pace. He didn't like what he was about to say. "First and foremostly, the Brothers are here. They intend to take you back to Clavell Hill when you are well enough to travel."

Roane truly had no idea how badly he was injured. "When will that be, by your estimation?"

The priest shook his head. "Weeks at least. Your chest wound was very bad. Though a rib deflected it from doing any real damage, you lost a great deal of blood and a moderate infection followed. Had Alisanne and Edward not stayed up day and night drawing the poison from you, you would surely not be here."

Roane's eyes drifted to Alisanne's sweet face. "How long have I been unconscious?"

He had directed his question at her. "Almost eight days," she said softly. "We didn't think you would ever wake up, Roane. You were so very sick."

He squeezed her hand and turned back to Joseph Ari. "We must think of a way to stall them. I must be stronger if we are going to escape them."

Joseph Ari didn't say anything for the moment. Edward, standing at the foot of the bed, spoke up. "It is more complicated than that, I am afraid."

Roane looked at him. "Why say you?"

Edward cleared his throat, trying to think of the proper words. He thought mayhap that his brother-in-law should tell him, but Joseph Ari seemed unwilling or unprepared to move forward. The priest lingered beside the bed, his head bowed and his attention diverted. Edward could see, at the moment, that he had no support from him.

"We cannot go with you should you flee," he said finally. "At least, my daughter and I cannot. But you can take my brother. I encourage you to do so."

Roane's expression immediately hardened. "I am not leaving you or your daughter behind. There is no question that when I go, I take all of you with me."

Edward scratched his head wearily. "It simply isn't possible, Sir Roane. Believe me when I say I would like nothing better than for you to take Alisanne away from here, but it is infeasible. She cannot go."

Something low and disturbing rumbled through Roane's chest. The growling, anxious surge gave him the strength to push himself onto one elbow, his eyes blazing with challenge.

"She is going and you will not stop me," he rumbled.

"Roane," Joseph Ari found his tongue. "Please understand that there is more at stake now. Alisanne must stay here."

Ill or not, Roane would not take no for an answer. He glared daggers at his old friend. "She is *not* staying here. I'll kill anyone who tries to stop me."

Edward and Joseph Ari passed glances. At Roane's side, Alisanne suddenly burst into low, body-wracking sobs. Startled, Roane struggled to put his arm around her without passing out from the pain. "What's wrong, love? What is it?" he whispered to her.

Her hands were over her face as she caved like a weakling onto his shoulder. "They're right, Roane," she gasped. "I cannot go with you."

His face was in her hair. He could sense something terrible but intangible, unable to put his finger on the source of their mystery and pain. "Why can't you?"

She pulled away from him; it was the hardest thing she had ever had to do. More than anything she wanted to give in to his strength, his life, but she knew she could not. She could never again depend on him, as sweet as the dream had once been. Now she was resigned to a life that would be as terrible and desolate as she could imagine. She tried to stop crying.

"Because I am Dodge's wife," she whispered.

Roane stared at her. As pale as he was, he paled further and his body began to shake with horrible, fitful jolts. "What?" he demanded in a short, painful breath.

"Bordeleaux married them on the day they wounded you," Joseph Ari said bitterly. "She has been Lady de Vere for over a week now."

Roane didn't say anything. In truth, he wasn't sure what he could say; there were so many horrible thoughts roiling through his mind that it was difficult to grasp just one. In spite of that, he knew exactly what he must do. Pain and threat of death aside, there was no other solution open to him and in a burst of horror-fed energy, he shoved himself into a sitting position.

"I need a sword."

The voice coming out of him sounded surreal. It wasn't Roane at all, but some avenging angel determined to bring death and destruction. Alisanne shrieked, stumbling in his direction.

"Roane, *no!*" she cried "You can't do anything about it. Please lay back down, let me…."

He ignored her, grabbing hold of Joseph Ari with a grip like iron. "Find me a sword. Do it now."

"Roane, Roane," Joseph Ari pleaded. "You'll only succeed in getting yourself killed. You can't do anything about it!"

Roane began looking around the room as if a weapon would miraculously appear. "I can make her a widow."

"I cannot allow it," Joseph Ari said with more conviction than he felt. It was difficult to be brave in the face of Roane's rage. "You'll condemn yourself."

"I am already condemned."

Alisanne put herself in front of him. "Roane, please," she begged softly. "There must be another way, but murdering Dodge is not the answer."

"Murdering Dodge is precisely the answer," he tried not to bark at her. His searching gaze came to rest on her pale face and, as always, he felt himself soften. He touched her cheek to let her know that he was in no way angry with her. "Nothing will keep me from you, Alisanne, not Dodge nor the Hospitallers nor God himself. I fear this is the only way to remedy the situation."

She wasn't convinced. "You against all of those men? Do you really think they'll all stand by while you kill Dodge?" She grabbed him by the shoulders, forcing him to be still and think. "Of course they won't. They'll kill you. And then I shall be at the mercy of Dodge forever and you will never be able to help me. Is that what you want?"

His rage tempered. His fury had affected his thinking until all he could see was blood. Now he was cooling and coming to see reason somewhat. They were right, all of them. He suddenly felt very exhausted and toppled back over onto the bed.

"I cannot stand by while he... as his wife, he can...." He couldn't finish his sentence. There was suddenly a lump in his throat.

Alisanne sat down beside him, soothing him gently. "He hasn't consummated the marriage," she said. It was a rather embarrassing subject, but one he must know. "He hasn't touched me."

Roane looked at her. "Why not?"

She flushed again, clearing her throat. "I... I told him it is my woman's time."

"Is it?"

"No, but he believes me for now."

The mystery of life deterred most men and Roane was infinitely grateful. He squeezed her hand, bringing it to his lips for a kiss. "Then there is still a chance," he looked at Joseph Ari. "What about an annulment?"

The priest shook his head. "Not a chance, unless we could prove that Dodge was a follower of Satan or that he was demon possessed. Anything that has to do with the immortal soul would be considered, but nothing earthly. You know that, Roane."

He had, but he had asked anyway. Desperate men didn't think clearly often times. As the mood of the room cooled, Roane lost himself in thought. He ran scenarios through his mind over and over, holding Alisanne's hand, feeling her trembling warmth. Nothing was more important than being with her, married or not.

"Then I'll simply take her away from here," he said quietly. "We shall go to Gargrave Castle."

Alisanne's eyes grew large. "We are going to Gargrave?"

"Indeed," he thought on the great castle, lodged on a rocky promontory in a dominant position over the Yorkshire countryside. "I've not seen my home in some time. 'Tis time to make amends to my brother and rejoin the family. I've been the prodigal brother long enough."

Alisanne was hopeful. "Do you think he can protect you from the Hospitallers? If they discover he is your brother, they'll track you...."

He waved her off gently. "We have discussed this before. My brother can withstand far worse than what the Hospitallers can throw at him, or even Dodge should he be stupid enough to follow us. We shall be perfectly safe, forever."

Joseph Ari, shaking his head, interjected. "Roane, you'll be living in sin with another man's wife. How can you...?"

"I think it is a good idea," Edward declared. "If Baron Coniston is his brother, nothing could be more perfect. De Vere wouldn't dare tangle with a powerful warlord, nor would the Hospitallers, if they were wise."

The priest looked at him. "But the Hospitallers are a godly sect and the Baron, not even the king, would refuse God's messengers if they were to demand Roane's return."

Edward's features twisted irritably. "Joseph Ari, you know as well as I that the Church does not support the Hospitallers, just as they do not acknowledge the Templars. The church would not intervene."

"But they would intervene if Dodge demanded his wife back."

"De Vere has what he wants, Kinlet and her lands. Alisanne means nothing to him."

It was true. But the priest did not give up. "Then you are telling me, in essence, that you condone your daughter living in sin with another man?"

Edward was deadly serious. "Given the choice of my daughter living honorably as the wife of a dishonorable man, or living with an honorable man dishonorably, I shall choose what is best for her. In this case, it is the morally lesser of the choices."

"Living in sin like an animal?"

"Aye."

Joseph Ari shook his head again; it wasn't that he didn't agree. But as an emissary for the church, he must take the moral stand. Throwing up his hands, he moved away in a gesture of defeat.

"What do we do now?" Alisanne asked Roane.

He was quiet a moment as he considered their options. "The Hospitallers want to return me to Clavell Hill within the week, so we must leave sooner than that."

"But you are not well enough," Alisanne insisted. "You cannot travel yet."

Roane knew that. But he also knew that time was of the essence. "I can travel in a day or two," he said, though he wasn't at all sure. "But I cannot do it alone."

It was an open suggestion. Edward took the bait. "I'll help you," he said. "Have no fear, I shall do what I can."

"You are coming with us, Father," Alisanne insisted softly.

"Of course you are," Roane confirmed. He eyed the priest, pouting in the shadows. "So are you, John Adam."

Father Joseph Ari cocked an eyebrow. "And be a party to your sin? I think not."

"Would you rather stay here and face Dodge's wrath?"

Joseph Ari was silent a moment. He hung his head, chewed his lip. "You will take me back to my monastery," he said quietly. "I will be safe there. Dodge cannot touch me."

Alisanne rose from the bed, feeling her way across the room until she reached her uncle. She held his arm tightly. "You will not come with us?"

He kissed her on the forehead. "Truly, child, I cannot. My place is here."

"But you will help us, will you not?"

He could never resist her. "I will do what is necessary."

"Helping the morally depraved?"

He sighed and grunted at the same time. "I prefer to think of it as assisting the cause of love. And that is, God has said, the greatest cause of all." He looked at Roane, lying flat on the bed. "You do love her, do you not? I'll not lift a finger to help you if this is just a passing fancy."

Roane knew that Joseph Ari knew him well enough to know that

Roane was not impulsive when it came to women. But the priest, for his own conscience, wanted confirmation.

"She has become my reason for living," he said quietly. "I was dead until I met her. She has given me a reason to go on."

The priest nodded his head at being told what he already knew. "Then I shall help."

Alisanne hugged him tightly. "Thank you, Uncle John."

He smiled at the use of his old name. He remembered long ago the beautiful toddler who spoke with a lisp. "You are welcome, child."

ॐ

IT WAS VERY late. Alisanne didn't know how long she had been asleep when strange sounds woke her. It was dark as she sat up in bed, her heart pounding in her ears as she struggled to gain her bearing. She was still, listening intently, when the sounds came again; the chair in a darkened corner gave way with a groan and she yelped with surprise, holding the bed linens up around her neck as if to protect herself.

"Who's there?" she demanded.

The chair popped and groaned again. "'Tis only your husband, Alisanne." Dodge was drunk; she could smell the alcohol that wafted on his breath. "It is perfectly within my rights to be here."

Horror filled her. She knew, without words, why he had come and she struggled to be strong. "Aye, it is," she said, trying to sound casual. "But I am exhausted. I'll speak with you come the morn."

"It wasn't speaking I had in mind."

His words were like a brutal blow and the mere thought made her nauseous. "I am still unclean, my lord," her voice was quaking. "You must give me time to recover my strength."

Dodge issued a frustrated sigh. "How much strength does it take? You simply lie there while I do all of the work. It's easy, really."

She swallowed hard, laying back down on the bed and turning away from him. "I... I feel weak and ill. I'll faint, I am sure. You must allow me to heal."

"But it's already been a week."

"Sometimes I take a long time."

"You couldn't possibly be stalling, could you?

"No, my lord."

Dodge was aggravated and drunk. Throwing himself on the bed, he pinned Alisanne beneath him and she gasped, flinching when he stuck his tongue in her ear in what was supposed to be a seductive move. He was heavy, and his weight was crushing her.

"My lord!" she breathed. "I cannot... I cannot catch my breath."

He licked her cheek, slobbering on her delicate skin. "That shall be nothing compared to the breathlessness you will feel when I take you as my wife."

It was all she could do to keep from screaming. But to yell would only bring her panicked father and Roane, who would undoubtedly try to kill Dodge in his weakened state. And that would only lead to his greater harm.

"Please," she gasped. "You are hurting me."

Dodge licked her again before leaping off. He adjusted the bulge in his hose. "That is only a foretaste, my lady. I plan to hump you like a rabbit until you are with child. And when that child is born, I'll hump you again and again. We shall have lots of sons to fill this place, and I'll enjoy every bloody moment of the mating."

The idea brought tears to her eyes. Alisanne lay as still as stone, biting off her sobs, listening to Dodge's footfalls as the crossed the floor. The door opened and closed again. Then, and only then, did she let the tears come aloud. When she was positive Dodge had gone, she stumbled out of her room and into the corridor.

Roane was sound asleep when something burrowed beneath his covers. He was still considerably weak as a result of his injury and, weaponless, he threw back the covers to see what possible threat could have entered his bed. It didn't take him long to deduce that Alisanne was hovering against him, shivering like a terrified child.

"Alisanne," he hissed. Instinctively, his arm went around her and pulled her close. "What's the matter, love?"

She was sobbing. "Dodge," she sniffed. "He… he came to me."

Roane was filled with horror. "What happened?"

She could hear the fury in his voice. "Nothing," she whispered, burying her face against his bandaged chest. "But I cannot hold him off forever. He said that he is going to fill me full of children, and that he is going to enjoy every minute of our mating."

Roane sighed, struggling to stay calm. But he had expected nothing less. He pulled her closer, protectively. "We shall be free of this place before that can happen," he assured her. "It will never come to that."

"But what if it does?" her head came up, her unfocused eyes full of tears. "Roane, I can't *see* him to fight him off. I can't run away because I won't know where I am going. I am completely helpless against him!"

He shushed her softly, pulling her back down against him. "You are not alone in your fight against him, you know that. I am here, and I shall protect you."

She sniffled and wept until the tears finally cooled. She needed his reassurance desperately. Roane continued to hold her in the darkness, his eyes wide open and staring into the darkness. He knew that she could probably not hold Dodge off more than another day, but he was so terribly weak that it would make traveling extremely difficult. Yet there was no choice; they had to leave immediately.

"Where's your father?" he asked.

"In his chamber across the hall, I would imagine," she said. "Why do you ask?"

"Because it is apparent that we must leave tonight. We can't waste time waiting for me to regain my strength; to do so jeopardizes both of us. The longer we stay, the more chance there is of the situation taking a turn for the worse."

She sat up, looking in his general direction. "But to risk your health also jeopardizes us. You need to rest before we can…."

He cut her off gently. "I shall recover more quickly given the chance to move about. Besides, Gargrave is a good distance north. We must get a head start. Now, do you think you can make it across the corridor and tell your father of our plans?"

Her expression was dubious. "Are you sure?"

"Very sure, love."

"Very well," she said quietly. "Roane?"

"Aye?"

She swallowed hard, struggling to form the words. "I wouldn't normally ask anything of you, you know that. But I... I...."

He touched her cheek gently. "You may ask me anything. What is it?"

She fidgeted. "I was wondering... if it wouldn't be too much trouble, or wouldn't be too taxing, if you might consider laying your hands upon me."

He wasn't quite sure what she had in mind. "What do you mean?"

She put her hand to her face. "My eyes," she whispered. "Would you consider using your gift on my eyes?"

He was struck with the ironic horror of her statement, stunned into silence. He should have known that at some point she would have asked this of him, but in truth, it was such a terrible subject that he had deliberately pushed it from his mind. Alisanne mistook his quiet for disapproval.

"It's just that I feel so useless and vulnerable because it is so difficult for me to see," she said quickly. "With you wounded, I could be of more assistance to you if I could only see a little better. It would be the greatest miracle of all if you could only heal my eyes, just a little."

He was glad she couldn't see his face. He knew there were tears in his eyes. "Alisanne," he said hoarsely. "Nothing would give me greater pleasure. But I've not used my gift since the day it was given to me and... I don't... I don't believe I possess the power any longer."

Her expression passed between disappointment and surprise. "How do you know?"

Christ, how can I tell her? "Because I do," he said lamely, knowing it sounded as if he was being evasive.

Alisanne thought that mayhap he was nicely trying to tell her that he did not wish to heal her. A lump formed in her throat and she turned away from him so he would not see the anguish in her face. "I see," she murmured. "I am so sorry to have asked you, then. I did not know."

He knew what she was feeling; he was feeling it too. Reaching out, he grasped her so she would not slip away. "Believe me, love, if I could heal your eyes, I would gladly do so. Nothing in this world would give me greater joy. But my so-called gift is gone."

She was shaking when she turned to him. "How do you know?"

He had to tell her. He had no choice. "Because I tried to use it once before."

"When?"

"On you, a week ago, while you were asleep," he almost choked on his guilt. "The morning you awoke with your sight so much worse was the morning I had tried to heal you."

She thought back to that day when she woke up to a very blurry world. "You tried to heal my eyes then?"

He wouldn't have blamed her if she left him forever. "I tried," he tried not to sound like he was begging for her forgiveness. "But it did not work. When you awoke, you were worse than ever. I... I thought not to tell you what I'd done."

"Why not?"

"I did not want you to hate me for worsening your condition."

She looked at him quizzically. "Roane, why would I hate you for trying to heal me?"

"Because I ruined you," he whispered. "It's the most difficult thing I've ever had to live with, Alisanne, believe me. What I've caused is unforgivable."

"You didn't cause anything. My sight was already going bad."

"I think I helped it along."

"That's madness."

He shifted on the bed, burying his face against her supple breasts, feeling her heat and life against him. "Can you ever forgive me for what I've done?"

She stroked his hair. "There's nothing to forgive, darling. You tried to help me. It's not your fault that it went awry."

"You are far too gracious."

"Would you prefer that I hate you?"

He laughed softly, relief flooding him. "Not really." Her breasts were against his face and, instinctively, his lips found the soft swell. He kissed her, gently. "I would prefer that you remain as sweet and gracious as you are."

Alisanne continued to caress his hair as his mouth tenderly worked the roundness of her breasts. His hands cupped each globe, kneading them gently as he suckled her flesh. In the darkness and privacy of the chamber, her gown fell down from her shoulders and Roane tasted the sweetness of her nipples as if they were the most delectable, succulent fruits. In his heated grasp, Alisanne groaned her pleasure.

Roane lay her down on the end of the bed, ignoring his weak and dizzy body, as he slid the gown further and further down her torso. He kissed her tenderly over every inch of her velvety flesh, sliding her gown off the rest of the way and finally tossing it aside. He was painfully engorged, but he patiently spent his time acquainting her with his touch.

"Roane?" Alisanne whispered.

"Aye?"

"I want you to take me now, this night," she hissed. "I want you to fill me with your son so that Dodge will never have the chance to do so."

His head came up from her abdomen and he gazed at her in the very dim light. "He will never get the chance as it is. We are leaving tonight."

"But we are not gone yet," she ran her fingers through his short, soft hair. "Until we leave… until I know we are well away from Dodge, I still fear that we might fail."

He knew she had a point. He would be damned if Dodge de Vere would touch her, much less fill her with his child. It seemed like an immoral thing to do, deliberately impregnate her so that Dodge would never have the chance. But the emotions he held for Alisanne told him that his desire to procreate with her were natural, not immoral. He loved her with every fiber of his being. Whether or not she was married to him, whether or not they would ever be married, she was already his wife in his heart. He believed God intended such things to happen when earthly circumstances were less than ideal.

"We will not fail," he said. "As long as we are together, we shall never fail. As I take you now, I do it because of the love I have for you, not the contempt I hold for Dodge."

Alisanne's unfocused eyes were moist. "I love you as well. With everything I am, I am yours."

He kissed her tenderly, his body aching with emotion. "As I am yours," he whispered. "Are you sure you want to do this? There is still time to stop, to wait."

"Wait for Dodge to take me first?"

He signed softly. "I don't want this to seem like we are two dogs in heat, mad to be the first one to deposit his seed. There is far more to it than that. But I must be honest and say that I feel the need to claim you for my own more strongly than I've ever felt for anything. To think of Dodge touching something that, heart and soul, belongs to me...."

He couldn't finish. Alisanne put her fingers to his lips. "Then wait no longer. I want my first, and only touch of intimacy, to be from you. Fill me, Roane, as only you can."

His hose came down and he thrust into her quivering body, breaking her maidenhead and hearing her whimper beneath him. He regretted that it was necessary to do it so quickly, so boldly, but the brief flash of pain was over and now he could concentrate on showing her how lovemaking was meant to be. Alisanne clung to him, a new and frightening experience rapidly turning into something heated and wonderful.

As he moved, she moved with him, their hips grinding together, lifting their passion higher and higher. There was a wonderful friction building, a fire spreading from her loins and into her limbs like river of flame. Roane touched her, kissed her, whispered heatedly in her ear to fan the flames into a wild blaze. Suddenly, the inferno in her body erupted, sending her into gentle convulsions that dimmed her hearing and laid waste to the world around her. And somewhere in the midst of her sweet madness, she heard Roane softly grunt her name and knead her buttocks furiously until his passion, too, seemed to come to rest.

Alisanne thought time had come to a halt. Nothing seemed to move in the darkness of the chamber except her thumping heart and Roane's loud breathing. They were heated, sweating, wrapped in each other's bodies. Alisanne never wanted to let him go, feeling Roane against her, his fingers gently caressing her head. Of all the things she had imagined lovemaking to be, it had never been this wonderful.

"Are you well?"

Roane's voice floated down to her in the darkness and she turned toward him, pulling his head down for a kiss.

"Never better," she murmured. "Thank you."

He returned her heated kisses. "I am sorry it had to hurt, but it is like that the first time for a woman."

"The pain was well worth the price."

Roane didn't know what to say. He was, in truth, overwhelmed by the entire experience. Never had it been so wonderful for him and he thanked God for His blessing in bringing Alisanne to him. For a man who had been a loner his entire life, now he couldn't stand the thought of being a single individual again. Alisanne completed him, a piece of him that he never knew was missing.

"As much as I would like to lie here all night, savoring your sweetness, I fear that time is of the essence," he murmured. "The sooner we leave this place, the better."

She nodded. "I know."

"I hate sounding so callous after so wondrous an experience."

"You are not callous, you are truthful."

With a final kiss, Alisanne sat up, feeling around for her gown. Roane found it for her, lying on the floor beside the bed, and helped her dress. He even put her slippers on for her, as difficult as it was for him to move at all. Alisanne appreciated the gesture.

"I'll go and tell my father now," she said. "Father Joseph Ari, too."

"Let your father find John Adam," Roane said. "I don't want you wandering the halls with Dodge and his men lurking about."

"As you wish," she said. "I'll return as quickly as I can."

"I'll be waiting."

She stumbled toward the door and he rose from the bed, naked, to help her find the panel. No sooner did he touch the latch than the door flew open in a swift, popping rush.

Alisanne stumbled back, startled. Roane instinctively put himself between the open door and the lady, his massive nude form proud and imposing. The corridor beyond was lit with smoking torches and Dodge stood in the threshold, a host of mercenaries lingering behind him. They snickered lewdly when they realized what had most likely happened, but Dodge wasn't amused at all.

"I knew she would be here," he snarled. "Damnation, I knew it!"

Roane remained calm. "For once in your life, you were correct."

Dodge glared daggers at him. "So you are not as wounded as we have been led to believe," he said. "You are apparently well enough to take what does not belong to you!"

Roane would not acknowledge his assertion. He was more concerned with how he was going to get them out of this mess.

"You took what did not belong to you to begin with," Roane growled. "She was always mine, de Vere. 'Tis time you realized that."

"She's my wife, you arrogant bastard, and these walls within you reside are also mine," he turned to the men behind him. "Tell Father Bordeleaux that his prisoner is well enough to travel. Tell him to get this thieving whelp out of my castle!"

Alisanne, forcing herself from stunned silence, pushed forward.

"Dodge, no! He's still too weak to...."

Dodge made a move to grab her, but Roane flattened him with one swift blow. Alisanne could hear men rushing him and she began to scream, begging Dodge and his men not to hurt him. She pushed forward into the melee to somehow protect him and she could hear Roane begging her to get away. But she could not, would not, listen; sighted or not, she had to help him. Before she could get close to him, however, someone grabbed her from behind and hoisted her up, carrying her from the room.

Alisanne could hear the sounds of scuffling fading as she was carted further and further down the corridor. She fought and kicked, screaming Roane's name and hearing his desperate calls in return. But it was of no use; Roane was overwhelmed, and so was Alisanne. Dodge clapped a sweaty hand over her mouth the last few yards of the corridor before throwing her into her chamber and bolting the door from the outside. Alisanne cried and beat against the door furiously, but the panel remained solid.

Desperate, she put her ear against the crack in the door, listening for any sounds from Roane. For all she knew, they had killed him. Weeping, heartsick, Alisanne sank to the floor, her hands on the door, praying that Roane was alive and well. She couldn't even imagine what Dodge would do to punish him. But that paled in comparison to the fact that the Hospitallers were now going to take him back to Birmingham and Clavell Hill where they would try him for heresy and, even worse, witchcraft.

The worst possible thing she could imagine had happened. She had feared it all along, as if a premonition had been warning her. Alisanne cursed God for letting her have one brief, sweet taste of immortal love, then in the next breath she begged him to help Roane. Short of a miracle, she didn't know who else could save him except God.

Or, mayhap, Baron Coniston.

CHAPTER NINE

Nine days later

"MY LORD, I come for one who cannot come," Joseph Ari said. "I beg audience with the Baron. 'Tis a matter of life and death for his brother."

The great hall of Gargrave Castle was a cavernous room with a great vaulted ceiling and a gallery surrounding the entire chamber, cut with lancet windows for light and ventilation. The walls were of red stone and two massive tapestries hung at either end. The castle itself was over one hundred years old, a Norman structure built on top of an earlier, possibly Roman, fortification. The sight on a hill overlooking North Yorkshire was perfect defensively and aesthetically.

There were a few people in the great hall, most of them servants loitering in the shadows. A pair of well-dressed men lingered before Joseph Ari, one of which had announced himself as the majordomo of the estate. The other man, mayhap nearing forty years of age, had auburn hair and wide shoulders and never uttered a sound. He sat in a large oak chair while the other man did the talking. At the mention of Roane, however, both men seemed to show a great deal of interest. In fact, mentioning Roane's name had gained Joseph Ari access to the castle in the first place.

"Who sent you?" the majordomo asked.

"The Lady Alisanne de Soulant," Joseph Ari couldn't bear to call her by her married name. He eyed the two men carefully, hoping his words would gain him further credibility. "She and your brother wish to be wed."

The majordomo looked at the man in the chair. "Roane is to wed?"

he repeated with awe. The other man looked equally surprised. The majordomo turned back to the dirty, worn priest in a flash of arrogance. "Who is this woman that she is worthy enough to be betrothed to an heir to the House of De Garr?"

"Her father is the Baron Craven," Joseph Ari said with thinning patience. He was so exhausted he was ready to drop; riding non-stop for nearly a week had brought him to Gargrave Castle and the point of collapse. He didn't want to stand here and argue. "The de Soulant family is old and distinguished. Edward de Soulant, the lady's father, served King Henry in his personal guard."

The man in the chair had been listening intently. It was obvious that he was very interested, yet he seemed unnaturally restrained. "Who are you to this family, priest?"

"I am the lady's uncle. And one who served with Sir Roane in the Holy Land."

The man eyed him dubiously, though it was difficult to tell exactly what he was thinking. After a moment, he spoke again. "Why do you say that you come for one who cannot come? Why can't the lady travel in important matters regarding her betrothed?"

Joseph Ari wouldn't lie, but he could twist the truth just a bit. "She is... ill, my lord. It is extremely difficult for her to travel."

The man in the chair accepted the explanation. "Then tell me why you have come in her stead."

Joseph Ari was astute enough to realize that he was addressing the Baron. Other than the fact that the man was well dressed and possessed a definitive air of authority, he also faintly resembled Roane. "My lord, are you aware of the history of Sir Roane's troubles?"

The man tried to remain neutral, pretending not to know that the priest recognized him. But his façade was for naught. "I've not heard from Sir Roane since he joined that foolish sect and traveled to the Holy Land years ago. What troubles do you speak of?"

The priest's eyes glittered. "Then you know nothing of his gift."

"What gift?"

Joseph Ari moved closer, the reverence in his voice evident. "Sir Roane was blessed with a great gift whilst in the Holy Land. God gave him the ability to give sight to the blind; I myself was blinded in one eye and healed by the touch of Roane. The Hospitallers refused to believe that Sir Roane could perform miracles and denounced him as a sorcerer. For three years, Roane has been hiding from the very sect that once embraced him. Now they want to prosecute him for heresy and witchcraft. Thanks to a bounty hunter, the Hospitallers now have him. Lady Alisanne has sent me to his most gracious and powerful brother to ask for help."

The man in the chair changed expressions as the story sank in; he went from interest to disbelief to rage in a matter of seconds. Suddenly, he was rising from his chair, his handsome face taut. "Are you telling me that those idiot Hospitallers are trying to kill my brother after he gave up everything for their foolish notions of healing and devotion?" he boomed. "Once they bled him dry of every bit of wealth he had, they decided he was a heretic?"

Joseph Ari shook his head. "It wasn't the money they took from him. It was the fact that in the Holy Land, God blessed him with a miraculous gift, one that follows the precise directive of the Hospitallers. Roane was given the gift to heal, my lord, and the others feared him for it. They think he is possessed."

Bowen de Garr, third Baron Coniston, took on an expression of disgust that much favored his younger brother. "Rubbish," he growled. "I don't know about any damnable gift from God, but I do know that my brother is no more possessed than I am. In fact, I would wager to say that Roane has finally come to his senses by leaving the sect and finding a decent woman to marry."

Joseph Ari could feel hope bloom in his chest. "Then you shall help your brother?"

Bowen glanced at the majordomo as if seeking guidance or permission or mayhap both; it was an odd, silent exchange. But the majordomo merely shrugged. "It was your father's wish that..." he began quietly.

"I know what my father's wish was," Bowen snapped quietly as he ran his fingers through his auburn hair. He didn't appear indecisive as much as he appeared stunned. Had his father been there, however, there would have been quite an attitude of refusal. Mayhap that is why he had sought some sort of approval in the majordomo, a man who had faithfully served his father. Old habits were hard to break. But Bowen was most assuredly not his father; he and Roane had always been close and he had missed his brother terribly. Now was not the time to let bygone bitterness between his father and brother affect his decision.

He looked at the priest. "You know that Roane was disinherited when he joined the Hospitallers."

"I know."

"My father cried many hours over his errant son, though he would never let on."

"A father never loses love for his son."

"He demanded that his name never again be spoken within these walls."

"Will you leave him to his death, then?"

Of course he wouldn't. Bowen shook his head slowly. "I am not my father," he said softly. "But I'd be lying if I didn't say I feel the anger of his presence at this moment, knowing that I am about to help him. Do you know where they have taken Roane?"

Joseph Ari felt a wave of relief; for a moment he thought things were going to work out differently than he had hoped. "Clavell Hill, on the outskirts of Birmingham, is the Hospitallers' lair," he replied. "They are most likely, at this moment, going through the mockery of a trial, condemning Roane for crimes he has not committed. Because they are crimes against God, they will undoubtedly find him guilty and execute him by purification."

Bowen seemed to pale; in fact, the ambience of the entire room chilled, a stir of terror at the thought of such a horrible death. Purification was the most hideously painful death known to man, the agony of the human body thought to also kill the spirit of the demons that possessed it. Time was of the essence, for every second ticked away the remaining minutes of Roane's life.

"Stupid bastards," he rumbled. "They shall wish they had never laid eyes on Roane de Garr, for now in my anger they shall feel the wrath equal to that of God's on earth." He turned to the majordomo in a fit of fury and purpose. "Zander!"

The man's body went taut with anticipation. "My lord?"

"Rouse the troops. Assemble all but fifty men in the outer bailey within the hour. We ride for Birmingham!"

The majordomo fled. Instantly, the great hall turned into a hive of chaos as the servants scattered, preparing to send their army on a well-supplied mission to save their native son. Joseph Ari watched the commotion, murmuring fervent prayers of thanks to God for the Baron Coniston's determination. He could only hope they would not be too late.

ೞ

Eleven days later

"I SHOULD NEVER have listened to you," Edward hissed. "This is the most foolish, insane thing I've ever done!"

Alisanne ignored her father's ranting. He had been ranting the entire trip from Kinlet Castle and she was long accustomed to it. "How close are we to Birmingham?" she asked casually.

"On the outskirts," her father growled. "We should not have come, Alisanne. We can do nothing for Roane. We can only pray that John Adam was able to convince the Baron to come to his brother's aid. We can do no more!"

Alisanne was resolute. "I cannot rely on the fact that the Baron will be convinced. If he does not come, we must be here to help Roane in any way we can."

Edward shook his head in frustration. "How?" he snapped softly.

"We can do nothing against the Hospitallers!"

"I can only trust that we will know how to help when the time comes," she said firmly. "In any event, I do not intend to leave Roane to face this alone."

Edward knew that; he sighed, his anger softening. The only reason he had come with his daughter was because he knew she would have come to Birmingham with or without his help, and he certainly could not let her go alone. Dodge and his men had been on a drinking, eating and hunting binge for over a week, lavishly spending the reward from Roane's capture. Their frequent and long absences had made it possible for Alisanne and her father to slip away unnoticed, but Edward knew their luck wouldn't hold out forever. When Dodge came out of his stupor, he would realize his wife was missing and it would be no mystery as to where she might have gone. Time was growing critical. He would come after her with a vengeance.

"I don't know what we can do," he repeated, with less force in his tone.

"The first thing we can do is gain entry to Clavell Hill," she said. "We shall worry about the rest when we get there."

Edward lifted his eyebrows in resignation. Birmingham was a sprawling, dirty city filled with all of the characters one might expect in such a town. Edward and Alisanne rode into the southernmost outskirts of the berg, and were immediately swallowed by the bustle. People were everywhere, the dust from their travels heavy in the air.

Alisanne could smell the stench, hear the commotion, but it was difficult to make out anything of detail. All seemed to be one big, colorful blur. Edward directed the old horse through the crowds, careful not to run over anyone. The last thing he wanted was attention. He paused once, to ask a shopkeep where he might find Clavell Hill. The toothless old man pointed to the north, explaining the location of the monastery. They were half way through the town before Edward spoke again.

"Now that we know where we are going, have you any plans yet?"

he asked.

"I told you I would know when we got there," Alisanne said.

Edward was silent a moment, watching a young girl, not unlike his daughter had been long ago, play in the dirt. "You are going to see him, aren't you?"

"I did not come all this way not to."

"Are you hoping he'll help you plan his own escape?"

"Roane is a brilliant man. He'll think of something."

Edward shook his head with defeat and frustration. "That has been your plan all along, hasn't it? To see Roane and have him orchestrate his own escape."

"Is that so wrong?"

"No," Edward said softly. "I am just not sure what we can do against one hundred Hospitallers. Alisanne, I am not even sure if they will let you in to see him. What if they don't?"

She was more determined than he had ever seen her. "Then we shall find a way," she said. "We *must* find a way, father. I did not come all this way to be turned back."

Edward didn't say any more; in truth, he wasn't sure what more to say. His daughter was determined and he couldn't shake a distinct sense of foreboding. If the Hospitallers didn't punish her for attempting to help a prisoner escape, then Dodge would surely punish her for coming to Clavell Hill. Either way she was damned. But he could not reproach her in good faith; he had known, once, what it was to be young and insanely in love. And it had been clear, even to him, that Alisanne and Roane had something special.

When it finally came into view, Clavell Hill wasn't what he had expected. Mayhap he didn't know exactly what *to* expect, but it was nothing as he imagined. A former Roman fortress, the Normans had repaired the crumbling walls and keep, leaving it a strange mixture of architecture and building materials. An ancient Roman and Christian graveyard, combined, lay against one of the rocky slopes. The shape was boxy, ugly, and as Edward gazed upon it, thought it looked more like a prison than a church. There were no battlements, at least not as he knew them, but he could see people lingering within the guarded courtyard.

A small town, including a big Norman church, had grown up around the fortress. It was busy, full of people, who milled about on the main avenue, conducting business or conversation. As they lingered on the edge of town, studying the hell they were about to plunge into, Edward was coming to feel ill.

"We are here," he said to his daughter. "'Tis looming before us like a great beast."

Alisanne's senses heightened; concentrating, she could smell a coldness, a rot, drifting on the wind, but she couldn't see much but a big dark mass in the distance. Her body flushed with fear. "Is it so horrible, father?"

"Bad enough," he said. "Now, how do you propose we get into this place?"

She thought a moment. "We shall tell them that I am his sister. Surely they cannot refuse his family."

Edward shrugged. Alisanne, sensing his disapproval, struggled to concoct something more believable. "Mayhap...mayhap if we seek employment as servants. Tell them that our farm was destroyed in some Biblical disaster, like pestilence. Mayhap then, as men of God, they would feel sorry for us and take us in."

It was plausible, but Edward was still doubtful. "What if some of the brothers recognize you from Kinlet? They'll tell Father Bordeleaux and your game will be ended."

Alisanne thought furiously. "Then we must disguise ourselves. Mayhap some dirt on our faces, a cloak around our head, and surely they will not know who we are."

It was as good a plan as any, but that wasn't saying much. A quarter of a mile from the structure, Edward reined the old steed to a halt and pulled his daughter down. "Here," he plopped some mud in her hand from a puddle on the side of the road. "Put this on you."

Alisanne could smell the urine and she balked. "But this... this is...!"

"There's nothing else, girl!" Edward snapped. "Besides, they'll not want to get a close look at you if you smell like a gutter rat. Now put it on!"

He was right. Alisanne groaned as she smeared the mud on her body, dirtying the peach colored dress Roane had purchased for her. It nearly killed her to do it. Before long, both she and Edward were appropriately filthy and swathed in their cloaks. Edward put her back on the horse and began leading the animal down the road.

"Now we shall see how stupid the brothers are," he mumbled.

Alisanne hoped they were stupid enough.

CHAPTER TEN

H E WASN'T ACCUSTOMED to feeling such hopelessness. Even in his darkest hour, there had always been a ray of light to convince him that all was not lost. But not now; Roane gazed up at the tiny window at the top of his cell, more of a drain and an air hole than an actual window. But it was big enough to let some light through, just enough to tease him. Around him was unimaginable filth, the oldness of the ancient Roman fort more evident here than anywhere else. He sat, daydreaming, wondering what other prisoners had languished here before him. He wondered if they had met their fate as bravely as he was expected to meet his.

Death by Purification. The thought of it didn't make him queasy as it did yesterday when his sentence had been announced. Oddly enough, now he was rather resigned to it. He'd seen death by purification before, an indescribable act of horror and pain all in the name of God. He didn't think God would approve much of these things men attributed to him, but his opinion didn't matter. God apparently didn't care for many things these days. All that mattered was that in three days, after the event of the Sabbath, Roane was to die.

A rodent ran across the floor of his cell, disappearing into some hole in the dark recesses. Roane was in an inverted vault, a bottle-shaped cell with the sloping sides and the narrowest part at the top. It was a good eight feet to the trap door above, a heavy panel that opened on occasion when the brothers felt like feeding him. In a week he'd hardly had more than the ingredients to comprise one decent meal. And he knew all of that food, scraps of bread and a few dried bits of cheese, had come from his old friend Albert. As weak as he was from his chest injury, the lack of food and squalid conditions were making recovery very difficult. But he had no real desire to fully recover if they were simply going to execute him.

His thoughts drifted from his impending death to visions of Alisanne. In truth, he'd thought of little else since his imprisonment. She was Dodge's wife now and he blocked out all of the horrible things Dodge had probably done to her by now. Her sweet body, her beautiful face, and her tender soul all at the mercy of that animal. If Roane thought too long on it, he began to sweat with rage. He was helpless to aid her and he knew it. He could only pray that Dodge would grow tired of sporting with her and leave her alone; it was the one great hope that kept him from going completely insane. He swore the first thing he would do after he died was to come back as a rat and chew on Dodge in the middle of the night and give him an infection that would leave him a drooling idiot the rest of his life. He drew some strange satisfaction at that thought.

The trap door over his head opened and the light streaming in, as weak as it was, was enough to blind him. Roane blinked and held up a hand to shield his eyes from the brilliant rays. Instead of food being thrown into his pit as expected, a rope suddenly dangled from the hole and a body squirmed down it. Startled, Roane struggled to rise to his feet.

"Sir Roane," a small man hit the floor of the vault and rushed toward him. "We have come for you!"

Roane stared at the man, unrecognizing, until realization abruptly dawned. A surge of hope and excitement hit him so hard that he nearly collapsed, grabbing the man by the arm to steady himself. "Edward de Soulant!" he hissed. "What in the hell...?"

Edward shook his head in a quick, cutting gesture. "No time, Sir Roane, no time. We must get you out of here!"

Roane was beside himself. "But I can't... I don't understand. What in the hell are you doing here?"

"I've come to get you out," Edward said as if Roane was a simpleton. "I've waited eight days to gain the proper time and access, and God has finally shown me the way. But time is of the essence."

Roane gazed at him as if he didn't believe a word the man was saying. "How is it that you have managed to accomplish... *this*?" He gestured to the rope, the trapdoor, the room in general.

Edward flashed a grin. "I am now a servant to the Hospitallers. I've been serving the prisoners and guards of the vault their meals for nearly a week in the hopes that somehow I would discover a way to free you. Did you not get the food I threw you?"

"Then it was you?"

"Aye."

More was becoming clear to Roane's shocked mind. "What of the guards now?"

"They're sleeping. Ale with a draught of sleeping potion in it."

"Where did you get the sleeping potion?"

"I stole it from one of the priests. I heard him say that it causes him to sleep for hours."

"Christ," Roane breathed. "If that is true, then they will be asleep for quite some time. But I can't simply *walk* out of here. Everyone knows me!"

"You can walk out unnoticed if we conceal you," Edward insisted. He began to rummage around in the layers of clothes he was wearing and Roane realized the man had brought several garments with him, wrapped around his body. Edward began throwing things at him. "Put this on! And this! We must hurry!"

Dumbfounded but not senseless, Roane struggled to put on the articles of dirty clothing. "What of Alisanne?" he demanded as he struggled with a tunic. "How is she?"

"She is well enough," Edward, in truth, was terrified. He kept watching the trapdoor for signs of movement. But the ale he had brought the guards was working its magic well; they had been in a drunken stupor when he last saw them. "She's here, with me, and...."

"Here?" Roane nearly toppled over in his surprise. "You brought her *here*?"

Edward fixed him in the eye. "She is the reason I myself am here," he said. "She was going to come with or without my help. I could not let her come alone."

"Damnation, where is she?"

"Working in the kitchen. Where do you think I got all of the extra food to throw to you? The brothers were not providing for you at all, so Alisanne has collected the scraps."

"But what of her sight? She cannot see very well and the kitchens are a dangerous place for her."

"They keep her from the fire. She churns butter, kneads dough, things like that."

The reality of the danger they were in was not lost on Roane, more so now that Alisanne was involved. He found he could hardly breathe. "Christ," he hissed again. "I should have known... certainly she knows I would do the same for her in any given situation. But what about Dodge?"

Edward shook his head, helping Roane to finish dressing when the man faltered. It was obvious that he was still very weak. "He is the least of our worries at the moment. He probably does not yet realize we are gone. It is your friends of the brotherhood I am concerned with."

Roane nodded in mute agreement. "And John Adam?"

Edward came to a halt, his hurried manner wavering. "I knew naught what else to do, Sir Roane," he said as if apologizing in advance for his actions. "Alisanne and I sent him to your brother to ask for help."

Roane's eyes softened with approval. "To Gargrave?"

"Indeed."

"How long ago?"

"Almost three weeks now."

Roane sighed, heavily, as if a great weight had been lifted. "My brother is mostly likely already on his way here." He put his hand on Edward's arm, in appreciation. "The Hospitallers cannot hold out against my brother. Bowen will destroy them if they resist in releasing me."

"You are sure?"

"I will stake my life on it. And I have."

"But Alisanne told me of the bad blood between you and your father. Are you quite sure…?"

"My father is dead. My brother does not hold the same grudge, I assure you."

Edward finished helping him dress in the peasant garb that stank like manure. "Forgive me for saying so, but mayhap you should not put so much faith in your brother's appearance. We are not even certain that Joseph Ari made it to him; mayhap something befell him along the road. There are so many uncertainties."

Roane's confidence subdued somewhat. "But one can hope for the best."

"Yet one cannot depend on the uncertain."

"Is that why you are determined to smuggle me out of here? In case my brother does not come?"

Edward gazed up at him, suddenly looking very old. "Alisanne is my only child. I would do anything for her happiness. I have already failed her with this horrific marriage to de Vere, but I will not fail her where you are concerned."

Roane's gray eyes twinkled. "You do not mind that your daughter and I will be sinners, living and loving together without the benefit of God's blessing?"

Edward shrugged. "Living and loving together is no worse than a sham marriage to a man who would only humiliate and beat her. I cannot imagine God punishing you for loving a woman enough to save her from what the Devil has brought about."

"You make a good argument."

"I make no sense at all."

They laughed after a moment, softly. Edward sobered. "Where do you plan to take her when all of this is finished? The two of you cannot stay in England."

Roane shrugged. "My family has holdings in France. Upon my return from the Holy Land, I passed through many beautiful places in Italy. I could build her a house in the warmth of the sun somewhere. It does not really matter so long as we are together."

Edward knew he had made the right decision in risking his life for this man. Anyone who loved his daughter that much couldn't be the demon everyone said he was. But time was wasting as they dreamed of the future. Edward helped Roane to the rope just as it was yanked from his grasp.

The men in the pit stared, startled and confused, at the trap door above. There were figures milling about and Edward immediately sank into despair.

"My God," he gasped. "We have been discovered!"

Roane, too, felt his hope dash. But he would not show an ounce of outward fear. He stood under the trap door, gazing steadily into the murky gloom above until a face finally came into focus.

"Roane," Albert shook his head sadly. "Do you realize what you've done, man?"

Roane was steady. "It is a prisoner's right to attempt escape, Albert. One can only try. I did force this man to help me, however. He had no choice and is completely innocent of wrongdoing. If you would be so good as to help him out of the pit, I would be grateful."

Albert was truly sorrowful. "I cannot do that, Roane. He is as guilty as you are now."

"He is not. Lift him out immediately, my friend."

"I cannot," Albert hissed. "The guards are drugged and bound, the lock to the door is destroyed. It was only a matter of time before someone happed upon your scheme. Did you truly think you could escape?"

"I can if you help me, too."

Albert paled. "Don't ask me that, Roane. You know that I...."

He didn't finish his sentence before he was being roughly shoved out of the way, and Roane recognized one of the knights who had sat upon the panel that had convicted him of sorcery. He was a thin-faced, nasty looking man and immediately, Roane knew the situation was bleaker than he could have ever imagined.

"So I see you have used your sorcery on this poor servant to manipulate him into aiding you," the knight snarled. "So be it. He has chosen his path to follow you and therefore he shall follow you in death as well!"

The trapdoor slammed before Roane could say another word. In the corner of the vault, Edward hung his head and cried.

◌ঃ

ALISANNE HAD BEEN churning butter for the better part of the morning. It was practically the only thing she could do that didn't require an inordinate amount of sight. Surprisingly, the Hospitallers had been very good at allowing her to work. Mayhap they felt sorry for her, as if God had burdened her with blindness and they, being messengers of God, were obliged to help her. She had been terrified at first that the men who had come to Kinlet would recognize her, but a week later that had yet to happen. So she sat quietly, though somewhat restlessly, in the warm and steamy kitchen, churning butter and helping wash off vegetables while her father tried to ease his way into service in the vault.

It had not been as easy for Edward to gain access to the Hospitallers' compound as it had been Alisanne. Edward wasn't crippled, after all, and they didn't need any more help. But Edward would not let Alisanne enter the compound without him and finally the priests relented, though Edward suspected their reluctance was more due to having the girl's father chaperone her in the midst of men who were supposedly celibate. Edward and Alisanne had immediately volunteered for kitchen duties, thinking that would mayhap be the best way to find their way into the vault. After all, even prisoners needed to be fed. Fortunately, their hopes had come to fruition.

Edward had hoped to free Roane very soon. He'd not yet seen him, for they were keeping Roane in an inverted bottle vault, a hole, and it was difficult to talk to the man. The last she saw of her father, he had somehow wormed his way into the gang of servants that fed the prisoners and those brothers who were living in solitude, and Edward had loaded himself with baskets of bread to be distributed. He had a plan, though he'd not told his daughter much about it.

He'd kept his head down, doing as he was told, but his gaze sought out his daughter just before he'd disappeared from the kitchens although she couldn't see much of his facial expressions. She couldn't see the silent farewell or the hopeful countenance he tried very hard to keep concealed, but she knew he had glanced in her direction simply by the way his head was turned. Alisanne had been very aware when he had left the room, her heart racing as she prayed for her father's success. Everything depended upon it.

From that point on, it was a waiting game. She continued to churn the butter, turning cream into the soft white paste for the priests' tables. Because of her red and crusty eyes, no one paid much attention to her but the truth was that today, oddly enough, her vision seemed to be better. She was seeing details, for example; the features of someone's face when they drew close to her or the details of the kitchen surrounding her. It was extremely encouraging and she felt a good deal of joy over it. Still, she couldn't see anything at any length and everything seemed to have a fog or halo around it, but it certainly was an improvement. She felt better than she had in weeks.

But Alisanne didn't let on that her vision had improved, fearful that they might kick her out of the kitchens to do more difficult labor. Therefore, she kept her head down, working endlessly over the butter churn until her hands were numb and her arms felt as if they were about to fall off. Eventually, the morning passed into the afternoon and the kitchens grew busy as the cooks prepared for the evening meal which would take place after Matins, the sunset service. Alisanne kept to her corner as servants shuffled around her and, eventually, she finished with her buttery task so they put her on kneading bread.

The kitchens were hot and not very well ventilated, but every time someone came in or out, she could see the kitchen yard beyond and smell the animals and hay. She could also see what time of day it was, or at least how bright the sun was, and she was acutely aware when the sun began to set and still her father had not returned. It was a struggle not to become frightened.

Night fell. The meal had been served to the priests and knights, the battle-hardened men who served the priests and protected the facility, and Alisanne could hear their conversation and laughter in the great hall that was adjacent to the kitchen. When she had finished with a loaf of bread in an endless line of bread loafs, one of the cooks gave her a tiny bowl of vegetable stew with some kind of grain in it and a small hunk of bread.

She was ravenous, shoving the bread and stew into her mouth and hardly able to chew because her mouth was so stuffed. Sitting on a stool next to the hearth, she was quite warm and cozy as she ate her bread and stew. With every new voice or every movement near the kitchen door, she kept looking for her father to appear and her anxiety was on the rise. She was no longer able to keep it entirely at bay and when the cook finally dismissed her for the evening, she wandered out into the kitchen yard with fear clutching her heart. She didn't want to entertain the prospect that something had happened, but it was becoming increasingly evident that something had.

Alisanne and her father had commandeered a small corner in the storage area near the stables as their temporary home. They shared it with a few other servants; a pair of red-haired sisters and an older woman with one bad eye who snored like the devil. The shelter smelled strongly of horses but it was dry and warm. Alisanne could see the stables, vaguely, as her gaze perused the wide yard area but it was difficult to see much in the moonlight. She had difficulty seeing in dim light, anyway. She thought mayhap that she should simply return to the storage area to wait for news from her father but the ringing of bells from the church caught her attention.

Turning in the direction of the low, squatly built church with the three-story tower, she could just see the tip of the tower over the roofline of the great hall. Silhouetted against the night sky, she could see flickers of light in the tower, torches that the bell ringers carried in order to accomplish their task. It began to occur to her that she should like to pray for her father's safe return and for Roane's release. Mayhap God would hear her prayers and for once allow the winds of fortune to blow in her direction. The truth was that she was too nervous to return to the storage area just yet; she felt as if she needed to do something more. She had to ask God for help.

Pulling her cloak tightly around her body and pulling the hood up to provide her with some warmth against the cool night air, she made her way out of the kitchen yard and out of the complex, heading towards the church. Other people were wandering towards the structure as the bells rang out, echoing cold and shrill against the dark sky, calling the faithful to worship.

Alisanne followed the masses, losing herself in the crowd as it filtered into the church. Once inside, however, she was too fearful to venture deeply into the dimly-lit room. She remained back by the doors, lingering with uncertainty.

The church was as cold and dark as a tomb, smelling of unwashed bodies and cheap tallow candles. The priest, a hairy man with pig-like features, had begun to drone in Latin and the congregation bowed their heads and crossed themselves. As the service began, Alisanne removed her hood, her damaged eyes peering into the darkness and having great difficulty seeing in the soft candlelight. As she followed the Mass, she didn't notice a big knight standing near the entry to the church.

He was watching her intently.

CB

ALBERT HAD FOLLOWED Alisanne inside the church. He had seen her emerge from the kitchen yard, a woman in a dark woolen cloak with the face of an angel, and he thought he recognized the face. In fact, he was sure of it. He'd only seen it once but it had been enough to impress him. He knew who she was.

Putting aside thoughts of the warm meal that was waiting for him, he followed the woman into the church and stood back by the entry as she lingered several feet away. She was praying, following the priest as he recited the liturgy, but the knight wasn't following the priest at all. He was following the lady. When there was a break in the service as the priests switched out duties and a new one began to sing the mass, the knight slipped up behind the lady and grasped her by the arm.

"Not a sound," he hissed at her. "Come with me."

Terrified, Alisanne's natural reaction was to turn to the source of the muttered threat and her eyes beheld a face that was vaguely familiar. Like a faint dream or a memory that was too distant to be plucked, she couldn't quite place the big man with the black beard but when he tugged on her arm, she had no choice but to follow. He was bigger and stronger than she was, and she knew he meant business. As he dragged her out of the church, she was stiff with terror.

The knight hustled her through the worshipping peasants and out into the night beyond. Still, he continued to pull Alisanne along until they were down the entry steps and onto the street. Until that point, Alisanne had gone along without a word but when he tried to pull her into a smaller, darker avenue that bordered the east side of the church, she balked. She was terrified that he was going to do something unspeakable to her. Yanking her arm from the knight's grip, she turned to run but he easily captured her and dragged her into the shadows.

"Stop, lady," he commanded quietly. "Cease your struggles and listen to me. I mean you no harm."

Not strangely, his words didn't ease her. "Let me go!" she cried.

His response was to tighten his grip. "I swear upon our Holy Father that I mean you no harm," he said. "Please, my lady, be still. You are Roane de Garr's companion, are you not?"

She came to a stop and cast him a fearful gaze. "Why... why do you ask?" she demanded, verging on terrified tears. "What do you know of him?"

"I know a great deal."

"Then tell me your business before I scream my head off!"

The knight loosened his grip but he didn't let go; he could see how genuinely frightened she was. "My name is Albert," he said quietly. "I was with Father Tertious Bordeleaux when he came for Roane at Kinlet Castle. Do you not remember me, my lady?"

Alisanne's struggles came to a halt as she eyed the man suspiciously. Truth was, she couldn't see him very well in the darkness. "I... I am not sure," she admitted, her gaze darting about nervously. "There were so many men and my eyes... well, I do not see very well at times."

He could tell that was true simply by looking at her. She had beautiful eyes in shape and color, but they were very red and irritated. It was truly a pity, too; a woman like this, in fine health, could command a prince for a husband.

Albert studied her in the darkness, contemplating his next move. He'd truthfully only come to warn her off and tell her to leave because of Roane's impending sentence, but now he found himself questioning his very motives. After the events of the afternoon with Roane and the servant who had tried to help the man, Albert was beginning to question everything. He looked at the quivering woman before him, dirty and disheveled, and his thoughts began to shift.

"When was the last time you had a decent meal, my lady?" he asked, his tone considerably softer.

Alisanne could not seriously recall. "I... I am not sure," she said, confused by his question. "Why would you ask such a thing?"

Albert still had her by the arm. This time, he tugged her back towards the avenue with its dirty people and desperate businesses. "Come along," he said quietly.

"Where are we going?" she asked, dragging her feet.

"Some place warm."

Alisanne struggled against him, continuing to demand that he let her go, but he continued to ignore her. Only when she realized that he had taken her to the stoop of the nearest inn did she stop her struggles, and that was only mostly out of curiosity. She'd never been to an inn before and the strong smell of smoke and roasting meat had her attention.

Albert was able to drag her into the inn without a fight.

CHAPTER ELEVEN

ALISANNE HAD NEVER had pickled pears before but found very quickly that she liked them very much. In fact, she ate an enormous helping of them along with everything else at the table – over-cooked mutton, turnips and carrots, as well as a steaming bowl of beans and peas and onions. She was so hungry that it was difficult to pace herself. She'd never seen so much readily-available food in her life.

Albert watched the woman eat as if she hadn't eaten in weeks, strange emotions rumbling in his chest. He'd seen plenty of starving women, and plenty of beautiful ones, so it was difficult to surmise why this particular woman had his attention other than she was Roane de Garr's lover and Roane was in a particularly precarious situation.

Up until an hour ago, he had sided with Father Bordeleaux on Roane's sentence purely because he had no real choice in the matter. Roane had been a hunted man for his acts against God for three long years. But Albert supposed that, in his heart, he knew that Roane was not a sacrilegious man. Roane had been more pious than most of them. And Bordeleaux, as they all knew, could be less than holy in thoughts and actions. Such was the stain of power that marked him.

So he watched the Lady Alisanne eat as he wondered if there was a way to remove Roane before he was scheduled to be purified. *Purification.* That's what the Hospitallers called that horrific act. It was torture on a main scale, an event so barbaric that it made most hardened men weak. And they were going to do such things to Roane. The more Albert thought about it, the more he knew it wasn't right. Roane had been a good friend to him, once. Mayhap it was time for him to take a stand and help his friend. Mayhap it was finally time to take the lead and cease to follow the collective brotherhood. He had his own opinions about such things and Roane didn't deserve the hatred that had been cast against him.

"Will you tell me your name now, my lady?" he asked quietly.

Alisanne looked up from a piece of bread with a great slathering of butter and honey. "I am the Lady Alisanne de Soulant," she said. "My father is Baron Craven. Have... have you seen him today, too?"

Albert shook his head. "I do not remember your father, my lady," he said. "He has come with you?"

Alisanne nodded, thinking mayhap that she shouldn't tell him what her father's purpose was here, so she lowered her head back to the pears. "You said you are a friend of Roane's," she said, shifting the subject. "If that is true, then why did you let the Hospitallers take him? You know the man is innocent of those foolish charges."

Albert took a long drink of his ale. "I knew Roane well, my lady," he said quietly. "What they accused him of... it does not seen possible. But I saw the proof of his gift with my own eyes."

Alisanne's head snapped up, her irritated eyes fixing on him. "How would you have seen it?" she demanded. "Were you there?"

Albert held his ground in the face of what sounded like an accusation, which mayhap implied that he was just as guilty as Roane was if, in fact, he witnessed such a thing.

"The man he cured," he said. "I knew him. He had one eye that was bad and suddenly... his eye was healed. He said it was a miracle and that Roane had performed such a thing."

"Then you did not *see* Roane do anything."

"I did not. But the man he cured swore it was Roane that did it."

Alisanne was exasperated. "Roane was in the Holy Sepulcher when these things occurred," she said passionately. "Is that not what your Order seeks? Signs from God and the presence of miracles? Why was Roane immediately cast in a demonic light when this happened? I do not understand how such an Order who can profess to serve God could be so blind to His miracles?"

Albert looked around, making sure no one heard her as she spoke.

He held up a hand. "Quietly, please," he murmured. "Surely you know that if your association with Roane is known, you will be facing execution along with him and those who have tried to help him."

Alisanne was preparing to retort but something in what he said caught her attention. "Those who have tried to help him?" she repeated. "Who else has tried to help him?"

Albert toyed with his wooden cup as he gazed at her. "A servant he evidently enlisted to aid him," he said. "The man is now in the vault with him. Both will face execution."

Alisanne's face paled. "Execution?" she breathed, stunned. "I... I had not heard this. Of course, I have not asked anyone about Roane and I've not heard the servants speak of him... in fact, I have heard no one speak of him. My father and I had to... well, it does not matter what we did. You say that he is to be *executed*?"

Albert could see the painful distress on her features which only served to fuel his own distress. "Aye," he responded. "Two days from now."

She stared at him. No longer hungry, she pushed her food away and hung her head as the tears began to come. Fumbling, she pulled on her cloak and tried to stave off the flood of sorrow.

"I... I thank you for the information," she whispered. "I must go now."

Albert reached out and grasped her wrist. "Where must you go?"

Alisanne pulled weakly as she tried to move away. "I must find my father."

Albert wouldn't let her go so easily. "My lady, please," he said. "Do not go. Please remain."

Alisanne shook her head, wiping at the tears that were falling. "Although I thank you very deeply for the meal, I must find my father. He must know what Roane's fate is."

Albert maintained his hold on her. "My lady," he said, his voice soft but firm. "Please sit. I... I want to know why you are here."

She paused in her haste to leave, looking at him dubiously. "What do you mean?"

"Surely you did not come to Clavell to see Roane perish," Albert said quietly. "It would therefore stand to reason that you have come to free him somehow."

Alisanne didn't want to give away her intentions, fearful that this was somehow a trap. "How would it be possible for me to free him?" she asked, though it was a weak argument. "I have no means to do this."

"You said your father was here. *Where* is he?"

"I do not know," she said honestly.

"Surely he is not simply ambling about, aimlessly, while your lover faces execution. Surely you both came here with a scheme in mind."

Alisanne stiffened, one of courage and indignity. "We do not scheme. I will not deny that helping Roane escape has been in our thoughts but, as you can see, we have not the means nor the opportunity."

Albert regarded her carefully. "What have you been doing since you came to Clavell?"

"Working in the kitchens."

"Is it safe to assume that your father was working in the kitchens, too? Or, mayhap, in the stable? Working as a servant would give him access to almost anywhere in the compound."

She stared at him, seeing that his logic was much the same as hers. *He knows*, she thought. *He knows we have been posing as servants to get close to Roane.*

"Why do you ask me this?" she wanted to know.

Albert's gaze lingered on her a moment longer before reaching for the earthenware pitcher of ale and pouring himself another cup. "Because you heard me mention that a servant was captured trying to assist Roane," he muttered. "It may have been your father. I did not get a good enough look at him, but for his efforts, he too is slated to be executed along with Roane. It is possible you are all alone in this now."

Alisanne suddenly wasn't so willing to depart. She stared at Albert, trying not to feel bone-crunching agony at the thought of her father's failed attempt to free Roane. It was true that Albert had mentioned a captured servant; she never thought twice that it had been her father although she should have. She began to feel sick and weak.

"Oh…," she murmured as she sank back into her chair. She gripped the sides of it, her expression dazed as she thought on what he had told her. Her shoulders slumped. "Aye, you did mention that. You said a servant had attempted to free him?"

Albert nodded. "He put something in the food and drink he served the guards. When they went to sleep, he tried to free Roane but was caught by me and another knight who just happened to be in the area at the time. We found the guards drugged and followed the trail to Roane's cell."

Alisanne had known her father was up to something although he'd not said much about it. She could tell by the way he was acting, however, that he had something mapped out. Now she knew what it was and she was genuinely speechless. The man had failed and unless she could think of a scheme to save both him and Roane, they were both going to die. Despair clutched at her; she had no idea what she was going to do.

"What would you have me say to all of that?" she asked with soft resignation.

"The truth."

"So that you may throw me in the vault with them and execute all of us?"

"Nay," he shook his head. "I will help you get them both to safety, but there is little time. You will have to learn to trust me, my lady. I know it is difficult, but I cannot say that you have a choice if you want to save their lives."

Alisanne had all but lost her tears. She stared at the man, shocked. "You would *help*?" she sputtered. "I do not understand. You were there when the Hospitallers took him; why did you not help him then?"

Albert managed to pull her back into her chair. "Because I would have been one man against fifty," he said quietly. "As great a knight as I am, even I cannot survive such odds. But now… I know where Roane is and how closely he is guarded. I know the strengths and weaknesses. I can come up with a plan."

Alisanne couldn't believe what she was hearing. For a moment, she was truly speechless. "Is this true?"

"It is."

She continued to stare at him, wondering if he was indeed sincere. She couldn't chance disputing the man and risk him withdrawing his offer. She was out of options and therefore had no real choice but to trust him.

"Then… then I do not know what to say except you have my eternal gratitude," she said sincerely. "But I am curious to know why you would do this now? You said you have known Roane for years. Surely you were there when he was first accused and when the brotherhood first put a price on his head. Why did you not help him then?"

Albert shrugged; it was difficult to maintain eye contact with her as he felt both guilt and confusion. "Mayhap I was too willing to listen to the head of our Order when he accused Roane of being in league with the devil," he muttered. "Mayhap I have been too willing to go along for fear of being accused of Heresy just as he was. But I know in my heart of hearts that it is not true; Roane would never side with Satan. He is too true and good a knight for such a thing. Having known John Adam and his failing sight before Roane was able to heal him, mayhap I have always known it was a miracle. Mayhap God did indeed choose Roane for such a gift and we have no right to dispute it."

Alisanne gazed steadily at him through the dim light and smoke of the inn; with her bad eyesight, everything, including Albert, had a halo about it.

"He no longer possesses the gift, you know," she murmured. "He tried to heal my eyes to no avail. He had no powers at all."

Albert looked at her, surprised. "Is this true?"

"Aye," she nodded. "Mayhap God only allowed Roane to perform one miracle and it happened to be on my uncle, for he no longer has the gift of light."

Albert was fixed on one particular part of her statement. "Your uncle?" he repeated. "John Adam is your uncle?"

Alisanne nodded. "That is how I came to know Roane," she said. "I wanted him to heal my eyes as he had my uncle but when he tried, he only made matters worse."

It was a stunning revelation. Albert's first reaction was that he should bring this to Father Bordeleaux's attention. Mayhap it would make a difference and Roane would be absolved. But in the same breath, he knew it would not. Gift or no, Roane was still a doomed man. Now, it was the principle of the situation – for Bordeleaux, to back out of an execution would make him look foolish, and the arrogant leader would not allow such a thing.

"Your eyes," he said after a moment. "They are very red. What is the matter with them?"

Alisanne shook her head. "A year ago they became as you see," she said. "They have only grown worse and my eyesight has dimmed as a result. A physic has said I will soon be blind. You see, it is my fault that he was captured by the Hospitallers. A bounty hunter used me as bait, hoping to prey upon Roane's innate sense of chivalry, but Roane fell in love with me and I with him. The bounty hunter was able to capture him and turn him over to the Hospitallers so that is why I must help him; he would not be here if it was not for me. I must help him escape or die trying."

Albert was coming to understand the relationship between the lady and Roane now. "So you and your father came here to try and find a way to release him."

"Aye."

Albert pondered the situation and the events at the small castle in Shropshire where they found Roane. "I seem to remember that bounty hunter at Kinlet Castle," he said. "A rather unpleasant fellow as I recall. Wasn't there something about a marriage?"

Alisanne nodded, ashamed. "The bounty hunter knew of the affliction of my eyes," she said quietly. "He demanded my hand and my father had no choice but to comply or face serious threat. Dodge saw in me an opportunity to gain lands and titles, and I was forced to marry him shortly after the Hospitallers took Roane away."

Albert lifted his eyebrows as if the seriousness of her situation was taking on new dimension. "And he let you come after Roane?"

"I left. I am sure it will not take him long to figure out where I have gone and come for me, so you see, Roane and I must leave here very soon or all will be lost."

Albert grunted. "I would say that is a fair statement."

Alisanne's gaze grew serious. "Now that you know everything, will you *please* help me?" she begged softly. "I ask not for myself but for Roane; you know he is not guilty of what they have accused him of. Would you see an innocent man come to harm, knowing full well of his innocence? It would make you as evil as those who have falsely accused him."

Albert sighed faintly as pieces to the puzzle came together. Now, he understood a great deal. Call it foolishness, or call it his own innate sense of chivalry and honor where a fellow knight was concerned, but he knew he had to help. It was increasingly clear that he had a job to do. He had to save a friend.

"I said I would help you," he said quietly. "But you must do exactly as I say. I know this Order and I know their habits. I will do all I can to save Roane and your father, but you must trust me. Speak to no one. Remain quiet and as obedient as you can, and hopefully I can get us all out of here alive."

Alisanne nodded seriously. "Do you already have a plan?"

His gaze lingered on her a moment, his dark eyes reflecting a myriad of possibilities. "Not yet," he said. "But something will come to me."

Alisanne could only trust him and hope he was sincere. The truth was that she didn't have much choice. Albert whistled over a bar maid and ordered more ale for himself and something warm for Alisanne. They sat in silence for a minute or two until the woman returned with warmed wine and more ale. Alisanne sipped the sweet and spiced drink gratefully as Albert downed his ale.

Now that a partnership of sorts was established between them, each was lost to their own thoughts. Men's lives hung in the balance. Unfortunately, the more Albert drank, the more the drink went straight to his head and after nearly an hour in the inn, he was well on his way to being drunk. Alisanne could tell just by the way he was looking at her. She cringed when next he spoke because he knocked over the empty ale pitcher and spit all over her arm as he spouted his words.

"I know a very good physic," he said with a good deal of alcohol induced self-assurance. "I shall take you to him and we shall see if he can cure your eyes."

Alisanne had to admit she was rather intrigued by the suggestion but she was sure it was the ale that was loosening his tongue. "Is that so?" she said, sipping at her wine and wondering how she could convince the man to stop drinking. "I think that mayhap sleep is all they need right now. Mayhap we should both retire and meet here in the morning."

Albert shook his head. "Nay," he said, reaching over to grab her hand. "I will take you to him now.

Alisanne pulled her hand from his grasp. "I must go to bed," she insisted, moving to stand up. "You should go to bed, too. I will see you here in the morning."

Albert opened his mouth to argue with her when the door to the inn suddenly flew open and several men pushed into the establishment. They began shoving people out of the way and generally creating a ruckus. Although Alisanne couldn't see them very well, she wasn't concerned until she heard one man in particular. He began to bellow.

"Barkeep!" the man roared. "Barkeep, present yourself! You will service me immediately!"

Alisanne knew that voice; dear God, she knew it all too well. Terror welled in her chest as she plopped back down on the chair and pulled her hood over her head, facing away from the sounds of the commotion.

"It is him!" she hissed at Albert. "He has come as I knew he would. It is Dodge!"

Albert, in his drunken state, had no idea what she was talking about. "Dodge?" he repeated rather loudly. "Who is that?"

Alisanne hushed him frantically. "The bounty hunter," she whispered. "The man who forced me to marry him. He has come!"

Albert began to grasp what she was telling him. None too discreetly, he looked over towards the entrance of the establishment and could see several heavily armed men near the door. The innkeeper, a fearful little man with hairy hands, was over speaking with them. They could hear Dodge's imperious demands for food and lodgings. He turned back to Alisanne.

"I recognize him," he said, not sounding as drunk as he had moments earlier. In fact, he sounded rather lucid. "We must remove you from this place before he sees you."

Alisanne could only nod her head urgently, keeping the hood down around her face. Albert stood up and took her by the hand.

"Come along," he said quietly. "There is a back way."

Alisanne clung to the man as he led her into the guts of the structure, past the smoky kitchen, and out through the gaping-hole back entrance. There was a yard beyond with a few horses tethered and a soft fire glowing for the servants who were working in the yard. Somewhere, a horse nickered and a goat bleated as Albert led Alisanne through the yard in a hasty retreat, and into the alley that backed up to the inn.

It was a panicked flight that wasn't over yet. The alley was very quiet, devoid of activity now that night had fallen and people were settling in for sleep. Avoiding the street that faced the entrance to the tavern, Albert took her down the dark avenue very quickly, kicking a dog out of the way that didn't move fast enough, putting distance between them and the inn.

It seemed as if he took her a great distance because they seemed to be running for quite some time until he abruptly came to a halt, and

Alisanne held on to him tightly as he pounded on a door. With her bad eyes and the darkness of the street, she could hardly see a thing and had no idea where they were. Still, it didn't matter – all that mattered was that she was away from Dodge, as far away as she could get. Her heart was thumping painfully against her ribs, her breathing coming in short gasps, when the door that Albert had been knocking on finally opened. She found herself thrust into a dark and warm hovel.

Alisanne was immediately hit by the smell of old and rotted things. It smelled awful and she pushed her hood back slightly to assess their surroundings; it was a single room filled to the brim with more clutter than she had ever seen, and she immediately spied a tall, thin man with long gray hair down his back. He was very old and clad in dirty brown robes. Albert was already standing in front of the man, whom he seemed to know very well.

"Ovier," Albert greeted. It sounded like *o-vee-ay*. "What have you done to yourself? What happened to your nose?"

Alisanne was trying to see what was going on through the dim light. The old man grinned ruefully as he brushed at his bruised face.

"A kiss from your friends in the brotherhood's guard," he said. "I did not move fast enough when Bordeleaux came down the avenue like a conquering emperor and they made their displeasure known. Albert, why do you sound so drunk?"

"Because I am," Albert said as he eyed the old man's blackened nose. He was often one of those roughing people up in the name of the brotherhood and Bordeleaux. "But I shall sober and heal, much like your nose."

"I should have lain down in the street in front of them."

"Then they would have killed you," he said, turning to indicate the small woman in the heavy cloak. "This is the Lady Alisanne de Soulant. My lady, this is my rebellious uncle, Ovier."

Alisanne timidly removed the hood of her cloak, nodding her head respectfully to the wiry old man. "My lord," she said.

Ovier's attention was entirely on her, inspecting her as one would inspect a prized mare. Nothing escaped his scrutiny as the yellowed eyes grazed her from head to toe. Just as Alisanne began feeling very uncomfortable, the old man spoke.

"My lady," he said as he made his way towards her, extending a hand. "Never have I seen such beauty. You must forgive an old man his admiration. When are you and my nephew to be married?"

Alisanne's eyes widened as Albert chuckled. "This young lady is spoken for many times over, I am afraid," he said in his drunken flourish, "and I am not one of them, unfortunately. Nay, uncle, we have come to you for help. Lady Alisanne has a... problem."

The old man was holding Alisanne's hand, his expression concerned. "Problem? What would that be?"

Albert briefly explained the situation, starting with Roane and the Hospitallers and ending with Roane and Edward preparing for execution. Hearing Albert repeat it in his inebriated swagger made Alisanne think it was a wild and sordid tale, indeed, an unimaginable tale of crisis and woe. The old man listened carefully, still holding Alisanne's hand.

"Then her lover and father are slated for Purification?" Ovier said when Albert was finished. "That barbaric and brutal end is a weapon of the devil. It is not right in any civilized world."

Albert nodded, eyeing Alisanne and noting her distressed features. "Nay, it is not, which is why I intend to help her free them," he said, sounding a little less drunk. "But there is more, Uncle; the lady has an affliction of the eyes. I was hoping you could examine her and see if you are able to help."

The old man immediately bent over to peer at Alisanne's eyes and she naturally recoiled from his proximity and intent expression. Albert saw her reaction and hastened to reassure her.

"My uncle is a physic, my lady," he said. "He is very skilled. He learned his craft in the Holy Land and knows many wonderful and mysterious ways of healing. You must trust him."

Alisanne wasn't sure about letting the old man touch her, realizing the smell she had first encountered upon entering the hut was coming from him. *He* smelled rotted and old. Resisting the urge to pinch her nose, she flinched with the old man reached out and lifted her eyelid with a gnarled finger.

"Hmmm," he said, studying both eyes. "Do your eyes pain you?"

Alisanne nodded fearfully. "Aye."

"Are they crusted over, especially in the morning?"

"Aye."

"How is your sight?"

"Bad," she admitted. "Everything is hazy. Sometimes it is very dim."

"Do you see better in sunlight?"

"Much."

Ovier inspected her a moment longer before dropping his hands and moving over to a large, chipped table with one leg that was held together with an old piece of rope. A fat brown cat nested beneath on a bed of scraps. The table was strewn with all manner of bowls and cups and phials, wax from burnt candles and burn marks marring the surface. Ovier collected an oil lamp in the middle of the table, bringing it over to Alisanne so he could better inspect her eyes. She watched his expression with some apprehension.

"My... my uncle had the same affliction," she said as the old man inspected her left eye closely. "He had one bad eye that was glazed over."

Ovier moved over to her right eye. "It was milky white?"

Alisanne nodded as much as she could with the old man peeling back her eyelid. "Aye," she said. "Our family has a history of bad eyesight."

"It was only in one eye?"

"Aye."

"Was it red and angry?"

"Not that I recall."

Ovier let go of her eyelid. "Then that is different from what you have," he said. "You have a great poison in your eyes. It looks as if it has been there a very long time."

Alisanne didn't know if she felt better or worse. "What do you mean?" she asked. "I will go blind with it, won't I?"

Ovier moved back over to the table and began busying himself. "If I can get the poison out, then I do not see why you should," he said. "But your eyes are damaged. I can see the injury on the surface caused by the poison. I fear your sight will always be poor, my lady, but I do not believe you will lose it."

Alisanne was stunned. "Then… then I am not going blind?"

"I do not believe so."

It was the first time Alisanne had been given hope for her eyesight and she was truly surprised. All of the things that Dodge had told her, that the physic had told her, came tumbling down upon her and she was starting to think that mayhap his physic from Worcester had not been a very good one. Mayhap it had all been part of a greater scheme for Dodge to obtain more land and wealth and titles, by telling a young heiress that she was going blind and marrying Dodge was her only hope of being cared for once such a thing occurred. Like fools, she and her father had allowed themselves to be coerced. Dodge's lies to a frightened young woman had gotten him what he wanted. She was coming to feel very, very stupid.

"I simply cannot believe it might be true," she whispered. "I have been told that I would be blind. And now you say it is not so?"

"It is not so."

Tears sprang to her eyes, tears of joy and relief and disbelief. "Then what will you do?" she asked, her voice choked. "Can you help me?"

The old man was banging around on his table. He put something into a wooden cup and poured hot water into it that had been boiling over the small hearth. He stirred it a bit with his finger before bringing it over to Alisanne.

"Here," he said, handing her the steaming cup. He pulled out a small three-legged stool from against the wall and directed her towards it. "Sit and drink this. It will make you feel better."

Alisanne obediently sat, sniffing at the wooden cup. It smelled of flowers. "What is this?"

Ovier was back over at his table, now indicating for Albert to assist him. "A warm brew of rose petals, nettle, mint, raspberry leaves, and petals from the flower of mercy. Drink it."

Alisanne did. It was a slightly sweet brew that was very warming and as she sipped, she watched Albert and Ovier fuss around at the table, evidently concocting something. Albert was attempting to help but he was still so inebriated that Ovier finally chased him away. The more Alisanne drank, the warmer and more languid she began to feel. She was having a difficult time keeping her eyes open, exhausted and weary from the trials of the day, but the brew was also having an effect on her. It was making her feel very strange and fluid. Finally, Ovier turned away from his table and approached her.

"Come, my lady," he said, taking her by the arm and pulling her up from the chair. "You will lie down while I apply this medicine."

Alisanne could hardly move. She felt very drunk. She practically fell onto the cot as Albert put her legs up onto it. Ovier rolled her onto her back and in the dark smelliness of the squalid hovel, he hovered over her with only the faint hearth for light. His profile had a surreal countenance in the weak light.

"Now," he said, taking the bowl of medicines he had been mixing. "You will lie very still, do you hear? You must sleep in order for this to be effective, so be very still and go to sleep."

Alisanne was nearly incapable of speech. She looked at the old man just as he took a long stick, dipped it into the bowl, and let the droplets from the end of the stick fall into her eyes. She flinched as it stung, closing her eyes. Ovier then dug his fingers into the same bowl and began smearing something cold and fragrant over her eyelids.

"Keep them closed," he murmured as he finished putting a paste over her eyes and began to wrap her eyes up with a piece of boiled linen. "You must sleep now. We shall see how your eyes are in the morning."

Alisanne couldn't argue with him; in fact, she couldn't move. Whatever was in the brew had her floating on a sea of languid bliss, warm and delirious and calm. Very soon, she drifted off to sleep, carried away by the strains of unknown narcotics. She never even put up a fight.

Ovier was aware when she drifted into the safety of deep slumber. Her body relaxed completely and her breathing steadied. He finished wrapping the linen around her head, binding her eyes, before setting the bowl down that held the remains of the paste. The cat crept out from underneath the table and began licking the bowl. Meanwhile, Ovier wiped his hands off on his dirty brown robe, watching the lovely lady sleep peacefully. Albert, who had been watching the entire thing from the end of the bed, glanced up at his uncle.

"What did you give her to make her sleep like that?" he asked.

Ovier's gaze lingered on his patient. "The flower of mercy has such an effect," he said. "It is most helpful for inducing sleep as well as relieving pain. She will sleep for quite some time."

"Flower of mercy?"

"Aye," Ovier replied. "I discovered it whilst in the Levant. It is a mysterious flower from the far east with great pain-easing qualities."

Albert understood, his gaze trailing back to Alisanne. "What did you put in her eyes?"

The old man stood up wearily. "Cow's milk," he said frankly. "There is a property to it that tends to rid the body of poisons. I have seen it many times. Then I put a mixture of herbs and milk on her eyes to help heal them. If it is truly just a poison that infects her, then this should help it substantially. We shall see come the morning."

Albert's gaze remained on the woman now sleeping deeply before him. "Mayhap it is best if she remains here," he muttered. "I must free Roane and her father and it would be much better if I did not have to worry about her. There is something else I did not tell you – the bounty hunter who forced her into marriage is in town. That is why we fled here; we saw him not a half hour ago at the tavern near the church. You must keep the lady here. Do not let her out of your sight; otherwise, that damnable bastard might find her and all will be lost."

Ovier nodded. "She will be safe here," he said. "What are you going to do?"

Albert drew in a long, deep breath. "I am going to see Roane," he said. "We have plans to make."

"But how are you going to free the man?" Ovier wanted to know. "It 'twill be impossible to free him from the vault. There are too many barriers and too many guards."

Albert was aware of that. "I have been thinking that the only opportunity to release him will be when they move him from his cell to the gallows," he said. "I can ensure that I am on the detail that escorts him to the executioner. Once I free him, it will be of little consequence for the two of us to kill the other five guards. Then we can flee."

"It is very risky."

"I do not believe there is a better alternative."

Ovier was serious. "What is this knight to you that you would risk your life so, Albert?"

Albert sobered, his jaw ticking faintly. "He is my friend," he said quietly. "I knew it was wrong when the brotherhood accused him of Heresy. I knew it was wrong when they brought him here and savagely sentenced him. I have known this was wrong all along but still I did nothing until now. I have much to atone for. I cannot see an innocent man, my friend, purified for no reason at all. I could not live with myself."

Ovier was pleased to see that the usually rigid young knight was finally developing a conscience. "Then you will need help."

Albert could see just by his expression that he meant he should, in fact, be the one to help. Albert grinned. "You?"

"I was not a bad knight myself, once."

"That was a hundred years ago, Uncle. Can you even hold a broadsword these days?"

"One does not need to hold a broadsword in order to fight."

Albert's smile faded; he was correct. The planning for Roane and Edward's escape began at that moment.

CHAPTER TWELVE

"**W**HO IS THAT fool at the gate?" the sergeant in charge of the watch could hear bellowing outside of the Clavell Hill's gatehouse. "Is that the same man who has been demanding to see de Garr?"

Albert was standing on the second floor of the gatehouse, watching the scene below. The man Lady Alisanne had identified as Dodge de Vere, her husband, was standing at the gate and commanding that he be admitted inside. It was a foggy morning, misty, and having left the lady at Ovier's hovel the night before so that he could return to his post at dawn at Clavell Hill, Albert had been listening to de Vere howl since before the sun rose. At first he thought the man was drunk but as time passed and the behavior continued, Albert simply thought he was an idiot. He didn't even know the man but already he disliked him intensely.

"Aye," he replied after a moment, he dark gaze never leaving the men below. "Mayhap I should go down there and find out why he wants to see de Garr so badly."

The sergeant grunted. "You can go down there and tell him I'll let the archers loose on him if he does not go away."

Albert liked that thought. It would solve at least one of his problems. With a grin, he headed down to the gatehouse entry, ordering the gates open. The portcullis was down, a massive fanged barrier made from iron and wood, and he approached it as the old gates slowly cranked open.

It was dank and dark in the passageway beneath the gatehouse, the path uneven and smelling of mold. Dodge and his men were waiting as the gates opened enough so that they could slide inside. However, when they saw the portcullis was down, the demands started anew.

"Open this portcullis!" Dodge ordered. "You will admit me immediately!"

Albert reached the portcullis, his patience already thin. "You do not give commands," he growled. "Who are you and what do you want?"

Dodge was incensed. "I am Sir Dodge de Vere," he snapped. "If that name does not mean anything to you, it should. I come from the House of de Vere. I am a son of Aubrey de Vere, the deceased earl, and you will show me all due respect."

Albert wasn't impressed. He eyed the man through the gaps in the portcullis. "I have never heard of an earl's son becoming a bounty hunter," he said. "The sons of nobility have more refined professions and do not make money capturing fugitives."

Dodge was outraged. "What I do is none of your affair!"

Albert was trying not to grin at the man's indignation. "Now I remember," he said. "You are the man who captured Roane de Garr. I would not think a son of Oxford to lower himself to deal with common rabble. Moreover, I seem to recall de Vere having only one son and his name is not Dodge."

Dodge seemed to lose some of his confidence but it quickly returned, shadowed by anger. "If you remember me, then you will open this gate," he demanded. "I must speak with de Garr."

"Why?"

"That is none of your affair!"

"It is if you want me to open this gate."

Dodge grew red in the face and began to huff. "That is between de Garr and me," he said. "Open this gate, I say!"

Albert cocked a dark eyebrow. "If you do not tell me your business with a prisoner, then you will leave immediately," he said calmly. "If you do not leave immediately, then I will order the archers to let loose upon you. Is this in any way unclear?"

Dodge and his men instinctively looked to the battlements, noting that, indeed, there were archers poised upon them. Startled by the knowledge, several of them retreated back to the horses in an effort to remove themselves from the range of the projectiles. But Dodge pressed himself against the portcullis as if trying to hide from the threat of arrows. He wasn't going to leave until he had satisfaction or until they dragged him away.

"My wife," he finally said, his gaze still glued to the archers above. "My wife has fled and de Garr knows where she has gone. He has everything to do with her disappearance, I tell you. He *knows!*"

Albert debated his reply; if he truly wanted to be rid of de Vere, now was his chance. Mayhap a story or two would send Dodge on a wild chase, far away from Birmingham and far away from Roane and Alisanne. It was worth a try. He was relying on the hope that Dodge didn't seem particularly intelligent.

"Your wife?" he repeated. "Why would de Garr have anything to do with your wife?"

Dodge was still eyeing the archers. "Because... because they were lovers before I married her!"

"How is that possible?"

Dodge looked at him, exasperated. "She was at Kinlet Castle," he explained as if Albert was a simpleton. "Her father is Baron Craven and she was at Kinlet Castle when you and your fellow priests came for de Garr. She was the bait I used to lure him out of hiding. Surely you remember her? A beautiful wench with brown hair and green eyes. She was the only woman in the damn castle!"

Albert lifted an eyebrow at his condescending tone. It was time to play the game, and play it well.

"Aye, I remember her," he said, pretending to think. "In fact, you are correct. She did come here. I saw her."

Dodge was electrified. "You did?" he gasped. "When? Where is she?"

Albert stroked his chin; he saw a grand opportunity here and he was not about to waste it. "I seem to recall seeing her with another man several days ago, in fact," he said. "I saw them in town, as I remember, and he seemed to be carrying her off on his horse. I remember a good deal of screaming."

Dodge looked at him, wide-eyed. "Screaming?" he repeated. "What do you mean?"

Albert shrugged as if he truly didn't know. "He was carrying her off. I did not give it much thought at the time, but as I think on it, it was possible he was taking her away."

Dodge reached through the slats of the portcullis and grabbed his arm. "Carrying her away?"

"Abducting her."

That only seemed to inflame Dodge. "Where did they go?"

Albert was casual; it seemed to enrage Dodge all the more. "They were heading south," he said. "The man rode a gray stallion and they were heading south. He was quite big and frightening looking. That is all I can tell you. Now, get out of here before I tell the archers to let fly."

Dodge released him and dashed off in the direction of his horse. He was yelling at his men as he went, waving his arms, and Albert watched the main vault onto his horse. He and his men seemed to be in a great hurry as they tore off down the road, the one that led through the main part of the town and back off to the southeast.

Albert watched them as they galloped off, plowing through anything that was unfortunate to get in their way, peasants included. He could hear screaming and shouts once they left his sight and entered the town. Lingering on the fact that he had just sent Dodge off on a fool's errand, he was feeling quite proud of himself as he turned away and ordered the gates sealed. He was just emerging from the gatehouse into the muddy mess of the bailey when the sergeant in charge of the watch approached him.

"Well?" the sergeant said. "What did he want?"

Albert was careful in his reply, trying to sound as if he didn't care a lick. "He was looking for his wife," he said. "It seems as if de Garr and the woman were lovers. Now she is missing."

The sergeant grunted. "As if we have time for another man's problems."

Albert nodded as if to agree. "He seemed rather concerned, however," he said. "I think I shall pay a visit to de Garr and see what he knows of the woman's disappearance."

"Why?"

"Because if he is a murderer as well as a blasphemer, then Father Bordeleaux should know."

The sergeant agreed and let Albert head off to the vault without further question. Keeping his pace slow and his manner even, Albert headed down into the bowels of Clavell Hill.

CB

EDWARD WAS SLEEPING heavily, snoring loudly from the illness in his chest he seemed to have developed over the past day. Being in the damp mold of the cell didn't help matters; the man was wheezing and coughing even in his sleep.

Roane was sitting against the cold and mossy wall, listening to the man struggle to breathe. He had no idea how long he'd been sitting there because time seemed to have lost all meaning. All he could manage to think about was Alisanne and how she was faring. Edward had said she was working in the kitchens as a servant but surely by now she must have realized something was very wrong. Her father was missing and she was all alone. It tore his heart out to think of her alone and vulnerable. He struggled not to go mad about it.

The only light came from the top of the bottle cell, extremely weak even in the best of times. He could hardly see a hand in front of his face. As he sat there and pondered Alisanne and her fate, the grate at the top of the cell shifted and opened, and a rope ladder fell through.

Startled, Roane wondered if they had come to take him to the executioner. He'd lost track of the days somehow. He sat still as stone, watching one boot on the rungs of the ladder and then a second boot. Someone was making his way down with a torch in one hand, carefully navigating the flexible ladder rungs. When he reached the bottom, he landed with a thud against the straw-strewn bottom. Roane couldn't quite make out the facial features until the man lifted the torch in his hand and his head was illuminated.

"Albert?" Roane said, peering at him as his eyes struggled to acclimate to the fire light. "What are you doing here?"

Albert moved across the uneven floor in Roane's direction. "Keep your voice down," he muttered. "I do not want the guards to hear."

"Hear what?" Roane asked, but he dutifully lowered his voice. "Why are you here?"

Albert squatted down beside him, eyeing Edward as the man awoke and began to stir. "Is that Lady Alisanne's father?"

Roane nodded, his brow furrowing with confusion. "How would you know that?" he asked, trying to keep his voice down. "Albert, what has happened? Why are you here?"

Albert sighed faintly. "Much has happened, my friend," he said, quickly and quietly. "Listen to me and listen carefully; I came across your lady yesterday when she was praying at church. We had a long discussion about the situation. Roane, I must ask for your forgiveness in this matter; I did not help you when I should have. You were always a faithful friend to me and you must forgive me for not rising to your defense when the Order accused you of Heresy. I was... foolish, I suppose. I knew you were not guilty of what they had accused you of."

Roane's expression was steady. Warm, even. "There is nothing to forgive," he murmured. "Had you defended me, you would have been in the same predicament I find myself in."

Albert shrugged weakly. "Mayhap that was my fear," he muttered. "I did not want to end up like you. But I find that I can no longer remain silent about this. After speaking with your lady yesterday, I have sworn to help you."

Roane's features grew serious. "How is Alisanne? I have been mad with concern for her."

"She is well," Albert replied. "I have taken her to my uncle for safekeeping so you must not worry. But you should also know that the bounty hunter – de Vere – has followed her trail to Clavell Hill. He was at the fortress this morning, demanding to see you because he is convinced that you are conspiring to keep her from him. I was able to send him away on a fool's errand but I fear he may return once he figures out that he has been duped."

Roane could only feel anger in his veins. "De Vere," he rumbled. "I wondered how long it would take him to show up here, looking for her. Thanks to God that Alisanne is safe from him. I owe you much, my friend."

"You owe me nothing," Albert said. "I have much to atone for and taking the lady to safety is the least I can do for you. But listen to me well for my time here is brief; if anyone asks, I came here to ask you what you know about the lady's whereabouts since de Vere made such a show of it this morning. If you are asked, that is *all* I asked of you and you told me that you know nothing of her location."

"Understood."

"Excellent," he said, speaking quickly and softly. "Now, there is nothing I can do for you while you are in this prison. It is too well guarded. The only opportunity I will have to free you is when they move you out of this cell and transport you to the executioner. I will make sure I am a part of the guard and at that time, I will release you. You must be ready to help me no matter what happens. You and I will have to fight our way to freedom, my friend."

Roane felt more hope than he had in three long years; three long years of hiding, of fear, of persecution. True, he was in the vault at this moment and awaiting his sentence to be carried out, but now he had help. He had hope. Someone was willing to help him from this hell and he was humbled and grateful. He had so much to live for now, that shining beacon of love and devotion known as Alisanne, and once he was free he would escape with her to France or points east and never look back. They would be free to live their lives and for the first time, he would be utterly happy. Alisanne was the greatest motivator in the world as far as he was concerned. There was nothing else. Reaching out, he grasped Albert's hand.

"I would fight my way through Purgatory if it meant freedom and Alisanne," he murmured sincerely. "I will be ready. Whatever comes, I will be ready."

Albert gripped his hand tightly. "Good," he whispered. "Then do not despair, for there is a way out of this. I will make sure of it."

"You have my eternal gratitude."

"You would do this for me if I was in the same situation, I would hope. In any case, I will do now what I should have done three years ago."

Roane nodded faintly as Albert let go of his hand and stood up. As he made his way towards the rope ladder, he turned to him one last time.

"If you know what's good for you, you'll think about what I told you and confess," he said loudly in case any of the guards happened to be listening. "The lady's welfare is at stake and even if you're about to meet a horrible end, you should consider the lady's standing and confess accordingly. You'll not want her soul on your hands as well."

He wriggled his eyebrows at Roane as if to silently emphasize that his words were for the guards' benefit only and commenced with ascending the rope ladder. Roane watched the man climb until he finally disappeared through the hole at the top of the cell and the light went out from the chamber completely.

It was cold and dank and dark again, he turned in Edward's direction although he could barely see the man. All he could see was the glimmer of his eyes when he moved them.

"And so it comes," he whispered. "Did you hear what he said?"

Edward was sitting up, huddled against the cold wall. "Most of it," he said, his voice raspy. "He is going to help us?"

Roane nodded. "He is," he murmured. "He says that Alisanne is safe."

Edward exhaled sharply, tears of relief springing to his eyes. "Thank the saints," he whispered. "My girl is safe. I have been so terrified for her."

Roane thought on Alisanne, on the future, and on what was to happen on the fateful day that approached.

"As have I," he murmured. "But now we know she is safe and can prepare for what we must do. It will not be simple, Edward, but I know you are a brave man. Your presence in this cell is indicative of that. You must continue to be brave, for Alisanne's sake. Can you do this?"

Edward nodded and began to cough. "I can. Of course I can."

"I am pleased," Roane said, eyeing the man who sounded worse than he had earlier. His illness was gaining ground. "This will all be over soon."

Edward hacked and coughed, finally lying back down again because he felt so poorly. "Not soon enough," he muttered.

Roane concurred. He couldn't wait for this to be over, either.

CHAPTER THIRTEEN

The village of Great Barr, England
Five miles north of Clavell Hill

"CLAVELL HILL IS wrought with more defenses than I've ever seen, my lord," the weary soldier was reporting to Bowen. "The Hospitallers must be very fearful that some great army will attack them. Or mayhap they are protecting their great treasure inside. In either case, the fortress is well-fortified."

It was sunset. In a cluster of woods outside of the small berg of Great Barr where Baron Coniston's powerful army was resting after their harrowed flight south, Bowen and Joseph Ari were listening to the scouting reports with great concern. Before they could question the scout, however, a second soldier spoke.

"We were in town, my lord, and saw the scaffold building," he said. "We asked what it was for and they said a heretic is to be executed on the morrow, a former Hospitallers knight who is in league with the devil."

Bowen sighed heavily as he glanced at Joseph Ari. "It seems that we have arrived here just in time," he said, raking his fingers through his dark blond hair as he spoke to his scouts. "Did they mention my brother by name?"

"Nay, my lord."

"Did they say what time the condemned was slated for execution?"

"It was my impression that it would be dawn, my lord. The scaffold was nearly finished."

Bowen pondered that a moment. "Did you have an opportunity to assess their strengths, then?"

The first solder shook his head. "Not much, my lord," he said. "The town does not seem to have the presence of soldiers other than near the scaffolding that they are building. Most of the army must be inside the fortress."

Bowen looked at Joseph Ari. "You've spoken much about the Hospitallers as well as my brother," he said. "You told me on the journey here that you were of the Hospitallers Order once, but you did not elaborate. Now, you will tell me your exact relation to them and what you know of their strengths. I've not asked you before but I will ask you now and you will tell me the truth."

Joseph Ari's gaze turned towards the south as if beholding the great and imposing bastion of Clavell Hill. He hadn't necessarily been hiding anything from Baron Coniston but he hadn't been entirely forthcoming about certain things, his relation to the Hospitallers included. Every time they got on the subject, he would turn to something else. Now, he had no choice but to speak of it because they were on the Hospitallers' doorstep and Coniston had to know everything.

"Clavell Hill, in ages past, used to be a hive for the Romans," he said. "There is a church that was built upon older foundations and the fortress itself has incorporated old walls and old structures that were once part of a Roman city. Parts of it are extremely old. The town, including the church, surround the northern and western side of the fortress, and the Order keeps to itself for the most part except when they open the gates to go to the church."

Bowen was listening carefully. "There is no church inside the fortress?"

Joseph Ari shook his head. "Strangely, no," he said. Then, he eyed Bowen and cleared his throat softly as he averted his gaze. "I left the order some years ago. You see, I had been a warrior priest with them for many years but since Father Bordeleaux has taken charge of the Order, some… distasteful and questionable things have occurred. False charges against your brother were one of many. I was forced to make the decision of either remaining with the Order and accepting how things had become, or leaving them for good. I chose to leave them for good and went to live with my brother, who is the father of your brother's intended."

Bowen was coming to understand a bit more about this quiet and mysterious man. Now, things were starting to make some sense. "But you are still a priest?"

"I still consider myself one," Joseph Ari replied softly. "I may not have an Order any longer, but I have lived my entire life as a priest and continue to do so. I have kept the name I took when I was ordained, Joseph Ari, because it honors Joseph of Arimathea, the man who prepared Christ's body for the tomb. I live a life of piety, chastity, and poverty although I am not associated with the Hospitallers nor the Catholic Church."

"Why not the Catholics?"

Joseph Ari looked at him, then. "They hate the Hospitallers," he muttered. "I tried to join them and they would not have me."

He seemed embittered about it. Bowen thought on that a moment but didn't pursue it. It didn't matter, anyway. He gestured towards the south.

"Tell me more about the fortress we are facing," he said. "Can we get into it?"

Joseph Ari shook his head. "Nay," he said flatly. "It is impenetrable."

Bowen lifted his eyebrows in an exasperated gesture. "Why did you not say so before?" he demanded. "I have brought eight hundred men with me. Are you telling me only now that I cannot breach that old Roman fortress?"

Joseph Ari stood his ground. "I was afraid if I told you that it was impenetrable that you would not come," he insisted. "Or, at the very least, that help to Roane would be delayed somehow as you decided what to do. Nay, I could not tell you. I needed you to come. Our best hope is to lay in wait for Roane when they bring him out to take him to the scaffold. The town is populated enough so that it would be possible to lose ourselves in the crowd and strike when the time is right."

Bowen wasn't as outraged as he had been moments earlier. True, he was frustrated that the priest hadn't been entirely forthcoming about the circumstances they would be facing, but he understood the man's reasons. It was possible that he was correct. In any case, he was intrigued by the prospect of covert operations. Besides, they might not have a choice.

"Mayhap," he muttered after a moment. "If the fortress is as fortified as you say it is, we could lay siege for days and never see any progress. But if they have to open the gates to move my brother to the scaffolds, it would be the easy way to get to him. Why go in when we can simply wait them out?"

Joseph Ari nodded. "My feelings exactly, my lord. If we want, they will practically deliver Roane to you."

Bowen was pleased with that idea. In fact, he saw it as an excellent way not to sacrifice too many men in a useless siege. He motioned for the scouts to go and get food while he and Joseph Ari head back to the bulk of the army.

"I will give the men a short while to rest and eat while we formulate a plan," Bowen said. "Since we cannot go charging into the town with all eight hundred men, I will have at least two hundred accompany us into town in disguises while the rest of the army waits here and sets up a defensive line. I can only imagine that once we free my brother, we will be pursued. We will set lines of solders to cover our retreat north, or at least delay the Hospitallers long enough to give us time to put distance between us and them."

Joseph Ari nodded in agreement. He began to glance around, noting the heavy forestation around them.

"If I may make a suggestion, my lord?" he asked.

"You may."

He began to gesture to the forest. "Put men into the trees," he said. "The Hospitallers will be caught by surprise by the ambush. It will slow them down more than a defensive line would. One cannot fight what one cannot see."

Bowen cast him a long glance. "You think like a warrior."

"I was a very good one, once."

"Let us hope that remains true because tomorrow at dawn, you will go into battle with me."

Joseph Ari wasn't displeased at the idea. He came to a halt, turning to face the baron. "I would ride through Hell's fury in the quest to aid your brother," he said quietly. "He is the greatest knight I have ever known and what has happened to him is truly despicable and tragic. I realize you have not seen your brother in many years, but believe me when I say there is no finer warrior in battle and no finer man of character. When you see your brother tomorrow, look at him through such eyes. His is a fine tribute to the de Garr name."

Bowen smiled faintly, remembering his bigger, stronger younger brother with much affection. "I have missed him a great deal."

"Then let us make sure you do not miss him permanently."

Bowen's smile faded. "Have no doubt; that is my intention."

⚃

ALISANNE AWOKE TO the sound of a crackling fire. She felt warm and languid, in that misty area between sleep and consciousness. She shifted slightly, turning her head and attempting to open her eyes but she was met by darkness. She panicked.

"My eyes!" she cried. "I cannot see!"

There was movement around her. She could hear joints popping and fabric rustling. "Steady, lady, steady," Ovier said. "Your eyes are wrapped. Allow me to unwrap them and we shall see how well you have healed."

It took Alisanne a few moments to remember where she was and what had happened. In the dark as she was, she was completely disoriented. A knight named Albert had brought her to a physic's hovel and the man had put something in her eyes. Aye, she was remembering more clearly now, and she clearly remembered the smell when Ovier drew close. It was pungent and offensive. He pulled her into a sitting position.

"Easy, lady," he said softly. Alisanne could hear him fumbling with something and suddenly, the bindings across her eyes began to move. "You have been asleep a very long time. How do you feel?"

Alisanne's fingers flitted around her face, touching the bindings across her eyes. "I... I am not sure," she said, still not over her fright of having awoken to darkness. "Well enough, I suppose. How long did I sleep?"

The bindings were loosening as Ovier cut them away. "An entire day and night," he said. "It is an hour or two away from the dawn."

Alisanne's thoughts turned away from her eyes and towards the coming day. Something horrible was filling her mind, something that threatened to restore the panic. "A day and a night," she murmured, trying very hard to weed through her sleep-hazed mind and remember something that Albert had told her. *In two days....* "Then... then it has been almost two days since Albert brought me here?"

"Aye."

Her stomach began to lurch, emotions of horror welling in her chest. "Where is Albert?"

Ovier pulled away the last of the bindings. "He shall be here shortly," he replied. "He has been out and about, making plans to save your lover. There is not much time now, so I am told. He is to be executed this day."

Alisanne could hardly breathe. She was in a state of utter despair when the bindings came away, so much so that she had her eyes closed, trying to stave off the torrent of emotion. But at some point, her eyes opened. It took her several long moments to realize that she could see the room; she could see the broken down table, the walls, and the old man sitting before her in great detail. The light wasn't particularly bright, but it didn't matter; she could see better than she had in over a year. Her eyes widened.

"Sweet Jesus," she murmured, holding out her hands and turning them over and over, noting the dirty nails and pale skin. "I can *see*."

Ovier was trying to gain a look at her eyes, reaching out to pull up an eyelid even as she was moving around, looking at everything around her.

"How *well* can you see?" he asked, peering into her right eye. "Are things clearer? Do they still have the odd halo around them?"

Alisanne was overcome; it was enough, for the moment, for her to forget about the coming horror. As she could see the detail in her surroundings for the first time in ages, she began to laugh hysterically.

"There is no halo," she said joyfully. "I can see the blisters on my hands and the cat underneath your table. I can see you, too, and you look to be as old as Methuselah!"

She was laughing as she said it, which made Ovier grin. "I *am* as old as Methuselah," he told her. "Now, be still, silly wench. Blink your eyes and tell me if you feel any pain or scratching."

Gasping with joy, she blinked several times and shook her head emphatically. "No pain!" she cried. Then, she jumped up and threw her arms around his neck, strangling him happily. "I can see without pain! You have performed a miracle!"

Embarrassed with her show of affection but pleased just the same, Ovier patted her hand as she kissed his dirty forehead. "No miracle, I assure you," he said, watching her wander off, visually inspecting everything in the room as if only now seeing for the first time in her life. "Your eyes had poison in them, poison that had been left to fester. It was simple enough to clear up."

Alisanne was in the process of picking up and studying nearly everything she could get her hands on. "But I have seen a physic," she insisted. "He said I was going blind from disease."

"He was an idiot," Ovier sniffed. "As I said, your sight may never be perfect, but at least we can clear out the poison that you have suffered from."

"What did you put into my eyes?"

"Goat's milk. There is something in it that rids the body of certain poisons. I have seen it many times."

She stopped inspecting his table and looked at him with an expression suggesting disbelief. "Do you mean to tell me that if the physic who originally examined me had put milk in my eyes, then I would have been quickly cured?"

"More than likely."

Alisanne struggled not to become angry to that. There was no use, anyway. All that mattered was that Ovier had been able to clear up what she had been told would blind her and her joy knew no limits. She felt as if she had been reborn. As she bent over to pet the cat, Ovier went to retrieve a pitcher of water and a bowl. He poured clean water into the bowl and took it to Alisanne, who was instructed to wash her face with it, especially her eyes. As she splashed water, the old man collected a polished bronze disc, blew off the dust, and held it up to her.

"Now," he said softly, "look at your eyes."

Water dripping off her face, Alisanne found a beautiful young woman with bright green eyes gazing back at her. It was the first time in her life that she had ever seen herself clearly and the moment was not lost on her. Tear pooled in her eyes as she took the disc from Ovier, staring at her reflection and seeing it with clarity and beauty such as she had never known.

"I have never seen myself quite so clearly," she murmured hoarsely. "'Tis rather shocking."

Ovier laughed softly. "Such beauty often is," he said. "Now you know why men are willing to live and die for you."

The smile faded from her face and she looked up at him. "Where is Albert?" she begged softly, wiping the moisture from her eyes. "Surely they are preparing to take Roane to the scaffold. What is Albert doing about it?"

Ovier patted her shoulder and turned away, shuffling over to a corner of his hut where a pile of possessions lay. He began rummaging through them.

"Do not fret," he told her. "He will be here."

"He should not be here," Alisanne said. "He should be ready to help Roane."

Ovier pulled something out of the pile and turned for Alisanne, extending the item to her. "He is," he assured her. "Here; this is a comb I made for my wife. It has not been used in thirty years. I do not believe she would mind if you used it."

With the mirror still in one hand, Alisanne timidly reached out to take the comb. "Thank you," she said softly. "Where is your wife?"

"Dead."

"Oh," Alisanne looked back at the crude comb. "I am sorry for you, but I appreciate your generosity. My possessions are in the fortress, including my comb."

"I know. Make yourself presentable, for Albert will soon be here."

"Are you certain?"

"I am."

He sounded so confident so Alisanne hastened to do as she was told. She ran the bone comb through her dark hair, all the while watching herself in the mirror. She was still coming to grips with the improvement of her vision, seeing things in the reflection of the mirror that she'd never seen before. Mirrors were precious and rare, and the one she'd had as a child, which had been her mother's, had been damaged long ago. Looking at it now made everything distorted.

Ovier had told her not to worry and that Albert had a plan to free Roane, but she couldn't help but worry. As she combed her hair, she thought on Roane and the hell he must have endured for the past several weeks. He had been injured enough when the Hospitallers had taken him from Kinlet, but weeks in a vault could do a lot worse to a man's health. Not knowing how he was tore at her and threatened to drive her mad. But soon enough she would know his health and soon enough, she would see him.

She had to trust Albert; she had no choice. She'd long stopped hoping for her uncle and Roane's brother to show up, like avenging angels, saving them all from the corruption of the Hospitallers. It had been weeks since Joseph Ari had gone in search of Baron Coniston. Mayhap he never found him; mayhap something had happened to him along the way. Whatever his fate, he was not here now and that was the only thing that mattered to her. Baron Coniston and his powerful army were not here to save Roane. It was up to her and Albert.

As she reflected on her fears, she noticed a strip of leather on the table top that was attached to the end of a dull knife, perhaps used to hold it on a belt or satchel. Untying it, she used the leather to tie off her hair into a long braid. Ovier was over by the hearth, returning to the table with a thick porridge that had been bubbling in a pot and finding a small bowl of crystalized honey on his cluttered table to sweeten it with. It was an unexpected treat and Alisanne hungrily slurped it down. Just as she was finishing with her bowl, the door to the hut lurched open and a big body walked through. The door slammed heavily behind it.

"I see you are awake, my lady," Albert said. He was dressed in full armor including a tunic bearing the colors of the Hospitallers sect, yellow with black. He looked rather fearsome as he pulled off his gloves and set them down. "How are you feeling?"

Alisanne was on her feet, her eyes wide at him. "Your uncle has cured my eyes," she said. "It is truly a miracle."

Albert peered at her eyes, looking better than he had ever seen them. With her combed hair, she looked quite beautiful and cared-for, certainly not the red-eyed waif he'd become acquainted with.

"They look very well," he agreed. "I am glad he was able to help you."

"So am I," she said. Her manner was very anxious and it was clear she didn't want to discuss her eyesight, at least not when heavier things were weighing upon her. "Your uncle says I have been asleep nearly two days. Is Roane all right? Have you decided what you shall do to free him?"

Albert cast a long glance at his uncle before answering her. "This shall be brief, my lady, as I am expected back at the fortress shortly," he said. His manner grew serious. "You understand that his sentence is to be carried out today."

She blanched but tried not to show how shaken she was. "I do."

Albert nodded and continued. "I have spoken with Roane. He is well, as is your father. In about an hour, Roane and your father will be taken from their cell and transported to the scaffolds near the square. I will be escorting them along with eight other soldiers and two knights. What I did not plan on was the fact that we have been ordered to keep Roane heavily restrained; he will be chained to a post because they still fear his omnipotent power. I did not tell him what you told me, that he no longer possess the power, because that would mean I have spoken to you and as far as everyone knows, you and I have never seen one another."

Alisanne looked very worried. "How will you free him if he is chained?"

Albert lifted an eyebrow as his focus shifted to his uncle. "I will need you in the crowd today near the scaffold," he said to him. "When the wagon carrying Roane approaches, I will need you to create a diversion of some kind. Anything at all in order to allow me to loosen Roane's chains. Once his is unchained, I will provide him with a weapon and we will run for our lives. My lady, this is where you will come in."

Alisanne was eager. "What can I do?"

Albert pointed a finger at her. "You will be carrying enough clothing to cloak me, Roane, and your father adequately so that we may blend in with the peasants," he said. "We will run to you and you must be in a place we can easily find you. Do you know the square near the cathedral very well?"

Alisanne shook her head. "Nay," she replied. "I have spent most of my time in the kitchens of the fortress."

Albert shook his head. "It is of no matter," he said, turning to Ovier. "You will take her to the corner near the well, the corner where the cobbler's business is located. Do you know which one I am referring to?"

Ovier nodded shortly. "I do."

"Take her there," he instructed. "Leave her with as much peasant clothing as you can find. My lady, you will wait for us there. Under no circumstances will you move. Is that clear?"

Alisanne nodded firmly. "It is," she said.

"Good," Albert replied, his gaze moving between the two of them. "About an hour ago, I took my charger and another steed I'd managed to steal and placed them in a livery on the outskirts of town. It is my intention to reach that livery and ride as hard as we can away from here. Ovier, once you create the diversion, you must retreat back to your home and remain. I do not want them to discover your involvement."

Ovier appeared much calmer than Albert or Alisanne. In fact, he seemed almost casual about it. "You needn't worry," he said. "No one will suspect an old man and if they do, well... I have lived a long life. I am not afraid of Bordeleaux's soldiers."

Albert cocked a stern eyebrow. "Try not to get caught, do you hear? I do not want to have to come back here to rescue your old hide from the scaffold, either."

Ovier waved him off. "You won't," he said. "What manner of diversion did you have in mind?"

Albert scratched at his forehead, partially covered by his hauberk. He was calm, methodical in his thinking, but it was evident that he was on edge. So much depended upon him that it was difficult to not feel apprehensive.

"A stampede?" he said, throwing up his hands as he thought aloud. "A fight? A fire? You decide, Uncle, for I cannot spare the time. I must return to Roane and we must all be clear on what is to happen. If one of us does not do as we are supposed to, then all will be lost. Roane and the lady's father will meet their death by purification and that is an ugly way to die."

Alisanne's eyes widened. "Purification?" she repeated. "What does that mean?"

Albert didn't have the heart to tell her if she didn't already know. He didn't want to frighten her more than she already was.

"It is a manner of being put to death," he said simply before turning to Ovier. "You should both be ready and in position by sunrise, for that is when we will be bringing Roane out of his cell. Do not delay."

Ovier nodded, as did Alisanne. Albert grabbed a piece of bread from his uncle's table, bread as hard as stone, and chomped it down as he pulled his gauntlets back on. Without another word, he quit the hut, leaving Alisanne and Ovier in the sudden and brittle silence. The weight of the approaching situation was not lost on either of them, although Ovier was much more in control about it than Alisanne was. As she stood there looking as if she had just seen a ghost, Ovier began to move.

"Come along, lady," he said briskly. "We must collect what we can to disguise the men in. I believe I have enough here to adequately conceal them but you must help me inventory it. Come along, now."

Alisanne began to move purely because he told her to, but her thoughts were running wild. "What are you going to do to create a diversion?" she wanted to know. "Albert said you should create a stampede!"

Ovier grinned as he moved about. "Albert wants me to create chaos, and chaos I shall," he said. "One does not need to create a stampede in order to do that."

"Then what will you do?"

Ovier began to pull pieces of material from a wadded pile under his cot. "Many years ago, when I was a young knight, I went on the second crusade to The Levant with King Louis of France. Oh, my lady, I was fascinated by everything I saw in my travels! The Levant is a land of great mystery and wonderment. It was during that time that I realized I was more interested in the mystic arts than in warring. Warring was simply a way to kill men and conquer countries; the mystic arts held the secret to Life itself."

Alisanne cocked her head. "Mystic arts?"

Ovier nodded as he pulled out more garments. "How do you think I learned to put fresh milk into your eyes?" he said. "The physics of The Levant know much more than we poor Christians do about healing. In the wilds outside of Jerusalem, I found a man who lived very much alone but who knew many wonderful and miraculous things. We became friends and I learned how to create pastes to draw out poisons, and how the body works against certain medicaments. But I also learned other things, like how to create fire that will burn even when water is poured upon it."

Alisanne's eyes widened with curiosity. "Truly?" she said, awed. "What manner of fire is this?"

Ovier finished tossing cloaks at her and stood up, stiffly, and made his way back over to his cluttered table. "Ingredients that the Arabs knew of but that the English are limited in," he said as he began to fumble around. "My mentor, Asharif the Good, taught me to make burning lime and *saltpetier* from wood ash. When mixed with bitumen, it can create a fire that will not be extinguished with water. It will burn anywhere. It is my intention to create a fire to distract the Hospitallers so that Albert can free your lover."

Alisanne was property impressed. She stood a moment, watching Ovier as he began to pull out bowls of ingredients, carefully filling small gourds with his mysterious mixtures. He seemed so very confident in what he was doing, which in turn fed her own confidence. With such great minds working to help Roane, surely there could be nothing less than success. She felt extremely grateful.

Still, she had her own work to do and she forced herself to continue with her tasks of assembling disguises for Roane and Albert and her father. Although fear continued to nip at her, she was determined and resolute; she had a job to do, something that would help Roane and her father escape to freedom. She could not, and would not, collapse like a frightened fool. The lives of the men she loved best depended upon it. But, God, she was so very frightened. She found herself praying steadily as she worked.

The time was upon them.

CHAPTER FOURTEEN

H<small>E HAD DIED</small> about midnight as far as Roane could tell. Edward de Soulant, Baron Craven, had succumbed to whatever cough and fever had him in its grip for several days and just before midnight, his breathing became labored and weak. Roane had held the man to comfort him and as midnight struck, the man had breathed his last in Roane's arms.

Roane was devastated on Alisanne's behalf, knowing how much she had loved her father. She had risked her life to save him once, even at the expense of luring Roane into a trap. But all of that was behind them now, bits of memories to join all of the other memories in their minds like stars blanketing the sky. There were so many good memories in that star band that they wiped out the early memories of the fear and distrust and suspicion he'd first had upon meeting Alisanne. Now, Edward felt like family and he mourned the loss deeply.

Roane had yelled up to the guards when Edward had passed away but he had been ignored, so as the night progressed and Edward's body began to stiffen, he rolled the man into the corner and covered him with damp hay to show him a small measure of respect. It simply wouldn't have been right to let him lie in the middle of the cell, his body cooling, as if he was no better than an animal. So he put him in a corner and murmured a few prayers.

The night passed and Roane contemplated what the morning would bring. He hadn't seen the sun in days, weeks even; he had seriously lost track of just how long he had been in the cell because he had no sense of day and night. He only knew that it was approaching dawn because he'd heard one of the guards overhead mention what he'd had for supper that night. Roane's head hurt constantly and the wound to his chest had been very slow to heal although, thankfully, it had never grown rancid. It was mostly healed now but lack of food and fresh air and adequate comfort had left him exhausted and weak. Still, knowing that Albert was ready to help him escape and that Alisanne was well had kept him alive. He would take on the devil himself if he thought it would help him escape these horrific bowels and into Alisanne's arms.

At some point, he must have slept because when next he realized, someone was lifting the grate on the top of his bottle cell and creating a bit of a racket. Instantly awake, with his heart in his throat, he watched as the rope ladder was dropped and armored men began descending. So the time had come. Still he sat, waiting, until the fourth man descended and they all stood around, looking at him as if waiting for him to rise up and throw lightning bolts from his fingertips. In fact, when he lifted his hands just the slightest, two of the men jumped in fear. He fought off a grin as a big knight with a no-nonsense manner about him broke from the pack.

"Enough with this foolishness." It was Albert and he reached down, grabbing Roane by the arm and hauling him to his feet. "Put your wrists together, de Garr. No tricks or you shall not like my reaction."

Roane had to make a show of distaste for Albert lest the others catch on that he knew the man and was partial to him. With obvious disdain, he held out his arms as slowly and reluctantly as he possibly could, as if irritated by the entire undertaking.

"So you come now," he said, his voice low like thunder. "I've been calling to the guards for hours. My cellmate has died during the night and must be removed."

A ripple of shock crossed Albert's features that was quickly gone. He slapped the shackles on Roane's wrists and began to twist the tightening screws. "I am not concerned about a dead animal in the corner," he said. "All I am concerned with is you. Will you come peacefully and with honor, or will we have to bind you and cart you from this place like a caged beast?"

Roane couldn't help but notice that the shackles weren't tight at all;

in fact, he could easily slip his hands from them. "I will come peaceful-ly," he said evenly, "but only if you tend to this dead man and give him a proper burial."

He could tell that Albert was confused; *is Roane serious? I don't have time to bury the lady's father!* "I will see that he's tended to," he said after a moment. "Will you come peacefully now?"

"I will."

Albert led Roane to the rope ladder and, rather roughly, shoved him at it and forced Roane to climb. He did, surprisingly deftly considering his wrists were shackled, but as he reached the top, more guards grabbed his arms and pulled him out of the hole. He ended up tripping onto his knees and as he struggled to get up, a voice he knew very well filled his ears.

"De Garr," Bordeleaux said, a hint of sinister to his tone. "So the day of reckoning has come for you."

Considering he'd spent weeks in darkness, even the dim light of the upper level of the vault was bright to Roane and he blinked his eyes rapidly as he focused on Bordeleaux. It was the man who had pursued him across deserts and mountains, into England, still always in pursuit as if Roane was the most dangerous and vile criminal ever known. He was still tall, slender, and resembling Christ in dress and appearance. Tertious Bordeleaux was a horrific excuse for a priest, more demon than angel.

For a brief, electrified moment, they simply stared at one another. Roane seriously considered lunging at the man and throttling him, but he fought off his natural instincts. To make a move would be to completely negate his chance for escape. They would probably kill him on the spot. Therefore, he simmered.

"It has," Roane said after a lengthy pause. "As it will come for you as well, sooner than you think. Tell me, Bordeleaux; when you stand before God in judgment, what will be your excuse to him why you threw the label 'heresy' on any man who did not allow you to do as you pleased, or any man whose piety and devotion to the Order was greater than your own? Do you think God will forgive you of your most deadly sins of envy and greed?"

Bordeleaux's smug expression faded. "I do not have to answer to you, de Garr," he said. "Worry about yourself for you will meet God much sooner than I."

"Mayhap," Roane replied, almost casually. "If I do, I will make sure to tell him everything I know about you so that when you finally meet, you will have much explaining to do."

Bordeleaux had lost his humor completely. He reached out and grabbed Roane by the arm, his fingers digging into his cold and dirty flesh.

"You are an instrument of the Devil," he snarled. "I will take great pleasure in your death today. Long have I waited for this moment."

Roane didn't reply. He met Bordeleaux's seething gaze with his usual steady resolve. Roane knew what the man was about, his corruption and wickedness, and Bordeleaux was aware of de Garr's knowledge. He was a threat indeed, in more ways than one, but mostly, he seemed to be a threat to Bordeleaux himself.

"Get him out of my sight," he growled. "Take him to the scaffold where we will purge his dark innards and lay him open for all to see. Today is a day of deliverance for the holy and righteous of England. Today we do away with Satan's right hand!"

He was being dramatic, as he usually was. The man had a big mouth and a loud voice. Albert shoved Roane away from Bordeleaux, grabbing his arm as he yanked him up the narrow flight of steps and into the daylight beyond. It was raining outside, a fine mist coating the land, as Albert dragged Roane to a wagon that was strewn with damp and musty hay. As he forced Roane to his knees, two soldiers came up with a heavy piece of wood between them, about six feet in length, and they lay the wood across Roane's broad shoulders.

Albert took the lead in strapping Roane's arms to the pole, making sure the ropes looked tight but in reality, they were quite loose. He wouldn't let anyone else tie Roane down, instead, keeping up a steady stream of curses as he strapped the man to the pole, spewing hatred and blaming Roane for the general failings of mankind. Bordeleaux had followed them up to the bailey to watch the prisoner loaded and was pleased by Albert's attitude and general roughness towards Roane.

But it was all an act; by the time they loaded Roane into the wagon, Roane had to hold on to the pole because the bindings were loose enough that the pole might slip from them if jostled too much. That would end the charade far too quickly if that was to happen. He had to make a show of it.

As the mist turned into rain and the wind began to pick up, Bordeleaux and two other priests climbed into a fine carriage to precede Roane's wagon from the compound. The gates of Clavell Hill were open and the portcullis was up as Bordeleaux's carriage headed out, making the sharp left turn that would take them directly to the square and the scaffold. Roane in his wagon, surrounded by eight soldiers, with two knights in the lead and Albert bringing up the rear, lurched from the gatehouse and followed Bordeleaux's carriage into town.

It was dawn and people had turned out to see the heretic brought to justice. The weather seemed to be keeping the crowd size down as the wet and weary stood along the muddy avenue, watching the procession pass by. Roane kept his head down, trying to appear as if he was penitent and frightened, when in fact he was trying to locate Alisanne among the sopping peasants from the corner of his eye. It was cold, with rain dripping off his pink nose, when they passed by a group and he swore he saw his brother's face beneath a dark hood. But he couldn't gain a clear look and they passed by before he could make a second try.

The storm was increasing and a bolt of lightning streaked across the sky. It was enough to chase more people inside, the lure of a good execution not strong enough to keep them out in the elements. Roane was soaking wet, feeling cold and miserable, but more than alert and prepared for what needed to be done. He couldn't see Albert but he knew the man was around. His body was tense, waiting for all hell to break loose. He knew it was coming, too. He had to be ready.

Something hit him on the temple and he staggered, seeing stars dance before his eyes. Looking down at the hay around him, he could see a cold wet rock glistening in the rain. He could also feel something warm trickling down the side of his face and he knew it was blood. So he tried to keep his head down, not wanting to get knocked out by frenzied peasants before he had a chance to escape. He doubted Albert would be able to lug his unconscious body to safety.

More lightning lit up the sky and he glanced up, noting that the rain was falling heavier now. They were passing through a narrow part of the avenue and the buildings were close; people were hanging out of the second floor windows to watch the solemn procession roll by. Roane shook the water from his eyes and as he did so, he noticed the town center up ahead and the dark shadows of the scaffold. He could feel his pulse quicken as his gaze beheld the tall, narrow lines of the scaffold; whatever was going to happen had to occur soon because the platform for his death was upon them.

He labored to remain calm, his innate sense of knightly control feeding his manner. He kept his attention focused on his surroundings, on Albert, and on Alisanne. He knew that she must be nearby; he couldn't see her but he could feel her, that sweet heart of warmth that he'd missed so terribly. He had no idea what her role was in all of this but he knew that she would be participating somehow. He couldn't wait to see her, praying that everything worked out as it should and very soon they would all be on their way to safety. It was the only thought that kept him going at the moment.

Hurry, Albert! Whatever you're going to do, do it soon!

CHAPTER FIFTEEN

"THERE HE IS," Bowen muttered from beneath his heavy hood. "Do you see him?"

Joseph Ari's dark eyes were fixed on the beaten figure of Roane as they paraded him down the street like a prize buck. The rain was pounding, the wind whistling, and some in the crowd were throwing objects at him, mostly clumps of mud. Someone actually hit him in the head with a sharp or hard object and the blood ran. Joseph Ari heard Bowen growl.

"I see him," the priest replied. "It looks as if the Hospitallers have not been kind to him."

Bowen's jaw ticked. "I can only imagine what they have done to him," he murmured. "Even so, he is still a very big man and, even in his weakened state, I would imagine very powerful."

Joseph Ari was well aware of what Roane was capable of. The man had the strength of Samson. "The men await your signal, my lord. You should not wait too long. Once he is on the scaffold, it will be more difficult to retrieve him."

"I am aware of that," Bowen said. "The men are waiting for me to throw back my cloak and lift my sword. It is my sense that it will be easiest to take him when they try to remove him from the cart. We can rush them then and overpower them."

"Agreed, my lord," Joseph Ari whispered anxiously. "They are nearing the scaffold now. We should move forward so we are closer to your brother."

Bowen began to move. As he did, men in the crowd, cloaked men against the elements, began to move as well. There was an entire sea of men moving towards the scaffolding, men who were burdened with heavy armor and weapons beneath their rain cloaks. Bowen had brought two hundred and eleven men with him into town, all of them concealed for what was sure to be a vicious fight. Hospitallers were warriors as well as priests and from what Bowen could see, there were more than a hundred of them surrounding the scaffolding and monitoring the crowd. Coniston's men easily out-numbered them, which was a mark in their favor.

As Bowen and Joseph Ari neared the scaffold, a bolt of lightning clipped the church that was off to their left about a dozen yards away. The crowd cried out in fear as a piece of the bell tower chipped off and fell to the ground. Many peasants were scared off by the display, which filtered out the crowd and created a clearer path between Bowen and his brother. The odds in their favor were increasing and Bowen continued to push forward.

The wagon carrying Roane began to slow as it neared the scaffold. Bowen was close enough that he could see the details on his brother's lowered head. His body tensed as he prepared to act but he wanted to wait until Roane's guards were in motion before he did anything so that there would be more confusion and more of an opportunity to wrest Roane away from the guards. Chaos would be to his advantage.

Bowen glanced over to his right and saw several of his men gathered a few feet away; all of them had crossbows slung beneath their cloaks. Since the village hugging the perimeter of Clavell Hill wasn't walled, it had been easy to slip in with weapons because there hadn't been any check points. If was evident that the Hospitallers felt very safe in their old Roman fortress, so much so that security for the village was lax. In fact, all of Bowen's men were heavily armed. They were ready for a fight.

The wagon came to a halt and the villagers began to surge forward, crowding around the cart as the guards yelled at them and shoved them back. One guard in particular jumped into the wagon bed with Roane and grabbed the big pole across his shoulders to turn him around. It was clear that he was preparing to take him off the wagon. When

Bowen saw this, he knew he could wait no longer. He made sure he was making eye contact with the group of his men several feet away when he tossed back his hood and flashed his broadsword. The group of soldiers collectively raised their crossbows and projectiles began to fly at the guards surrounding the wagon.

In an instant, chaos ensued. Screams went up and people started to scramble. Several men were hit by the arrows, including Albert. Hit in the shoulder, he lurched sideways and fell off the cart completely, and Roane was unable to grab him. As the lightning flashed and the thunder rolled, Roane heard himself screaming in anguish.

"*Nay!*" he cried.

His focus was on Albert but in short order he realized there was a vicious fight going on around him. Men in armor and weapons were charging at him, fighting off the Hospitallers guards, and suddenly a man he recognized was leaping onto the wagon. The man was moving so fast that he nearly knocked Roane over, his momentum nearly carrying them both over the side. Roane's eyes widened in astonishment as he focused on the familiar features.

"Bowen!" he hissed.

Bowen flashed a grin at his brother, slapping him lightly on the cheek as he went to release him from the shackles.

"You silly lad," Bowen grunted as he yanked off a shackle. "Did you really think I would let these idiots execute you? Did you really believe I would not come? God's Bones, why are these shackles so loose? You could have freed yourself!"

The chains came off and the big pole fell away. "I was going to," Roane said as he took the pole and launched it into the writhing mass of men. He took a brief moment to gaze at his beloved older brother appreciatively. "'Tis good to see you, brother."

Bowen grabbed him by the face and kissed his cheek loudly. "And you."

Roane couldn't help grin at his brother's show of affection, a moment of sweetness in the hell going on around them. "That knight you hit with your arrow was helping me," he said. "We must help him, Bowen."

As several of Bowen's men had leapt onto the wagon to defend both Bowen and Roane, a couple of them knocked the wagon driver off and took his place. Suddenly, the cart lurched forward and everyone standing on the wagon bed went down, including Roane. He grabbed hold of the sides to steady himself.

"Wait!" he bellowed. "We cannot leave Albert!"

Bowen was hollering orders to the struggling crowd of men they were leaving in their wake, commanding someone, anyone, to collect the Hospitallers knight who lay off to the side with an arrow in his shoulder. Roane couldn't see what was happening as Bowen's men turned the cart about and prepared to make haste towards the city outskirts. When he realized they were about to take him out of the village, he grabbed his brother.

"I cannot go yet!" he yelled. "I must find Alisanne!"

Bowen knew that. There was also the matter of leaving Joseph Ari behind, which he would not do. Somehow, he and the priest had gotten separated. He began to look around frantically.

"Where is Joseph Ari?" he demanded, to anyone who could answer. "He was with me a moment ago. Damnation, *where is he*?"

No one could answer him; the soldiers on the rear of the wagon were fighting off more Hospitallers who had come rushing down from the scaffold and were now trying to jump onto the wagon. Roane, seeing that they were about to be swamped, noticed the broadsword hanging from the hip of the wagon driver and he lunged for it, grabbing the weapon off of the man, and goring a Hospitaller who was trying to climb over the side of the wagon. As the mortally wounded Hospitaller was kicked away, Roane turned to his brother.

"Alisanne is around here somewhere," he said, yelling above the noise and bedlam. "I have to find her!"

Bowen opened his mouth to reply but he was interrupted by a column of fire that suddenly exploded next to them. Heat and flames roared, and the horses pulling the wagon panicked. The cart toppled over on its side, spilling everyone out across the wet and muddy ground. Roane rolled across the mud and scrambled to his knees just as another burst of fire hit the ground several feet to his right and shot up into the heavens. He could feel the heat of the explosion, even through the cold and the rain.

At first he thought it might be lightning strikes, but he had never seen lightning such as this; it was like balls of flame exploding, spraying those nearby with bits of flaming debris. The flaming debris would then stick to whatever it happen to land upon and continue to burn. Nay, this wasn't lightning. This was something else entirely and it only added to the pandemonium going on around them.

"Satan's followers!" came a booming voice from the roof of the building directly in front of him. "Demon soldiers who call yourselves men of God! Here me now! God will punish you for sentencing Roane de Garr, do you hear? He has given me the power to destroy all of you if you do not let him go!"

Over the wind and thunder, the man's voice still carried astonishingly well. Both Roane and Bowen craned their neck back to see who was shouting such curses from the rooftop when they saw the man launch another projectile. This one sailed over their heads and hit the ground very close to the scaffold, bursting into a giant ball of flame. Some of the flame splashed on to the relatively dry underbelly of the scaffold where it clung fast and ignited the wood. Smoke began to rise as the great wooden scaffold began to burn.

"Evil doers!" the man roared. "Sinners, all of you! Judgment is coming for you and you shall all perish in the lake of brimstone!"

By now, the entire town center was a writhing quagmire of frightened and fighting men. The villagers had long since fled, leaving a battle in their wake. Bowen's men were engaging more Hospitallers who had poured from the old Roman fortress and were now rushing to join the fight. While the majority of the men Bowen brought with him were occupying the Hospitallers, Bowen and several soldiers were huddling around Roane, shoving him away from the engagement.

"Who is that old man?" Bowen demanded, pointing up to the roof top.

Roane shook his head, going along with the group as he continued to search frantically for Alisanne. "I have no idea," he said. "Evidently someone who hates the Hospitallers as much as I do."

"I would agree with that."

"Those bursting flame projectiles were most effective. I have never seen such things."

Bowen didn't particularly care about the bursting bombs of flame; he was more concerned in removing his brother, who was quite unwilling to go. "Whoever he is, his intervention is most welcome," he said, trying to get his stubborn brother to move. "Roane, we must leave. The longer we remain, the more chance of you being captured again."

"I am not leaving Alisanne," Roane said, struggling against the men who were pulling at him. He realized they were moving him away, heading for the village edge, and he began to bellow. "Alisanne, where are you? *Alisanne!*"

No reply was forthcoming and he fought off his rising panic. There was no way he was going to leave without her. He knew she was here, somewhere; *he knew it.*

"Alisanne!" he cried again. "Alisanne, answer me!"

"Roane!"

He heard the distant scream and he froze, as did the men around him, all desperately trying to search out the direction and source of the cry. The rain was intensifying, falling in great silver sheets and seriously compromising visibility. As they all strained to see, the cry came again and through the crystalline wall of rain, a figure emerged on the square near the main well. It was small and slight, fighting through the rain as it approached.

It was Alisanne.

Roane could see her through the mist, a few dozen yards away. She was waving her arms frantically, rushing towards him, and he broke away from his brother and began racing towards her.

"Alisanne!" he bellowed.

"Roane!" she cried in return, slipping on the mud and ending up on her knees.

Roane saw her go down but it wasn't a terrible fall, simply slippery. The hood of her cloak came away, rain falling upon her silky brown head. Roane was straining with every fiber of his being to reach her, to get to her and bring her to safety. He had to hold her, touch her, and smell her. Only then would his soul be healed. Only then would he be whole. Dashing across that mud was the longest run of his life.

A run that was brutally interrupted, his hopes and dreams dashed in one horrifying moment. Out of the mist, like a surreal demon, came Bordeleaux, who had been at the base of the scaffold when the chaos broke out. He had been watching everything, moving in Roane's direction to stop the man from fleeing when he saw the lady emerge from the rain. She had been calling Roane's name and the more Bordeleaux looked at her, the more he recognized her from Kinlet Castle. He had married the woman to the bounty hunter, remembering how she had wept through the entire ceremony. But now she was here. Somehow, someway, she had come for Roane. Bordeleaux was convinced the woman was behind his prisoner's escape. He could not let that happen.

He had to stop it.

Bordeleaux reached Alisanne before Roane was able to get close. With a slender, wicked-looking dirk in one hand, he grabbed Alisanne and put the dirk against her torso, the threat and implication obvious. He wound his fingers in her hair, listening to her scream in pain. It was empowering. He yanked again and she screamed louder. With his screaming captive, he faced Roane.

"Another step and she dies!" he cried. "Throw down your weapon, de Garr! Tell your men to throw down their weapons or I will kill the lady right in front of your eyes!"

Roane came to such a sudden halt that he skidded on the slippery ground and went down on one knee. There was utter, complete horror to his expression and the broadsword in his hand clattered to the mud.

"Nay!" he gasped. "Do not hurt her, I beg you!"

Alisanne was terrified and overwhelmingly disappointed at having been caught by the evil bastard who had spent three years pursuing Roane. She could hardly believe it. Out of sheer fright, she began to fight and twist, feeling the sharp dirk poking at her side.

"Let me go!" she demanded, struggling to pull away. "Let me go, I say!"

Bordeleaux was distracted with her fight. She was surprisingly strong and he yanked on her hair to force her to stop, but Alisanne wouldn't back down. She screamed when he pulled her hair but then she tried to kick him.

"Cease!" Bordeleaux commanded her. "Do you hear me? Stop it or I shall gore you, I swear it!"

Alisanne was crazed with fight. She managed to twist around in his arms and grab at him with clawed hands. The first thing she came into contact with was his hair and she pulled as hard as she could.

Bordeleaux yelled in pain and the dirk was dislodged by the lady's flying elbows. As soon as the dirk fell away, Roane rushed the pair, tackling Bordeleaux. They went hurtling to the ground, as did Alisanne because Bordeleaux still had his hand wound up in her dark locks. She screamed in fright and pain as she was pulled to the ground and the men began to fight.

Hands, many of them, were reaching down, trying to free her from Bordeleaux's grasp. Roane was on top of the man, one hand around his neck as the other hand grasped the wrist that held on to Alisanne, squeezing so hard that he heard bones crack. Bordeleaux screamed in pain and his grip loosened, enough for Bowen to pull Alisanne free. Bowen thrust her at his men for safekeeping as he swooped in to assist his brother.

But Roane needed no assistance. He had Bordeleaux exactly where he wanted him, his hands wrapped around the man's neck and squeezing the life from him. Three long years of persecution, of pain and fear, were finding a release as he choked the priest to death.

It was the moment he had dreamed of during all of those lonely days and months and years he had spent isolated, fearing for his life, praying he would have the opportunity to end his torment once and for all. At this moment, his torment was very close to being over. But before Bordeleaux lost consciousness completely, Roane had a few things to say to the man.

"For every pain, every fear, and every moment of despair you caused me, you will feel my wrath until the end," he seethed. "For every false accusation, you will breathe a little less. For everything you took from me – my dignity, my reputation, my possessions, and my honor, your eyes will dim and you will draw your last breath by my hand. When you meet God, as you shortly will, I am certain he knows of every horror you have committed against me and against Mankind in general. Men such as you are the antithesis of reason and goodness. You are an evil abomination, and I thank God that my face is the last one you will ever see upon this earth. Look into my eyes and see how much I hate you."

With that, he used both hands and crushed Bordeleaux's windpipe. The neck bones cracked and Bordeleaux's panicked expression glazed over, gradually fading. His body twitched and an odd exhale expended from his lips, and as the rain fell and the lightning flashed, Father Tertious Bordeleaux fell still.

Roane didn't move; he kept his hands wrapped around the man's neck as if fearful of letting go, fearful the man would rise up again and once more Roane would be on the run. This had to end and he would make sure of it. He squeezed and squeezed even when it was clear that Bordeleaux was dead. Finally, Bowen bent over him.

"Roane," he murmured hoarsely, his hands on Roane's wrists. "He is dead, Roane. Let go."

Roane squeeze harder, feeling more snapping and grinding in Bordeleaux's neck. "Not yet," he grunted. "Not yet."

Alisanne, standing back with Bowen's men, watched the scene with shock and horror. The entire circumstance was horrific but one thing occurred to her; it wasn't over yet. Men were still fighting all around them and they had to leave. She was terrified that the Hospitallers would capture Roane again so she rushed up to him, kneeling beside him in the mud. There were tears in her eyes as she spoke.

"Roane," she whispered, a soft hand on his arm. "Please... let us leave. We must get out of here!"

Her soft and gentle voice seemed to break through his state. His grip loosened and he looked at her, only to notice almost immediately that her brilliant green eyes were not red and crusty as they usually were. They were clear, as clear as he had ever seen them. She looked radiant. His thoughts immediately shifted from Bordeleaux to Alisanne, and his heart bloomed full with the joy of seeing her before him, safe and sound. He was overwhelmed with it.

"My beautiful lass," he murmured, the hands that had so recently been clutching Bordeleaux's throat now moving to touch her face. He was trembling. "Are you well?"

"Very well, my love."

"Your eyes... they look so clear," he said, awed. "Can you see me?"

Alisanne could see the happiness in his expression and she laughed softly, tears of utter elation rolling down her cheeks.

"I can see you very well," she assured him as he ran a quivering hand over her forehead as if to make sure she was whole and healthy. "Albert's uncle healed my eyes. He is a wonderful healer. He has done so much for us, my love, so very much. There is so much to tell you but we must leave here immediately. Are you well enough to run?"

Roane stood up; he didn't give Bordeleaux, lying dead in the mud, another thought. The man was dead and that was all he cared about. Now, he could get on with his life and live without the fear that had haunted him for three long years. The force behind that fear was at his feet. He had killed the fear; that was the way he saw it. He had taken that fear and destroyed it.

"I am well enough to fly if you wish it," he said, cupping her face and taking a moment to gaze into those beautiful features. All he could feel was the fluid warmth of emotions that made his heart sing, loving her so much that it was difficult to verbalize. "I love you, Alisanne. You and no other, for all time."

Alisanne touched his face, watching him kiss her hand reverently. "And I, you," she whispered reverently.

They both heard Bowen sigh heavily beside them. "I hate to interrupt this touching repartee, young lovers, but we must collect all those who should not be left behind and desert this village," he said, his hand on Roane's shoulder. "You two can have all the time in the world to tell each other of your undying love once we've reached a safe haven."

Alisanne and Roane turned to Bowen, who was looking rather serious. Alisanne broke into a grin. "Greetings, Bowen," she said. "It is my greatest pleasure to finally make your acquaintance."

Bowen fought off a smile, seeing in that instant why his brother was so mad about the truly lovely young woman. She was sweet and charming.

"And you also, my lady," he said. Then he turned to his men. "Find Joseph Ari and find that Hospitallers knight that was attempting to aid my brother. He has an arrow in the shoulder so he should not be difficult to miss. Meanwhile, I am taking my brother and his intended out of here. We shall meet up in Great Barr, so give the retreat order and clear the men out. We have what we came for."

A few of the men began moving to carry out his order but Alisanne interrupted. "And my father?" she asked anxiously. "Please do not forget him. Where is he?"

Roane cast his brother a long look and faintly shook his head before grasping Alisanne by the arm, preparing to escort her out. "We will never forget him," he murmured, avoiding her question and praying she didn't press him at the moment. "Come along, now. We must leave before I end up on the scaffold and you along with me."

It was evident by Roane's expression that the lady's father was not to be recovered, at least by Bowen's guess, so he sent his men about their tasks as he grabbed his brother and, with the escort of a few armed men, began dragging him along as they headed out of the square. Roane had a strong grip on Alisanne, pulling her with them as they ran. Together, the group of them raced through the rain and thunder, down the narrow avenues, until they reached the outskirts of the village where several horses were tucked away in a dense copse of trees.

There was no longer a sense of panic among them but the air of urgency was still strong. They still had to get away, and get away quickly. As Roane and Bowen untethered the horses from the trees, a lanky figure in brown robes emerged through the wet shrubbery. The men drew swords, startled by the appearance, but Alisanne could smell the figure before she ever saw it. She turned with surprise to see Ovier coming through the leaves. She gasped and ran to him.

"Ovier!" she cried. "Are you well?"

The old man nodded, putting a hand on her shoulder to calm her. "Very well," he said. "I thought, mayhap, I might find you and your lover out here on the edge of town. It is a perfect place to gather, shielded from the road. I see that my instincts were correct."

Alisanne nodded eagerly. "We must leave now," she said, her eyes soft on the old man who had done so much for her. He had, in every sense of the word, saved her. He had given her hope again. "Will you come with us? I should like it very much if you would."

Ovier patted her shoulder. "Nay, my girl," he said. "Although I will miss you a great deal, my place is here. It is my home. But you must promise to send for me if you ever need me; I will come."

Alisanne was disappointed but she understood. "Of course I will," she said softly. "Thank you. For everything you have done for us, I thank you."

"There is something familiar about you," Roane ventured, interrupting their tender conversation. "Weren't you the one who threw the flaming projectiles?"

Both Alisanne and Ovier turned to him. "I was indeed, my lord," Ovier replied. "A little something I learned whilst on Crusade in The

Levant."

Roane grinned. "A worthwhile acquisition," he said. "You must also be Albert's uncle."

"I am."

"Then I owe you a great deal," he said, his features softening. "Alisanne tells me that you cured her eyes. I have not yet learned how you accomplished such a thing but truly, it is a miracle. You have my undying gratitude."

Ovier looked at Alisanne and they smiled at each other. "It wasn't such a miracle, as the lady will tell you," he said. Then he took her hand and led her over to Roane. "Now, you two must flee. I only have a few flaming projectiles left and I intend to use those on any Hospitallers that attempt to follow you. It will bring great joy to my life, you know; burning up Hospitallers. I have not had such fun in years."

Roane laughed softly as he helped Alisanne mount a leggy brown steed. Weak and weary and cold as he was, he nonetheless had the strength of the angels as he mounted behind her. He was at the end of a horrible three year journey and all he could see on the horizon was the joy of a wife and children and a limitless future. All he could see was hope.

"Burn up enough of them to help us get far away," he told Ovier. "We shall be in your debt."

Ovier simply waved them on as they spurred the horses through the trees and out into the road beyond. His smile faded as he watched the group disappear into the mist, wondering if, indeed, their paths would be smooth from now on. He hoped so; it seemed as if they had suffered through so much together, the knight accused of Heresy and the lady with the eye disease. He prayed their journey in life from this point on would be a smooth one.

Ovier was disappointed when he didn't get to burn up any more Hospitallers that day because none seemed terribly apt to pursue Roane and his rescuers. With Bordeleaux dead, there was anarchy and confusion in the air, so he saved his projectiles for another time.

Mayhap to use on a day he was feeling particularly ornery.

CHAPTER SIXTEEN

I N THE LATE evening and after the flight from Clavell Hill, Roane, Alisanne, Bowen and his army ended up in the berg of Stafford, a larger town where it was a relatively simple thing to hide an eight hundred man army. Bowen broke his men up into three separate armies to better conceal them rather than in one great mass. If the Hospitallers decided to march against Coniston's army, it would be less clear to them who, exactly, the enemy was if they were to only find smaller armies and not one big one. Bowen was done with the engagement and he wanted to keep it that way.

While his men camped all within a few miles of each other and enjoyed massive sides of beef that Bowen had purchased from a local farmer, Bowen and Roane had found lodgings in a large tavern called the Skull and Sickle on the edge of town. Joseph Ari was with them as was Albert, with a shoulder wound, who had caught up to them and had spent the evening being tended by a local physic. In the early morning hours, he too slept heavily.

The inn was two-storied and of newer construction. At the rough, stained table that sat in front of the smoldering hearth in the great room, Roane sat with Bowen and Joseph Ari in the early morning hours before people began to seriously stir for the day. In fact, there were several travelers strewn about the room, sleeping with their meager possessions, but Roane and Bowen and Joseph Ari paid them no mind. They were enjoying a loaf of fresh, hot bread, butter, a warm brew made from lavender, apple juice, wine dregs, and cinnamon, and the first peace they'd known in weeks. It was like the calm after the storm.

"After the frenzy of yesterday, it still seems hard to believe that I am finally free," Roane said as he sipped his brew. "Even as I sit here now in the peace and darkness of the dawn, I still feel edgy somehow, as if expecting Bordeleaux to burst through the door at any moment."

Joseph Ari, with a huge bruise on his cheek and a bandaged left hand, also sipped at his brew. There were big dark circles around his eyes. "You spent many years living in fear of the man," he said quietly. "You cannot expect to overcome what has become your nature overnight. Those feelings will fade with time."

Roane shrugged faintly. "I suppose," he said. "It still seems odd. *Peace* seems odd. I've not known much of it."

Bowen was chewing on his bread. "You will," he said. "As the priest said, you must give it time. You will live with me at Gargrave until you decide what to do with your life. I can use you, Roane. 'Twould be my greatest joy to have my brother back in the fold, the most powerful knight our family has ever produced. I would be proud."

Roane glanced at him, smiling faintly. "I certainly cannot return to Alisanne's home, Kinlet Castle," he said, sighing. "That belongs to de Vere."

Bowen picked at his bread. "What do you intend to do about that situation?" he asked the question they were all wondering. "She is married to another man, Roane. What are you going to do?"

Roane sat back in his chair; he'd been contemplating that for the better part of the night. When he wasn't sleeping like the dead, short as it had been, he had been pondering his future with Alisanne. He didn't like that they would be living in sin, living and loving as though they belonged together before God and the law, even though she was married to another. He wanted her married to *him*.

"I wonder where de Vere even is now," he muttered. "Albert said he sent the man off on a fool's chase when he came to Clavell Hill on the hunt for Alisanne, knowing she would have come to me. He could be half way to London by now in the hunt for her."

Joseph Ari grunted. "He is not *that* much of a fool," he said. "He managed to hold my brother and I hostage, force Alisanne to act as bait to draw you out, capture you, and then marry Alisanne to collect the barony. Don't count him out, Roane. He will eventually figure out that he has been duped by false information and when he does, he will return to Clavell Hill in search of you and in search of Alisanne. Mark my words; men like Dodge de Vere do not give up. They are dangerous."

As Roane reluctantly conceded the point, Bowen spoke. "And he is your lady's husband," he reiterated quietly. "I asked you once before but you did not answer – *what* are you going to do?"

Roane was contemplative a moment as he pondered that serious dilemma. "According to Alisanne, they never consummated the marriage," he said. "If the marriage has never been completed in every sense of the word, then mayhap it can be annulled. Moreover, they were married by a Hospitaller and not an ordained priest of the Catholic Church. If the Church does not recognize the marriage, then it is not valid."

Bowen nodded. "Excellent point," he said. "We must find out. There is a priest in Gargrave whom I know well. We will ask him when we return."

Roane liked that idea; it gave him hope. "I am most anxious to get her within the safety of Gargrave's walls," he said, reflecting on the childhood home he'd not seen in many years. "It will be good to go home."

Bowen looked at his brother; he'd not had much time to talk to him yesterday in the midst of their harrowing adventure, but now that the situation was relatively calm, he looked forward to coming to know the man again. Much had happened in the past fourteen years.

"Things have changed since last you were there," he said, draining the last of his brew. "To begin with, I married about ten years ago. I have four sons and the eldest two are fostering at Newcastle. You will like my wife, Roane; Estelle is a wonderful woman. Half-Spaniard, you know. When we argue, she screams at me in Spanish and I cannot understand a word of it. It makes it easier to walk away."

Roane grinned. "Congratulations on your marriage and your sons," he said, lifting his cup to him. "I, too, hope to have such fortune when Alisanne and I marry. I hope to be the father of many sons."

Bowen tipped his cup against his brother's, accepting his accolades. "Speaking of father," he said, "how did Alisanne take the news of her father? Surely you told her."

Roane's warm expression faded. "I had to," he said, toying with his cup and looking somewhat saddened. "When Joseph Ari caught up to us last night, and Albert subsequently found us, she became almost frantic for news of her father and I had to tell her. She wept hysterically until I plied her with enough wine to put her to sleep. She is sleeping still. She is exhausted."

"Can you tell me what happened to my brother?" Joseph Ari wanted to know; his expression was wrought with sorrow. "All I was told is that he died but I was not told how."

Roane looked at him. "Edward became very ill while in captivity with me," he said, his tone laced with sympathy. "Whatever affected him settled in his chest. He could not breathe and he ran a fever for days. In the end, it was just too much for him. I held him as he died and promised to take care of you and of Alisanne. I believe I was able to give him comfort."

Joseph Ari nodded with some gratitude and averted his gaze. He was close to tears and did not want Roane or Bowen to see his weakness. He was exhausted like the rest of them, bruised and battered, and his brother's death weighed heavily upon him. But he was pleased they had at least managed to free Roane and collect Alisanne. So much of their objective at Clavell Hill could have gone wrong and, for the most part, all of it turned out for the best. Except for Edward's death; Joseph Ari knew it was going to take some time to come to terms with it. He knew it would take Alisanne time, too.

"Then I thank you for what you were able to do for him," Joseph Ari said as he cleared his throat. "His only thought would have been for Alisanne's safety and you have seen to that. He would be grateful."

Roane watched the man struggle with his emotions. "And you,

Joseph Ari?" he asked softly. "What do you intend to do now that Edward is gone and Kinlet Castle is in the hands of an idiot?"

Joseph Ari lifted his head, smiling weakly. "I thought to come with you wherever you go," he said. "I can still lift a sword."

Roane reached out and put a hand on his slumped shoulder. "You and I have had many adventures together, have we not?" he said, a twinkle in his eye. "Mayhap we will have a few more before we are forced to give up our swords and live our lives as old men."

As they laughed softly, the door to the inn flew open and loud, noisy men spilled forth. In fact, they were so loud that most of the sleeping bodies in the great room began to stir, disturbed by the cold rush of air and the booming voices. Abruptly, the peaceful conversation that Roane and Bowen and Joseph Ari were having was interrupted by rude and boisterous men.

It wasn't an unusual occurrence. Taverns were full of irritable and loud travelers. But this group was different; there was something about them that made Roane take a second look. He was sitting with his back to the wall and facing the door, watching the knights as they began to remove their gloves and helmets. His gaze lingered on the group a moment before, gradually, he began to stiffen. His eyes narrowed and his hands tensed up. Bowen saw his reaction and eyed him curiously.

"What?" he wanted to know. "What is the matter?"

Roane didn't take his eyes off the group commandeered a couple of tables and began to sit.

"De Vere," he hissed, hateful sound of unimaginable hazard. "Christ, that's *him!*"

Bowen's head snapped around to the knights now settling in and calling for food. He counted at least eight of them as they banged on tables and kicked sleeping men aside.

"I thought he was off chasing rumors?" he whispered loudly. "Didn't your Hospitallers friend say he was off running wild?"

Roane nodded sharply. "He did," he said. "But for some reason, he has returned. God's Blood... of all the damnable luck."

"Stay calm, Roane," Joseph Ari instructed coolly. "Do not do anything to attract their attention, at least not until we can arm ourselves."

Roane simply shook his head, the irony of the situation not lost on him. "I cannot believe what my eyes are telling me," he muttered. "Mayhap it is as you said – mayhap the man realized he was chasing phantoms and is returning to Clavell Hill to resume his search for Alisanne. But why this tavern, in this town? There are so many others he could have gone to."

Bowen wasn't going to wait to find out. He stood up swiftly and brushed past his brother. "I am going for more men and weapons," he muttered quickly. "Keep your head down until I return. Do not let him see you. Roane, do you understand me?"

"I understand you."

Roane's heart was thumping against his ribs as his brother fled the room, apprehension filling his veins. He wasn't frightened, but he was concerned. This was an unexpected and wholly unwelcome occurrence. However, as he sat in the shadow of the hearth and watched Dodge smack the innkeeper, he began to think that mayhap it was a very fortuitous occurrence.

Before him was the man who stood between him and Alisanne's marriage. He was the obstacle, the barrier that needed to be removed. Moreover, the man before him was the one who had turned him over to the Hospitallers so they could execute him for false charges. Dodge de Vere had tried to kill him in every sense of the word. He was very dangerous, and rather than run from danger, Roane would face it. He would face it and triumph. Roane had to eliminate the very threat to his life.

Aye, it was vengeance. It was *wholly* vengeance. But it was also for peace, for as long as Dodge de Vere lived, Roane and Alisanne would never know peace, and Roane wasn't going to live the rest of his life as he had the past three years as a hunted animal. Nay, he would end this now.

Fortunately, Dodge and his men were more interested in a morning meal than they were their surroundings. One inn was like another, sleeping drunkards and smelly walls, and they delved into the bread and ale the innkeeper brought them with gusto. Roane and Joseph Ari were able to sit back and watch the men eat, scrutinizing every move they made and assessing just how armed they were. Each man seemed to have numerous weapons on his body, which would be normal considering they had been traveling. Threats abound on the open road. As Roane began contemplating the horrible death he had planned for Dodge, a small figure on the stairs off to his right caught his attention.

Startled, Roane turned to see Alisanne descending the stairs and terror surged through him so strongly that he nearly toppled of his chair. *Nay!* His mind screamed. *Alisanne, go back! He will see you!* The woman was out in the open where Dodge could easily recognize her. It was just too terrible to believe, an appearance that was most unwelcome.

He had to stop her, or protect her at the very least. Unless he wanted to yell at her, which would only cast the light of focus on her even more, he had to get to her somehow. Instinctively, Roane leapt up from his chair and tried to make his way to the flight of steps without attracting attention. He moved swiftly in the dim light but Alisanne was oblivious to what was going on; her focus was on Joseph Ari over by the hearth and she waved at the man as she descended the steps.

The stairs were too wide-open to be missed by anyone, including Dodge, and Alisanne was half-way down the stairs when he realized the woman he had been searching for was right in front of him. As Roane reached the bottom of the stairs in a futile attempt to divert Alisanne, Dodge leapt up from his chair.

"You!" he screamed. "It is *you!*"

Alisanne heard the shout, turning with shock in the direction of the sound. True, she'd seen the group of men as she descended the stairs but the room was so dim she hadn't given them a second glance. Now, she was coming to regret that decision with shocking clarity because Dodge was on his feet, leaping over chair and kicking over tables in his haste to reach her. Alisanne was frozen to the spot as the man approached her like some hellish nightmare. She could only pray that she was still asleep and that was all this was – a nightmare.

But it was no horrible dream. It was as real as rain and twice as ominous. Fortunately for Alisanne, Roane was much closer to her than Dodge was. He mounted the steps two at a time and grabbed her, forcing her back up the steps.

"Get into the room and bolt it," he commanded. "Do not open it for anyone but me or Bowen or Joseph Ari. Is that clear?"

Alisanne nodded frantically and scrambled back up the steps as Roane shoved her, helping her move quickly. But Dodge was already on the steps, charging up with his men behind him like some great and awful human tide, and she screamed when she saw how close he was. Roane, hearing her scream, turned to see that Dodge was nearly on top of them. Lashing out a massive boot, he kicked Dodge squarely in the head and sent the man crashing back on his own men. All of them tumbled back down to the bottom in a heap of armor and flesh.

Roane, seeing that Dodge was delayed, at least for a few seconds, swung around to Alisanne.

"Go!" he roared.

Alisanne shrieked as she ran off, disappearing back down the narrow corridor to the room she had slept in. Roane heard the door slam and with that, he felt much better. At least he knew she was locked in and somewhat safe. Now, he could face Dodge without having to worry about her.

Dodge was on his feet amidst the pile of his men. He recognized Roane in an instant, fury and outrage evident on his face. For several long seconds, it was as if his mind couldn't grasp what his eyes were telling him. He just stared at Roane as if incapable of moving. The dead had arisen as far as he was concerned. A ghost was standing in front of him.

"You are supposed to be dead!" he finally bellowed. "Why did those bastards let you live?"

Roane was providing a very big barrier, albeit unarmed, between Dodge and the top of the steps. He looked dirty and disheveled, mayhap a bit thin, but he was still a very big man nonetheless. By far bigger than Dodge. But the fact remained that he was unarmed and until Bowen returned, Roane would have to hold off Dodge with wits and body alone. His sharp mind worked quickly, trying to think of a way to stall the man until the weapons arrived and it would be more of a fair fight.

"Surely you remember what they accused me of," he said to Dodge, sounding smug and calculating. "Heresy, among other things. You will of course remember that I was accused of using witchcraft to heal a man. Lightning shoots from my fingers. Or have you forgotten that?"

As he'd hoped, his statement gave Dodge pause. There was something in his expression that suggested he was at least contemplating what Roane had said. Aye, he knew what the man had been accused of. There was some fear and mystery to that.

"I had you for days and you never once showed any sign of witchcraft," he muttered. "If you are so capable, why didn't you use it on me and free yourself?"

Roane lifted an eyebrow. "My hands were tied," he said, lifting a big hand as if to show him an example. "Now they are free. If I were you, I would be very careful about my next move. I am here because the Hospitallers are dead, including Bordeleaux. They tried to execute me but, well… I was not agreeable to it. They have been duly punished."

He was flexing his fingers ominously. Dodge and his men couldn't help but take notice, glancing at each other nervously. It was true that when they'd first captured him, he'd been subdued and restrained, hands included. But now he was free. The apprehension surrounding them began to grow and a couple of Dodge's men actually backed away.

Dodge felt the apprehension but he wouldn't surrender to it, at least not yet. He was a proud man, too proud for his own good. He pointed a finger at Roane.

"You had the opportunity to use your witchcraft on me when first I saw you," he said accusingly. "On your mountaintop retreat you could have killed me with your lightning but you didn't. You let me go and it cost you. Will it cost you again? Now you have my wife and I want her. She is mine."

Roane wouldn't back down and now that Alisanne had been brought into the conversation, he would let them know he was quite prepared to kill them all in order to protect her. He lifted both of his hands and the majority of Dodge's men took a healthy step backwards, wary of his intentions. Roane wasn't quite sure what he was going to do if they charged him and he couldn't produce the lightning bolts, but for now, he had them sufficiently frightened. That would do until his brother could return.

"Your marriage is invalid," Roane said confidently. "You were married by a man who was not ordained by the Catholic Church; therefore, they do not recognize your marriage and it is invalid. Kinlet Castle does not belong to you, nor does Lady Alisanne. She will soon be my wife and the Craven barony will belong to me. All of your scheming and betrayal will be for naught."

Dodge's face flushed with outrage. "You are mad!"

"You haven't consummated your marriage yet, have you?" Roane said, a twinkle of mirth in his eye because he simply couldn't help humiliating the man. "She hasn't let you touch her, meaning even if your marriage had been conducted by an ordained priest, it still would be in danger of annulment. Face the facts, de Vere; nothing belongs to you, especially not the lady."

Dodge's face turned all shades of red. "You bastard," he snarled. "I shall kill you for this, do you hear? Your witchcraft cannot save you now!"

As he took a step towards Roane, the back door and front door to the establishment flew open and men with weapons began pouring in. Startled by the sudden rush of armed soldiers, Dodge and his men unsheathed their weapons and soon a full-scale battle was occurring in the middle of the great room. Chairs smashed and tables overturned.

Bowen, spying his brother half way up the flight of stairs that led to the second floor and sleeping rooms above, made his way over to him and tried not to get struck in the process.

"Roane!" he called. "Your weapon!"

He was extending a sword to Roane but Dodge, who was nearer to Roane than Bowen was, saw the exchange and threw out his broadsword, clipping Bowen on the wrist. It was enough of a strike to cause Bowen to drop the weapon and Dodge was able to punch the man in the face for good measure. Bowen dropped to the ground.

Furious, Roane began to come down off the stairs. He leapt on Dodge, throwing him to the floor as he began to pummel him furiously. Dodge screamed, trying to protect himself, but it was no use; Roane's fury was unleashed and he beat Dodge mercilessly. Every strike, every infliction of pain, had a meaning behind it; vengeance for his capture, vengeance for the marriage to Alisanne, vengeance for the pain and suffering Dodge had caused. All of it had a meaning, and Roane showed no mercy. It was a brutal beating.

Meanwhile, one of Dodge's men had made it onto the flight of stairs. Roane was so busy beating Dodge to death that he never saw the man slip up the steps and make a break for the sleeping rooms. As Roane beat Dodge into unconsciousness, the man managed to break into two rooms, the second of which contained Alisanne. Alisanne screamed as the man rushed into the room and grabbed her by the hand. But his grip slipped and he ended up latching on to her hair. Screaming and fighting, Alisanne was pulled from the room.

Roane heard the screams. Dodge was a bloody pulp at his feet and he froze, horrified at what he was hearing. About the time he rose to his feet, the soldier had Alisanne at the top of the stairs. She was howling something fierce, trying to fight the man but being prevented by the grip he had on her.

As Roane watched in horror, it appeared as if the man intended to throw her down the stairs and panic flooded his veins; he did the only thing he could think of. Lifting his hands as if by sheer force of will he could stop what was about to happen, he put every ounce of fear and pain and horror into one terrific shout. Everything he was, and everything he would ever be, was bundled up into that cry. It was the force by which Nature was moved. At this instant, Roane moved all of Nature.

"*Nay!*"

At the sound of his voice, something burst out from his hands, like invisible bolts of lightning, hurling up the staircase and crashing into the soldier that held Alisanne. The force of the strike was enough to cause the man to release his grip and he hurtled backwards, slamming into the wall behind him so hard that part of the wall crumbled and the soldier ended up half-in and half-out of the tavern. There was a big hole now where once had been a solid wall and the soldier who had created it was quite dead, his upper torso and head hanging out of the building before the dust had even settled.

It all happened in a flash. Smoke trailed up from the dead man, permanently smashed into the broken wall, and the entire body of writhing, fighting men came to a startled and fearful halt. Even Roane was startled at what he had done; he stood there, his hands still lifted, looking at the results of what his utter and total terror had caused. Alisanne had been in danger and all he could see, think, or feel was his horror at that prospect. There was nothing else in his heart at that moment than the desire to save her.

And he had.

Alisanne, gripping the banister from where she had fallen against it, looked at Roane with something more than complete shock; it was disbelief in its purest form. True, she had seen what had happened, an odd force of energy flying from Roane's hands and killing the man who was trying to toss her down the stairs, but she still couldn't believe it. In truth, mayhap she wasn't meant to believe it. Mayhap she was simply meant to accept it. Just like a full moon or the rise of the tides, there were some things that weren't meant to be understood but merely accepted. As she gazed at Roane, eyes wide, she knew this was one of those things she wasn't meant to understand.

In fact, no one understood what they had just seen, least of all Roane. He tore his eyes from Alisanne, looking at his hands, feeling that his fingertips were very, very hot. Mouth hanging open, his gaze found Alisanne again as if to say…

… I guess I do still have the power!

Power, indeed. Men around him began to back away, forgetting their fight as they struggled to move away from him. Dodge's men grabbed their bloodied and beaten liege, making haste out of the tavern before de Garr turned his awesome power on them. No one wanted to be cast down by a man who had powers beyond their comprehension. It was the most astonishing thing any of them had ever seen. And it was utterly terrifying.

Bowen had seen all of it. He rose stiffly from the floor, his features a mask of shock. Timidly, he touched his brother on the arm, getting his attention. Roane was torn between looking at his brother and still inspecting his hands, trying to figure out just how he had managed to accomplish such a thing.

"Roane?" Bowen ventured hoarsely. "What… what was that?"

Roane shook his head helplessly. "I truly don't know," he muttered, awed and breathless. "All I could see was Alisanne's death and every corner of my soul was determined to prevent it. I held up my hands instinctively to protect her and…."

He couldn't finish his sentence. He was as baffled as the rest of them. Bowen finally reached out and took one of Roane's hands, peering at it as if to note something different from ordinary hands. But they looked ordinary enough to him. He was stumped.

"This goes no further," he said, mostly to his men standing behind him who had witnessed the entire incident. "We will speak of this no more, is that clear? If word of this gets out, I will find out who spoke of it and punish the man accordingly."

"Dodge's men saw it," Roane said, gesturing to the dead soldier burrowed into the wall. "They'll speak of it. Mayhap they're already riding for Clavell Hill as we speak to spout it to anyone who will listen."

"If they do, no one will believe them," Bowen grunted. Then he threw up his hands in exasperation. "Who would? It's pure insanity to even entertain such a thing. But I must ask, Roane… when it happened… how did you do it?"

"I don't know!"

"But what were you thinking?"

Roane lifted his big shoulders, trying very hard to pin down what he had been thinking at that exact moment. "I am not sure," he said. "It was as if my entire mind and body joined together and… I cannot explain this other than to say the power I thought I'd lost evidently wasn't lost at all. I thought it was gone but clearly, it is not. I have no idea how I summoned it."

"You did not summon it," Joseph Ari stepped forward, pushing through a group of Bowen's men in order to reach Roane. His weary eyes glimmered at the man. "It summoned you and you responded in kind. Don't you see, Roane? God has given you a gift and through you, He works miracles. You used this gift on me once before and you healed me. Now you have saved the woman you love. Don't you see? God has given you what he has given no other; a touch to save and a touch to heal."

Roane looked at the man who had been there the day he had received his "gift", the day the lightning struck the slab in the Holy Sepulcher. His gaze lingered on him a moment before moving to the stairs where Alisanne still stood. His features softened as he focused on her.

"I couldn't let her come to harm," he murmured. "She is all to me."

"Your love saved her," Joseph Ari said softly. "Once, when you used your gift on me, it was because you loved me, was it not? We were the best of friends, in brotherly love."

Roane looked at Joseph Ari. "But I tried to heal her eyes once before," he said. "It did not work."

"Mayhap that was because you did not love her then. But you love her now."

Roane nodded, thinking that the man might have a point. He loved Alisanne more than anything in the world. "What I did... it was motivated by pure love."

The priest nodded confidently. "With love, you can move mountains, cure a blind man, or protect the woman you adore. Love can accomplish all things."

Roane was coming to understand now what it meant to love and be loved. This gift he had, feared for so long, was something only brought out or motivated by love. It was a true blessing from God in every sense of the word. He still feared it a little, but at least now he understood it. It was a part of him and he a part of it. It was a light unto his soul, making him what he was, and Alisanne was the seed from which that love was sprung. She was his shining star, his everything. He looked at Joseph Ari.

"What did you call me, once?" he asked, thinking back to that day in Jerusalem that changed his life forever. "The Lord of Light?"

Joseph Ari grinned. "You brought light into my life by healing my blindness," he said. "That is what you are to me; light."

Roane turned to Alisanne, who was coming down the stairs, approaching him. She no longer looked shocked, but warm and glowing. All of her glowed. Roane sighed as his gaze beheld her. For the first time in his life, and certainly for the first time in the past three years, everything came clear to him.

"That is what *she* is to me," he murmured. "*Light.*"

EPILOGUE

Year of our Lord 1200 A.D.
Kinlet Castle, Shropshire

"I AM NOT entirely certain why you are so reluctant, Roane," Bowen said. "The House of Penden is a very fine family. They are the Stewards of Rochester and also relations to the Earl of East Anglia. A marriage to the steward's heir would be a fine thing indeed."

Roane stood in the great hall of Kinlet, a fine place now that money and hard work had repaired the once-dilapidated castle. It was warm with a fire in the massive hearth, fragrant with rushes on the floor, and comfortable thanks to the fine furniture and tapestries that Roane's inheritance had provided. Bowen had given him half of everything those years ago, convinced that Roane was entitled to it. It had been a generous and selfless act, brother to brother. Now, Bowen was trying to produce another selfless act but Roane was resisting heavily.

Bowen had arrived an hour earlier, the end of a long trip from Gargrave Castle. He had come with one hundred men as escort, including Albert who was now the captain of his guard, and a message for his brother. Unfortunately, Roane didn't like the message.

"I am not entirely sure where you got the idea that I was prepared to betroth my seven year old daughter," Roane said, somewhat angrily. "Afton is much too young to be considered marriageable."

Bowen glanced at Alisanne, who was sitting by the fire sewing on a garment that was strewn across her lap. At her feet, two young boys, twins that were five years of age, played happily with a toy cart and pieces of sticks that they had built up into an imaginary castle. The baby was asleep upstairs, watched over by her nurse, while the eldest child, the daughter in question, stood silently next to her mother. Alisanne was focused on her sewing although she could feel the attention of the men upon her. She continued to sew.

"I believe what Bowen is suggesting is a marriage contract and not an immediate marriage," she said, finally setting her sewing to her lap. "We're not the royal family, for Heaven's sake, and we need not marry our children as babies in order to secure dynasties. But a contract with the Stewards of Rochester would be most advantageous for Afton. Who is the current steward, Bowen?"

Bowen scratched his head as he moved for the long, scrubbed feasting table and a pitcher of fine ale. "Sir Brac Penden," he said. "His son is eleven years of age and fostering at Lioncross Abbey."

"De Lohr's seat," Roane grunted. "He's the Earl of Hereford and Worcester. Christ, the man is legendary."

"We're off the subject," Alisanne said, looking over her shoulder at Bowen. "Did the Steward of Rochester seek you out to propose this marriage contract to your brother?"

Bowen nodded. "I knew the man's deceased father, Sir Hunt Penden," he said. "I only recently saw him and was able to offer my condolences when he brought up the subject of securing a good marriage for his eldest son. I mentioned my lovely niece, as I have only boys to offer, and he was most interested. It would be a very good contract, Roane. Afton will have to marry some time; why not marry into power?"

Roane had a permanent scowl on his face as he looked at his daughter, standing next to Alisanne. The Lady Afton Isabelle de Garr had his blond hair, her mother's beautiful face, and a personality that was all her own. She was brilliant, humorous, diligent, and manipulative even at her young age. She could make her father do anything with a sweet word and a bright smile. He was an idiot for her. Even now, she stood there looking at him with a completely innocent expression but he knew it was all for show. If she thought she could talk her father into anything, no matter what it was, she would do it. It was a game with her.

His gaze drifted from Afton to the twins, Dallon and Lynton. Even though they had been born together, they were miles apart in both looks and personality. Dallon was loud and aggressive while Lynton was more like he was, calm and calculating. They were strapping boys and he couldn't have been more proud of them. And the baby, Alexandra, was as sweet as she could be. He melted every time he held her.

Aye, Roane was exceedingly proud of his family. He was very blessed. But he was also very selfish and he didn't want to share them; he couldn't even think of a marriage contract at the moment for his darling Afton. But he knew, as they all did, that if Alisanne deemed it the correct and proper course, he would have to agree. She was his voice of reason, in all things.

"What do you think, Alisanne?" he finally asked because he was having difficulty making a non-emotional decision. "Tell me your thoughts, love."

Alisanne glanced at her daughter before speaking. "The House of Penden is a very fine house," she said. "Afton would be the steward's wife and well-respected. We could search the rest of her life and never find a better offer. Mayhap we should consider visiting the boy and making the judgment at that time."

Bowen grinned. "No need," he said. "I have invited the steward and his son to Gargrave next month. You could meet him at that time and discuss the arrangements."

Roane could see that his brother had things all planned out. "So speaking to me was only a formality?" he asked, outraged. "Why speak with me at all? You have already planned my daughter's future!"

Alisanne fought off a grin as she picked her sewing up and resumed. "Have no fear, my love," she said. "We will do the same to him. We will comb the countryside for the most obnoxious girl children we can find and bombard him with them. He will be pulling his hair out in agony."

Roane liked that idea. He pointed a finger at his brother. "You have four boys," he said. "Four obnoxious women."

Bowen scratched his head in frustration. "This is my reward for trying to do you a good turn?" he asked. "I would have done better had I stayed out of it and allowed your daughter to marry a pauper."

Alisanne giggled as Roane and Bowen grunted at each other. "Bowen, we appreciate your foresight, truly," she said. "And we would be very glad to meet the Steward of Rochester and his son. Afton will need to marry eventually and the steward's heir might prove a perfect match."

Bowen was triumphant over his brother, who was looking at his daughter. He went to sit in the chair across from his wife, a pair of chairs they kept before the great hearth where they could conduct conversation or sit and enjoy their children. He'd spent many an evening sitting in that chair, speaking with his wife or singing one or more child to sleep. Sitting heavily, he brooded pensively for a moment until he felt a warm body next to him. Looking over, he saw Afton standing next to his chair. Her big green eyes were focused on him.

"Dada?" she asked in her sweet little voice. "Why are you sad?"

Roane smiled at the child and pulled her onto his lap. "I am not sad," he said. "I am very happy."

"You do not want me to marry?"

His smile faded. "Of course I want you to marry."

"Then you do not want me to go away?"

"Nay, I do not want you to go away."

Afton's little brow furrowed. "But I must go away, Dada," she said. "I go to Trelystan Castle to foster soon. Mama says so. She says I will learn a great many things there. Are you not happy for me, Dada?"

Roane's smile was gone completely at the thought of his daughter being sent away to foster. He didn't want her going anywhere. "I am sure it will be a great adventure," he said glumly. "'Tis simply that I will miss you, that's all."

Alisanne had been watching the exchange carefully. When she saw that Roane was sliding into sorrow, she clapped her hands briskly.

"Children," she said, setting her sewing aside and standing up. "Uncle Bowen must be very tired from his ride. Take him up to his chamber, if you please. Dallon, ask your uncle if you can carry his baggage and Lynton, you will ask him if you can help tend his horse. Afton, escort your uncle upstairs and make sure he has everything he needs."

Alisanne had a very calm but sweet manner with the children and they immediately moved to do her bidding. Lynton, who had been playing with a toy cart, stood up with it still in his hand, gave it over to Bowen without a word, and then took his uncle's hand and began leading him out of the great hall. Bowen had no choice but to go with him, holding the cart in one hand and Lynton in the other. Afton and Dallon wandered after the pair, leaving their mother and father alone by the fire.

When the hall was empty and still for the most part, Alisanne turned to her husband. He seemed so forlorn and sad as he sat pensively in his chair. She went to him, a gentle hand on his head.

"What is the matter, my love?" she asked softly. "Does the thought of Afton's marriage bother you so much?"

He frowned as he took her hand and kissed it tenderly. "Nay," he muttered. "It's the fact that she is growing up so quickly. I look at her and I still see that fat-cheeked baby I was so in love with. Do you remember?"

Alisanne knelt next to the chair, grinning as he continued to nibble on her hand. "Of course I do," she whispered. "From the moment Ovier delivered her, you never let her out of your sight. She couldn't have spent more than a few hours in her bed for the first few months of her life. You carried her around constantly. When she would cry, you would panic."

He looked somewhat chagrined. "I had never been around an infant before," he admitted. "She was so sweet and perfect. I do not like the prospect of losing her, not even to marriage."

Alisanne sighed faintly. "She is due to foster in two months," she reminded him gently. "Roane, she must grow up. Dallon and Lynton must grow up, as must Alexandra eventually. You *know* this. You must prepare yourself for it."

Roane sat, staring into the flames, his wife's hand against his lips. He seemed so very pensive and distant.

"When I was growing up, it was just me and Bowen," he said softly. "My father was not particularly attentive to us since my mother died. When Bowen and I went to foster, we were separated and I was alone. When I was swept up with the Hospitallers Order and decided to join, again, I was alone. Until I met you, I was alone nearly my entire life and now I have the most wonderful wife and children a man could have. We have such a perfect world, Alisanne. We have fought hard to achieve it. I suppose… I suppose I simply do not ever want to see it end, and that includes sending my children to foster or watching them get married."

Alisanne understood somewhat. "We cannot deny them the opportunities we had," she said, stroking his blond hair. "We had the opportunity to learn from others, to make our own mistakes, and to marry someone we loved. Would you take that away from them simply because you do not want them away from you?"

He caught her eye, making a face because he knew she was right. Alisanne laughed softly and kissed his cheek. "We have beautiful, intelligent children, Roane," she said quietly. "Let them make their mark on the world as you have. Let them achieve their happiness."

Roane kissed her hand, her cheek, and finally her lips, losing himself in the deep love and admiration he had for her. His light, as he had once called her, was his greatest shining star and he thanked God daily that she had been brought into his life. When Bowen returned to the hall some time later, he and Roane sat at the great feasting table and made plans for the meeting with the Steward of Rochester. Alisanne had deemed that he should, so he did.

The Lady Afton de Garr was married to Sir Titus Penden ten years later in a lavish ceremony at Rochester Cathedral and eventually became mother to the future heir of Rochester. Dallon de Garr became a great knight for young Henry the Third and his brother, Lynton, went on to become a powerful priest in the Catholic Church, nurtured in his early years by his pious great-uncle, Joseph Ari, who had been a great role model for him. Lastly, the Lady Alexandra de Garr grew up to marry a son of the great Christopher de Lohr, Earl of Hereford and Worcester, linking the House of de Garr with the House of de Lohr. It was a long and beneficial association.

The Lord of Light never used his powers again. It was something that faded into family lore, told from one generation to the next, until it became a fable and foolishness that some reckoned. Surely no man, not even a treasured ancestor, had the ability to shoot lightning bolts from his fingers. Surely it was simply a story to make a great man seem greater. In any case, it made for a wonderful story that became more legend than truth.

The legend of the Lord of Light and his lovely lady fair.

☙ THE END ❧

Author Notes

Lord of Light is a story that took a long time to come to fruition. It was a partial story when first submitted to an agent about fifteen years ago, but when the agent shot down the general premise of a knight who had been given a paranormal "gift" from a freak bolt of lightning, the author put it aside and figured it wasn't good enough to finish. When she was reviewing old manuscripts in more recent times, a few beta readers told her that it WAS good enough to finish – and here it is!

What was Alisanne's affliction? Pure and simple – advanced Pink Eye. There are homeopathic remedies for it, but back in the High Middle Ages, no one had ever heard of probiotics, which can be found in fresh and unpasteurized milk – human, goat, or cow. Ovier knew it because the art of healing in Arabia (and even China) was much more advanced than it was in England, France, and the like. So a few drops of milk in her eyes, an herbal soothing paste to help the healing process, and – voila! – her eyes cleared up.

And John Adam/Joseph Ari's problem? A cataract that Roane miraculously cleared up for him with his gift. It was a miracle, pure and simple. Yes, this novel relies on the belief in miracles, but who's to say there aren't any? The author thinks so. But you be the judge.

ABOUT KATHRYN LE VEQUE

Medieval Just Got Real.

KATHRYN LE VEQUE is a USA TODAY Bestselling author, an Amazon All-Star author, and a #1 bestselling, award-winning, multi-published author in Medieval Historical Romance and Historical Fiction. She has been featured in the NEW YORK TIMES and on USA TODAY's HEA blog. In March 2015, Kathryn was the featured cover story for the March issue of InD'Tale Magazine, the premier Indie author magazine. She was also a quadruple nominee (a record!) for the prestigious RONE awards for 2015.

Kathryn's Medieval Romance novels have been called 'detailed', 'highly romantic', and 'character-rich'. She crafts great adventures of love, battles, passion, and romance in the High Middle Ages. More than that, she writes for both women AND men – an unusual crossover for a romance author – and Kathryn has many male readers who enjoy her stories because of the male perspective, the action, and the adventure.

On October 29, 2015, Amazon launched Kathryn's Kindle Worlds Fan Fiction site WORLD OF DE WOLFE PACK. Please visit Kindle Worlds for Kathryn Le Veque's World of de Wolfe Pack and find many action-packed adventures written by some of the top authors in their genre using Kathryn's characters from the de Wolfe Pack series. As Kindle World's FIRST Historical Romance fan fiction world, Kathryn Le Veque's World of de Wolfe Pack will contain all of the great story-telling you have come to expect.

Kathryn loves to hear from her readers. Please find Kathryn on Facebook at Kathryn Le Veque, Author, or join her on Twitter @kathrynleveque, and don't forget to visit her website at www. kathrynleveque.com.

READ ON for an excerpt from the forthcoming historical novel SINFUL FOLK by Ned Hayes, with cover and internal illustrations by *New York Times* bestselling illustrator and author Nikki McClure.

ENDORSEMENTS:

"*Sinful Folk* is a work of art. I found the story fascinating, approachable, and powerful. Miriam's story is a raw and brutal and passionate tale, but her story touches the reader because it's a timeless story – the struggles of parents, and of justice for their children. She makes it all very human regardless of the time period, and it's a wonderful portrayal of medieval life. Highly recommended."

– Kathryn Le Veque
bestselling author of *The Dark Lord* and *The Warrior Poet*

"A pilgrim tale worthy of Chaucer, evocative, compelling and peopled with unforgettable characters artfully delivered by a master storyteller. Be warned: Dress warmly before beginning this perilous journey across a winter-blasted, medieval landscape of fire and ice. Your heart will shiver and not just from the cold. An excellent novel, *Sinful Folk*. A wonderful book."

– Brenda Rickman Vantrease
best-selling author of *The Illuminator* and *The Mercy Seller*

"Brilliant, insightful, unflinching and wise. Master storyteller Ned Hayes has created a fascinating tale of a woman who finds her voice in a brutal world determined to silence her. Mear's quest on behalf of her child will capture your heart. She demands truth after an unspeakable loss. She wins justice for innocents. Her courageous choices in the face of evil will offer redemption, even to those dismissed as *Sinful Folk*. This spellbinding mystery will keep readers turning pages until the last sentence. Remarkable."

– *Ella March Chase*, bestselling author of
The Virgin Queen's Daughter *and* Three Maids for a Crown

READ ON FOR A FIVE CHAPTER EXCERPT FROM
SINFUL FOLK by Ned Hayes

CHAPTER 1

I N THE END, I listen to my fear. It keeps me awake, resounding through the frantic beating in my breast. It is there in the dry terror in my throat, in the pricking of the rats' nervous feet in the darkness.

Christian has not come home all the night long.

I know, for I have lain in this darkness for hours now with my eyes stretched wide, yearning for my son's return.

Each night that he works late, I cannot sleep. I am tormented when he is not here—I fear that he will never return. I lie awake, plagued by my own fears of loss and loneliness.

But my fears have never come to pass.

So on this night, I tell myself that the sound I hear is frost cracking, river ice breaking. I lie to my own heart, as one lies to a frightened child, one who cannot be saved.

All the while, I know it is a fire. And I know how near it is.

First, I could hear shouts and cries. Then there was the sound of rapid running, of men hauling buckets of water and ordering children to help.

A house burns.

Yet always I fear to venture forth, for my fright has grown into a panic that gibbers in the dark. *What if someone started this fire to burn me out?*

What sport would they have, watching a mute moan as she turns on the spit?

A crackle and hiss in the distance. A heavy thud, and then the roar of an inferno. *Where is Christian? I must go, I—*

Scrambling out of the straw, I rush to the door in my nightclothes. Then I remember poor Nell, who died last spring. I do not forget her agony.

I blunder in the darkness, fumbling for the fireplace soot. I smear the smooth edge of my jaw, marking with trembling fingers a hint of beard on my soft upper lip and my chin.

Always, I must hide my true face.

As my fingers work, I grip hope to me, a small bird quaking in the nest of my heart. Desperately, I mumble the words of a prayer from my past.

O Alma Redemptoris . . .

My sooty ritual is perhaps my own strange paean to womanhood. Like Theresa of Avignon, that spoiled heiress of the French throne, who shared my vows at Canterbury, the world will see me only as I intend. It is a type of vanity: if I cannot be a woman, I will be as ugly a man as I can muster.

And in this ceremony, my dread subsides. My fingers stop trembling. I think clearly for a moment. Even now, perhaps Christian is one of those who carry buckets of water to fight the flames. Christian will be fine. He is strong, vital, alive. He is mine, and I am his.

All will be well. I repeat it in my head like a rosary. *All will be well.*

Then there are harsh shouting voices outside, men rushing toward the burning building. "Trapped!" they shout.

Now I quake with dread, for I am not finished. I should wrap my bosom tightly, bind the feminine shape of my body into that of a eunuch. But I lunge for the door, my bosom unbound, my heart full of fear for my son, and fear for my own flesh.

Even as my heart belies me, I pray that this fire is nothing. Nothing to do with my life, my secrets.

Across the village square, the largest house—the home of Benedict, the weaver—is consumed by flame. Every piece of wood smokes and bends in the fire. The roof seems supported not by heavy timbers, but by ropy masses of blazing smoke.

It is the home where my son is an apprentice.

The smoke chokes and claws at my nostrils and my throat. The roof catches in a roar of flaming darkness. The crowd churns in turmoil, seeking to save their village, their children.

Not one of the villagers pays the slightest heed to me.

I am an old man to them, and a broken, mute one at that—wiry as a starved mule, leathery with long labor. It is rare that any in this village look beyond the wrinkles and the rat's nest of chestnut-colored hair to see my face.

Tonight, I force them to see me. I seize each of their faces with my gaunt hands, turning them, staring quickly into each pair of wild, frightened eyes. Here is that layabout Liam's frightened pale face and red beard. He looks for his son too. Across the way is a boy wrapped in a cloak and hood. My heart lifts—is it Christian?

But when I meet that boy's eyes, they are black as night. It is only Cole, the orphan. I see my friend Salvius, the blacksmith. He runs past, throwing water on the flames.

Then I see Tom, who hangs back in the crowd. I clutch at him, wanting answers, but Tom pushes me away, his wide-set, cowish face full of fear.

I turn. I pull down another man's hood, and it is bald Benedict, the weaver who owns this house. He gives me a dark glance and pulls away, to lift a bucket of water.

I grasp a short man next, small Geoff, the carpenter, with the squint. "Where's my boy?" he shouts in my face. "Where is he?"

I turn about again, I seize on every person, look into every face. I hope for only one boy, I search for his blue eyes. My son.

Christian.

Is this really all the living folk we have? Frantically, I count on my fingers. All the women accounted for and most of the men.

Only a few are not here: Jack, whose foot was trampled by a cow, and Phoebe, who is about to give birth. Benedict's wife will be with her this night—Sophia is the closest we have to a midwife now, now that Nell is gone.

That accounts for three. *But where are the older boys?*

Desperately, I search each of these villager's faces again and again—going over old ground—until they push me away.

Men and women shout their children's names. "Breton! Matthew! Stephen! Jonathon!" The large boy who belongs to Tom. The son of the carpenter. Then the second son of the weaver. And the eldest son of Liam, the woodsman. But there is only one name that echoes in my mind, and no one shouts it aloud. My son, my only.

Christian—Christian—Christian—

The house falls half apart, split wide, a timbered carcass steaming and cracking in the winter frost. Salvius is always brave: he leaps up onto the smoldering threshold and uses a beam to batter in the smoking door. Then Liam steps into the smoke, wrapping his arms in a wet cloak.

I push my way through the milling villagers to see Liam and Salvius emerge, dragging out a charred body. Then another, and another. Five, in the end—all the missing accounted for.

My tongue forms his name, but I cannot speak a word. Instead, I give a cry—that meaningless animal groan that is my only language now.

The flames rise again, the west wind gusts strong across the heath, a demon roaring as it takes the building apart. The crackle is that of hell itself. The men run frantically with buckets of water to save the neighboring crofts.

The five bodies lie on the ground, black as broken shadows. They stink now of death. Burned flesh, scorched wool. It is a nauseating stench, yet despite myself, my mouth waters at the smell of flame-roasted meat. I am always so hungry.

A bit of metal glimmers faintly below one charred head. It is a thin silver chain. *Is that my chain? My boy's neck?*

I am pierced to the root then, all of my veins bathed in a liquor of terror.

CHAPTER 2

T HE DAY IS almost upon us, the houses and trees silhouetted by a faint blue light in the east. The burned croft is a smoking wreck, embers steaming in the dawn.

The wind dies now. In this winter, we have had several unfortunate fires, but this is the worst yet. The crowd slows its frantic work, as the danger fades.

Now I can hear them: the cries of children, the sobs of babes in arms. No doubt those cries were all around me for hours in the crowd. Yet I had ears only for one cry, and that cry never came.

The bodies are surrounded by their families. These youth were our bleak earth's brightest, our highest roll on Fortune's wheel.

I go to the dead. They are blackened and unrecognizable, each boy stretched out like a penitent against the raw earth. *These are other children, not mine, not mine.*

But I reach out my hand, I cross them with the holy sign. My mouth moves silently in the rhythm of that last rite, although I have not a whit of faith left in me.

If I still believed in such fictions, the souls of these innocents would be trapped in limbo for eternity. A cold God to condemn children to such punishment. And *my* blessing means nothing: we have no priest in this village, no sacrament of burial, no sacraments at all.

The world blurs as my eyes go wet.

A voice calls my name loud. "Mear!" I turn, blind and terrified, covering my tear-streaked face. Liam's voice is strained and hoarse. "Mear. Ah, Mear, there is no shame in tears. All of us have lost."

Liam is the poorest man in the village, and we have lived side by side so long that I have wondered if he and his wife Kate see through my soot-stained skin to the woman underneath. I stay apart from him as much as I can, but always he talks to me, despite my silence.

Most of the villagers act as if I am of no more importance than a beast. No one here ever pays me mind. There are few who know I am alive. I prefer it that way, for I want to be invisible.

Yet I would have taken my child and left long ago except for this man, Liam, and my friends Salvius and Nell. Salvius needs me at his bellows and his smithy—he values my labor and my friendship. And Liam at least helps me laugh.

But Nell—poor Nell—she is gone.

Now Liam puts an arm around my slight shoulders, holding me as I sob. There is no laughter in him after last night. His green eyes are full of water, and his red beard trembles.

"Oh, Mear, thank you for blessin' their souls."

Who else has seen me bless and cross the dead?

But Liam does not care that I make the sign reserved for priests and nuns. He mourns over his son, and then he turns to look at another body, close at hand.

"I think here's your lad. Seems to me it has to be him. He was the last one I brought out—the tallest and the furthest from the door."

And when he says this, I cannot pretend any longer, I cannot wish away this hard truth. The silver chain glimmers faintly in the dawn light—it does not lie. I fall to my knees. Here is my beloved, my son.

Liam bends down to his own firstborn son, burned and blackened on the ground. A groan comes out of the stricken father, an anguished sound to shake the earth.

Now the crowd swells and crests under the whip of a mad grief.

Tom is slavering out some half-remembered tale, a demonic vision. "This is the work of those who killed the Christ. They are cursed—infested with the devil's seed! They drink children's blood in the night!"

Everyone knows this is the third terrible fire we have had this winter. This time, it was Benedict's weaving house that burned, and some in the crowd move toward his family.

"Why were the lads here?" cries Geoff, the carpenter. "Why were they burned?"

"I didn't do it!" Benedict's voice is strained with fear. "They gathered at Vespers, I tell you the truth. They were only here to work on the grand tunics for Sir Peter of Lincoln."

"Where were *you* then?" shouts Liam, choking back a sob. "It's your house!"

"I was with my wife!" Benedict sweeps his hat from his weathered scalp and throws it on the ground. "I took Sophia 'cross the valley to see to Phoebe's birth."

The men stink of rage, like a pan of smoking oil before it catches fire.

"You're a liar!" says Geoff to Bene, pushing toward him through the crowd.

"Goddammit, I lost my son too," Benedict shouts. "I wasn't even here!"

Hob, the alderman, affirms that Benedict returned late, at Nocturns hour.

Most times the crowd will listen to Hob, but today they will not be stilled. Women scream at Benedict and his family, wanting his blood in payment. Small Geoff rushes at Benedict, to hurt him.

But Geoff can't get through the crowd drawn tight around Tom, who bawls out the sordid details of his imagined witchcraft. The Star Chamber, the White Tower, evil stories of Old Gods and black fairies. And that ancient villain, the Jew.

"Every child knows who does dark deeds in the night," shrieks Tom. "Every child knows we suffer now in this world because of that crime against our Lord Jesus Christ. Jews did this!"

Ripe nonsense. But the villagers want so desperately to believe there is a reason for this loss.

Tom tells them that there is a root out of which murder grows, a seed that can be plucked. The fires come most likely from an old chimney catching, or a load of hay that catches spontaneously. Yet no one has died from the previous fires. This time, the villagers want a cause, a goat to tie the blood to, an empty vessel to fill with hatred and bludgeon with their loss.

"The Jews!" calls Tom again.

There are a few of Jewish blood here—I know who they are, even now, years after they converted. *How long will it take the crowd to remember and find those who once were Jews in this village?*

"Damn the Jews to hell!" someone in the crowd shouts. "Make the Jews pay!"

No one notices when I rise from the ground and stagger to the smoking ruin. My mute questions will find no answers in gruesome children's tales. I know what will tell me the truth—the bare reality of the boys' deaths. I push through the crowd to the place they died.

What power held the door so the boys could not flee the rising flames?

With my foot, I stir the warm cinders. The door broken by Salvius lies in pieces, smashed flat. But there is a knot here, an unlikely twist of the rope that I must examine.

I can see now that this was the rope that held the door tight closed. I pick at it, pull out pieces of a rope still stretched taut across the door-frame. I have seen this curious binding once before. But no fairie tied this knot. No errant ghostly Jew. It is a triple knot, tied fast across a half hitch. It crumbles to ash under my probing touch.

"Trial by water," wails Tom. "Trial by fire. Kill the traitor Jews, save the innocent!"

Liam taunts Benedict. "Don't you know a Jew? Did you burn the place for her, Bene?"

"We are all of us the traitors to our children! Every man in this village," cries Benedict. "Every man stands accused, every one should suffer trial by water, I tell you. Every one of us!"

"Who do we drown first?" Liam's face is stained with tears.

"Hell, I know you did it," screams Geoff at Benedict. "You killed them. Drown yourself in the pond first!"

The people surge back and forth, panicked. My heart thrums, fear shrinking my bowels, quivering through my pulse.

The quarreling men bring back to me the chaos of my dying home village many years ago, when I made that last promise to my mother. I can picture the hands moving from gestures to fists, from sticks to sharp sickles. Quick as a breath.

"That's enough!" Hob's deep and lordly voice finally stills the milling crowd. "The blood of these innocents cries out, as our brother Tom tells us. Their souls plead for vengeance! I agree. But I tell you, drowning—or near drowning—half the men of this village won't bring our children back to us."

The crowd murmurs affirmation.

"What will bring them back is justice!" shouts Hob. "And there's one seat of justice here on earth."

"Kill them Jews," mutters Tom again. "Kill 'em now." But the crowd ignores him this time.

Hob cries out louder. "We will take the proof to our King!"

"To the King," echoes Salvius. His masterful tone is a herald's cry that cuts through the chaos. Salvius leaps onto Benedict's cart that stands near at hand and finds a common cause with the crowd. "Come, my friends, we will seek the King's justice!"

Some in the crowd move at this—the men who shouted loud against the Jews now lift the lifeless bodies from the ground.

Benedict and the orphan, Cole, load the body of Benedict's son onto the cart. The boy's corpse lands with a sodden thunk.

Geoff pushes past me, muttering. "If I cannot kill a Jew here, at least I will go with my son, Goddamn them, and tell the king what I think of his damn'd protection against Jews, much good it did us."

Liam lifts his own son's cold body. He places him gently on the straw in the cart. "I'll go with you, my boy," he says to his son, and shakes with weeping.

The wind blows a hard gust. There is a simmering argument in the crowd. When the harvest failed and the belts tightened in this starving season of ours, most were left too weak to search for food outside the village. *How can any of us take a journey now?*

My friend Salvius waves away the questions. "Yes, yes, we've got enough food, and we're taking strong men only. We'll make it all the way to London, by God's bloody Son!"

As the light bleeds into the sky, the feeling of the crowd shifts with it. The hunger for this journey jumps back and forth between the villagers, like the heat of a flame passing between them.

Geoff protests, his voice a thin reed of reason. "We should take them to somewhere close-at-hand. The Abbot at the Cluny Monastery—it is close on the King's road."

Salvius skillfully whips them all forward, turning them all toward a journey as a great beast is turned with a small prod.

"The Jews!" the crowd cries. "We seek justice against the Jews—and we will take this proof of their crime all the way to the King. The Throne will judge the Jews!"

The men bellow loud, they swear on their children's unburied bodies, they will go and find the truth. Hob and Benedict shout themselves hoarse, promising justice to their clans. I turn away—I cannot keep up with the arguments that shudder from the crowd. None of their moans and barks is worth a spit in the wind.

I look at my son, and I sink into grief. When they come to get the body with the necklace, I do not let go. I close my eyes, I can hear them all around, their voices a cacophony.

"Why do you hold on, old Mear?"

"Let the body go."

"He is the father."

"Show him pity. He canna speak."

Tears leak out of my tight-shut eyes. *I want my boy.* My soul is tied to his sweet body, the one stretched out as a tortured savior. I can feel his burning through my flesh, the choking smoke is in my own lungs. I will burn with him.

But however much I wish it, I cannot take myself out of existence. I open my eyes once more. My body still breathes, my heart pounds ignorantly in my bosom.

I will not let him depart from me. I will heal him, I think desperately. *I will care for his wounded body until he is well again.*

The men lift his body onto the cart.

They are taking him away. There will be nothing left to me. Not a body, not a token, not a grave.

I lift my face, stained with ash and tears. A baying sob breaks from my throat.

Years have passed, almost a decade, since I made a sound that the villagers could hear. Now, all turn toward me. Even the men loading the bodies on the cart heed me.

I make a motion. I will come with them, wherever they are taking my son; I will go too.

Tom points at me and mumbles more of his cracked vision. "Let 'im come along! Mear here, he'll find the truth, I tell ye. The angels done foretold it."

People look away from Tom, shaking their heads. Few believe that I understood the debate of the morning and all the decisions that have been made. No one believes that I can make the journey.

I stumble back to our tiny cruck house—wattled and daubed by Christian and me. I bind my bosom firmly this time and I pack what little I have. After the poor harvest this fall, there is no food for me to bring except one old loaf of dark bread and some dried mutton. I put on the tarnished silver chain that matches the one my son wore; and I search for but cannot find my ring. I have had it for years, but it is not in its hiding place under the hearthstone now. My heart plummets at this loss, but it is too late. I do not have time to hunt for it further.

I seize also the sheepskins and furs that make up our bed, and a small pot of soot, for my face in the night, and that is all.

When I return, Hob has ordered supplies from the meager stocks of the village. He asks for sacrifice from families here to sustain the men on the open road, and his appeal is met despite the larder houses that sit empty after the terrible autumn and the poor fields that yielded nothing. Geoff piles up wood and tinder; Benedict loads straw and fodder into the cart. Liam has brought an axe, while Salvius sends Tom the miller to retrieve the last remaining sack of flour from the mill.

The villagers are like the swallows I watched as a child at a cliffside near the sea—gathering, arguing, a swarm of rising fervor filling them. I remember the flock of birds moving as a mass—breaking, re-forming, ragged at the edges.

Finally, a few brave souls know that it is time to fly.

The men put their shoulders down and push against the cart. Every person in the village wants to touch the wood of it, as one would touch a baptized child. The outstretched hands seem to hold it back for a moment, and then, with a loud heave and the crack of breaking hoarfrost, the wheels roll forward. The shifting crowd gives a hollow cheer and surges in a mass.

It is a confusion of purposes. The cart is leaving the village, but at the same time, it is as if the whole village is going with us. There are dogs and small children underfoot, and mothers are wailing, their ululations echo against the trees.

CB

THE SMALL CHILDREN of the village who trail the cart are beginning to know that those dead are not coming back. The realization of their loss blanches them white—grief giving their cheeks and chins a gray pallor, corpse-like in this light.

Salvius leaps again upon the farm cart, his handsome face distorted by grief as he stands tall. His hair catches the dawn light, bright as wheat chaff. "We will not stop until we see the king—until we claim his protection and his justice. Our children's bodies will testify to the murder. We go to the king in London!"

"Aye," agrees Hob. "We take the bodies to the king—we seek justice, not vengeance!"

"What's the diff'rence?" shouts Geoff, and the crowd roars its approval.

There is one elation at the prospect of traveling, of going somewhere so far away it is almost mythical: London. The women pull the children close, keeping them away from the cart and its dangerous journey. Several stand up to Hob and Salvius and begin to badger their men to come home. They question Hob and Salvius openly, doubting this accusation against ghostly Jews in the forest, these will-o'-the-wisp murderers. Hob and Salvius do not deign to answer them.

For the spirit moves the men, just as it moves the wing'd creatures and rough beasts. I think of our first parents—Adam and Eve—as they staggered away from their paradise, thrust out of the garden by an avenging angel.

We are at the edge of the village commons now. After this point, we cannot turn back. We must find out who did this.

I am already weary, yet as I struggle to catch up with the cart, I know that I am really going because my son is going. I have no one else. My whole life is contained in that tortured, blackened husk. My child.

Where else would I go, but with him?

CHAPTER 3

S TARS STEAM AWAY as a pale sun rises, hot coal dropped in a watery
sky. Light seeps across the forest as the reedy shrieks of wood fowl
echo in the trees.

The valley where our village of Duns rests is surrounded by forested
hills. The path from our village to the King's Highway is no road at all;
it is a crooked line of mud rutted with cart tracks, a rough trough where
the dirty snow is stabbed through by the hooves of feral sheep. To the
east, that faint track leads up through the forest until it reaches, finally,
the open country and paths that lead to other places.

The flock of villagers around the cart thins now. At first, as we
approach the last house of the village, it appears Hob and Salvius might
be heading for the open ground of the graveyard, but then the cart
passes that turning. Hob is taking us beyond the bounds of the known
world, aiming for the White Road, the King's Highway.

Sophia, Benedict's wife, calls out to us. "Without a noble blessing,
you lot take your lives in your hands!"

I know she is right. Peasants should have a tunic from a Lord of the
Land, to show his blessing on our travels. Except for Benedict and his
family, the others here do not have my knowledge of how the world
works. I do not know if half of them have ever set foot outside the forest
around our little vale.

These men have set, grim faces. They push on despite the warning.
They are the fathers of the missing, and this drives them onward. And
always, they look to Hob for direction.

Hob is sinewy and grizzled and humorless: sharp-eyed as a black-
bird and possessed of the false merriment of one as well. Veins make
ridges and valleys on his forehead and the backs of his leathery hands.

Like maps, the lines on his hands point to destinations unreached.

Hob urges us on. The others need a leader as they stumble forward, nearly blind with grief. Near the front of our pack is stoic, brooding Geoff, the carpenter. His eyes remain as dull and remote as ever, but his hands move constantly now, touching the cart, his side, his hat. It is as if his hands are puppets on a string, plucked by someone else's mind. Beside him is that layabout Liam, his bright red hair all awry, his lips moving with silent words I cannot hear, curses or prayers.

I am surprised to see both Liam and Geoff continue with us. Both of them are poor and aimless in their ambitions. They have naught with them for the journey, but—like the other men—they ignore their womenfolk and push forward.

The women like Sophia know the truth of adventures like the children's crusades, when people—young and old—wander from their villages onto the open road, trusting in God's providence, often to their own perdition or ruin. So the women collect the old, the infirm stragglers, the random children, and the feebleminded. Those too weak to go should not be pulled into the current of our passage, enticed down a path with no certain end.

One who does not need their help is Tom the miller, bullheaded and massive, who seems to move the cart almost by himself. His arms are heavy with muscle from the millwheel, his hands horned with calluses. Yet despite his brawn, his mouth is still full of those empty blustering words, those accusations. I think he talks so he won't have to think.

The thinking is done for us by Salvius, the blacksmith, the kindly one who gave me the wood to build my hut. He looks back for me from time to time. He looks back perhaps also to find his ward—young Cole, the orphan—who Salvius says he did not see this morning.

Salvius does what he can to encourage us, even as he looks up and down the trail. Cole has not yet been found, even among the dead.

Benedict, who owned the burned weaving house, is trying to push the cart, but at every step he is pulled backward by his wife. He shakes

Sophia off time and time again, and in the end, she simply staggers after him, crying, no longer pulling at his coat.

I pass her slowly, my feet already wet and painful, weighted down by my solitary bag of rags and oddments. At this point in the morning, as the others fade away, Sophia is the only woman in the village still with the cart. I wonder if she is afraid of going back to the village alone. She is known to have Jewish blood—even though her family converted when she was a babe in arms.

As I pass, Sophia turns to me, her face wet and heavy with sorrow.

"Ol' Mear, this is a pilgrimage for fools—you can't go on this journey." She takes my arm gently. A few of the men nod in agreement, and look away.

But I lift my hands, I make gestures as forceful and angry as I can, trying to show them that I need to be with my son.

Still, she pulls me back toward the village. So I make a sound as only the mute would make. This time, as loud as I can muster: a keening howl. There is an argument, Sophia's voice high and strident, the men shouting back. Hob comes to us, muttering blackly under his breath. He sees my agonized face and makes the final decision. "Let 'im come. His only family lies here dead, isn't that enough for ye?"

Salvius and Benedict push the cart ahead while Hob is separating Sophia from me, so Salvius misses when Geoff speaks up. "Aye, Salvius is going too, even though young Cole is back in t' village."

When I am free, I push myself forward and I go to Salvius, I pluck at his sleeve, and Salvius follows me. I point at Geoff, and Geoff repeats what he said, and explains further: "Sure, I saw Cole this morning, with water for the fire. He's alive, in the village, I tell you."

Salvius starts with surprise, and then he wraps his own cloak around my shoulders for the road ahead, wordlessly thanking me. He takes his belongings from the cart. He will go to find Cole.

"Take 'er with you too, won't you?" says Hob. He points at Sophia, who is marooned in the road, standing like a weeping statue. Her beautiful black hair is caught by the breeze and whips around her face.

Her white skin seems paper-thin in this light, and her eyelids flutter, as if she is caught in a terrible dream.

I think it is more than grief that keeps her here. Her incessant need, her grasping desire, is to own or hold onto all that she can. She always wants to hold the reins, to have what she cannot keep. But for the first time, Benedict is pushing on without her, disappearing around the bend ahead, and she does not know what reins to seize.

Gently, Salvius takes her hands and turns her back toward the village. Sophia walks in a daze, but she will be safe with Salvius escorting her. Her face shines with tears as she stumbles backward, past us and down the road.

I see them go, and something quails in me, a cold thing turning across my grave. I am worried about us traveling on the open road without Salvius's sure confidence, his clear purpose, and his lordly manner. He directs men as few others do. We may be lost without him.

Fog lifts in the valley, rising as mist through the bare-limbed trees. Far below lies the deeping combe with our village in the heart of it.

My whole world for nearly a decade has been contained in that place—and now the village of Duns looks so small. I hold up my hand, form a circle with my fingers. The distant village, wreathed in mist, seems a child's plaything that I can hold in my own hand.

A great fallen yew with nurslings jutting evergreen from its broken body lies near our path. This is the very place at which I first saw the village ten years ago. The line of trees here on the ridge is unchanged, as if I came here only yesterday.

I waited in the quiet vale of Duns far too long. At first, it was a refuge, where I could hide my tracks and recover my strength after the vicious attack that drove me from my home and my books. Then I met Nell, and she gave me sanctuary, and in that comfort of her friendship, I remained for years.

Last spring, after Nell was killed, I knew the village was no longer safe: my haven was gone. But I had only a few months to wait until Christian was ten years of age, and then he could claim his birthright.

One winter more and then we would have left together.

But now my son is gone—alone, without me—where I cannot follow until my ending comes in its turn.

Breathing deeply, I try to still my fear as I stare down at my wet feet in rags trudging through the snow. I step onto the sunken, snowy track, and I move beyond the fallen yew. Past this point exists a world—a life—known to me years ago. Ahead of us on the King's Highway is a monastery, where lives a monk who spent much of summer beside me as I held my babe. He scribbled constantly, writing down the stories I told him. I wonder if he is still there.

Would any remember me now at that monastery on the road? And what of Canterbury Abbey far away? And the Court?

Do any remember my name, after all my years of silence and obscurity?

CR

THE CART ROCKS to a halt just before the crest of a long hill. The heavy weight of the bodies has sunk the cart deep into a rut, and a wheel sticks fast in slush and snow. Ice welds the cart hard to the hillside.

"Heave ho," shouts Hob. "All as one, push together. Now!"

The first thrust from our shoulders doesn't budge the cart. Not a bit. Benedict glares at Geoff and me. "Come on, even you weak ones there, you push too!" Geoff the carpenter, stares back at Benedict. He still holds resentment toward the man whose house burned.

Hob puts his shoulder down. "Come now, men. Heave ho! Can't you move it?"

But Liam mocks him, making a half-born attempt at a joke. "Oh yes, Hob—it's me who's holding it back. If I'd just lift my li'l finger, you'd move, you would."

There's a faint whisper of chuckling, but that dies quickly. No one dares laugh out loud at Hob. And these are our boys we carry.

Liam and Benedict push at the stuck cart. Hob and Tom lean their bodies against the heavy wooden wheels.

I come to the cart and take hold. I peer inside, I shuffle through the straw, trying to find more answers. The chaos I see slowly resolves into sense, like letters read in a forgotten language.

The bodies of our boys are thin and weak from the poor harvest this fall: I can see their bones. Yet these boys are clad in heavy cloaks and warm furs. They are wearing the most lordly clothes possessed by their families, as if they wished to make themselves look better than they are. These are the best garments of their meager homes.

The threads and fur are burned and tattered, so I know for truth that they wore such clothing to their deaths. Even as I flinch from the sight, that firm fork of logic seizes hard. *They were in a house, not on the road. No one had planned a journey, that I knew of. So why were these dead boys wearing furs and cloaks?*

The cart does not move, despite our efforts; instead, one wheel sinks deeper into the snow.

Hob bends down and digs with his hands. He barks hoarsely at us in his commanding tone. "You lot, find summat to wedge it out— branches, wood, straw—anything to get this wheel out."

Reluctantly, I leave behind the puzzle of the boys' clothing. We step into the forest and spread out, trying to find spare wood.

Sound carries far here in the trees. Snow slides off a heavy oak as some creature shuffles through the woods, and ancient branches snap. Out of the corner of one eye, I see the flash of colored feathers. It is a yellowhammer, black eyes flickering in a hedgerow, tiny breast plumped out in golden livery, streaked with colors rich and brown. It was calling in its winter song:

A little bit of bread and no cheese—
A little bit of bread and no cheese—

Moments later, the bracken flutters and the slight shadow of the bird darts into the woods. Deep in the forest now, I hear a low voice that wends back and forth, whispering in secret. It is one of our party. I edge my way closer, stepping quietly so I can hear.

"Why were they together that night?" In this close copse, I can hear the whisper louder by some trick of the woods. "It's a lie, I tell you—they're lying to us!"

It is the small carpenter, Geoff, speaking with a dour look.

I have always found him distasteful. Perhaps it is but the memory I have of Nell whispering to me of his father: a man who defiled his own son. On that man's deathbed, she said, there were running sores on his flesh, the price of Gomorrah. Nothing she could give would help him, and no one believed the rumors of him.

And she was killed for it.

Geoff, now a man himself, has his father's choleric looks. He bears the same harsh voice, the same dark flickering eyes. I wonder if his father's desires run in his mind, in the blood.

Geoff is speaking to Liam as they push their way through the woods, searching for loose branches. "Our lads were takin' a journey—they were dressed in warm cloaks an' furs!"

Geoff has seen what I saw.

But Liam isn't listening. Instead, he interrupts before Geoff can speak again. "You've got to promise me to tell no one of my crime. You know what I did. Benedict knows it too. But keep my secret, an'—" begins Liam. Then my footsteps through the rotten snow, and a branch cracks.

I tumble forward out of my hiding spot. Liam starts with sudden fear. He drops the wood he has collected.

But I stumble forward, keeping my face incurious, even while my heart churns. *What secret?* I wish Salvius were still here, to find the truth of this. He would know what to do. *What crime does Liam conceal?*

When they see it is only me in the snow, they pick up their wood again. Liam nods his head in greeting, gives me a wink. "Mear knows the truth of all things, dontcha know? Pity 'e can't talk."

Geoff grimaces. He stoops and lifts a pair of twigs out of the thin snow in this copse. "An' I'll ask you this—why the rush to get on the trail at first light?"

"Aye, an' we have no blessing for the open road."

"Why does that matter?" says Geoff.

Liam grimaces. "Without that, we can be taken, dontcha know? Any man can kill us."

I am surprised that Liam knows this. He is right that we have no sanction from the Lord of our County, Sir Peter of Lincoln, for this journey. And without an embroidered Lord's tunic, or some such blessing—some holy writ of Church or King would serve—we are prey, subject to any man's whim or greed.

"How do you know?" Geoff shakes his head.

"I've been out here before. I've seen it happen," whispers Liam. And this is a surprise to me too—for years, I have thought Liam was born and bred in the village of Duns.

"There's a liar here somewhere," continues Liam. "After all, the house with boys in it was tied shut, from outside. Salvius and I had to break the door to get the bodies out."

The knot. I have a sudden vision of the boys pushing helplessly on the door, striving to get out as the knot holds tight. Smoke overwhelmed them. My eyes fill with tears.

Liam rips a branch from a small tree, his hands shaking with anger. "Before this journey is done, I tell you, I will know why they were gather'd together. Why did this happen?"

"I blame Benedict," says Geoff. "It was his house, and the first fire this winter where someone died. I don't believe his story of the boys weaving—not for a moment. Here's my guess—what if the boys were seeing his wife already?"

My heart sinks. Sophia, even in her fathomless need, would not seduce boys so young, would she? Liam gives his face a sardonic twist, a leer that makes his grin unseemly. My skin goes cold at that look. It makes me doubt him more. Liam always has been at the bottom of the village bounty, scraping the dregs. What if his need finally broke him and he took vengeance on his betters?

A loud bellow echoes from far away, on the other side of the hill. It is Hob's voice. Liam and Geoff lift their heavy load of branches, and we start back.

The skewed cart lies like a foundered ship in the drift of snow. I take my turn digging wearily at the frost-hardened ground; then I reach down to rub my painful feet, and I see a boy in a hooded cloak. He stands on the other side of the cart, pushing alongside us.

For a moment, my eyes are bewitched. I see Christian standing alive and hale again. That moment lasts a long breath, and then it is gone.

The boy's hood drops off his head.

Raven-black hair. Sunken coal-black eyes.

It is only Cole.

He is Salvius's misbegotten ward, the orphan. But he is here alone.

Hob talks to him, asking of his "Uncle Salvius."

I cannot hear all they say, but it seems Cole was in the woods and found us on the trail. He points at the cart, gesturing toward his dead friends. Hob's face is hard and untrusting.

Cole has the curse of lying and of theft. Few folk trust him, least of all Salvius who often must punish him for his many misdeeds. And Cole's face is etched by the scars of ringworm. Such marks are said to be the mark of a devil or a witch, and those scarred are mocked and called by names, so as to torment the devil inside. I do not know the truth of it. I do not concern myself.

He is a gangly, overgrown orphan boy from the edge of the village, the one some whisper was abandoned by his own mother. Perhaps they said the same about my Christian.

In fact, Cole once helped me watch my son. He is a little older than the boys who died but always he drifts toward those younger than he. For Cole has a wandering stammer, and no one treats him as a man. His weak voice is the last echo of the tenderness I once saw in that lad.

Cole says he sought us out, hoping he would find Salvius here, wanting to honor his dead friends.

I think that Cole is like the other children—he will spend the heat of this winter day walking with us, but he will fade eventually, when he wearies of the hard track and the heavy cart. In fact, even now, I can see a few of the other children in the valley below, wandering back along the switchbacks toward the distant village.

"Cole can come with us," says Hob. "It's too late in the day to send for Salvius."

"Let's go back ourselves," says Geoff. "You're right. It's late—I'm damn'd tired."

"None of us are going back!" Bene seizes Geoff's head with his great weaver's hands. He turns Geoff, forces him to look up at the trail ahead. "Look at the tracks, I say, look at them!"

We all stare at the hillside. The virgin snow is spattered with bootprints that go out of sight.

"We're followin' the villain, can't you see?" says Bene. "The tracks are—"

Geoff wrenches his head out of Benedict's grasp. "To hell with yer tracks! My son is gone—he ain't comin' back."

"Push on," calls Hob, and Geoff's complaints are ignored. The cart tilts forward this time and out of the ditch. Red-haired Liam and I both hold now to the branches of the whippletree in front, guiding the way forward.

Hob moves behind me then, goading us to the work. He spits on the ground and slaps our shoulders. I am the only one to follow his gaze and glance behind us. He is staring into the distance, along our backtrail.

Deep in the vale, a large puff of steam or snow punches into the air. A rider. I watch closely. Some group of people—another cart—follows along the adjoining trail, but I cannot see them in the trees.

Hob touches Benedict's elbow and whispers low. Benedict's cheek twitches, and he scratches anxiously at his bald scalp. Hob glances back again, then he shouts loud, urging more miles before nightfall. I put my shoulder to the cart.

We are pushed onward by the force of their will.

CHAPTER 4

T HE DAY WANES until the sun is caught once more in the net of the darkening sky. I struggle ahead of the cart now, into the tracks. "Stay back," calls Benedict. "Come back to the cart!"

But I pretend the wind covers his words, that I cannot hear him. Ice cuts through the canvas rags on my feet, but still my curiosity compels me. I pretend to stumble, and I fall to the ground so my face is close to the trail.

The marks of boots and horses are here. That is true.

But the tracks go the wrong direction. There is no bootprint going out of our village, no horse going toward the deep woods. No one fled. Instead, some strangers came into our village. Three men and at least two horses, by the look of the prints. But who?

Our village is small, and we should have seen them, unless they came in the night.

"Come back, Mear," Hob calls out. "The bandits may be ahead."

I now know we chase no bandits, no Jews, no villain here at all. Yet from their vantage point, these footprints are unseen, and rapidly the steps are disappearing in the thawing snow. In less than an hour, it will not be possible to see which direction they came from, even up close.

Soon, the truth will melt away.

Christian would be asking for answers; even in his youth, my son had a penchant for inquiry. Always he wanted to stretch his wings. *Why am I trapped in this village? And why can't I go to Lincoln town this spring with the lads? Why not? Why?*

Always asking, Socratic in endless examination, until finally I would throw up my hands and shake my head in mute exasperation. In the night, he would murmur his questions to me again, and then I would answer as best I could, whispering back what I hoped was true. I imparted to him all I could of my secrets, of what my mother taught me.

I also gave him the tools of inquiry and debate. I murmured like a night animal, teaching Aristotle's endless coiling logic. In my ear, I can hear him now—repeating back to me the secret lessons, his sibilant whisper in my ear:

Every art aims at some good end. The end of the art of medicine is health; the end of shipbuilding a vessel; the end of strategy in battle that of victory; the end of economics, wealth. The ends of master arts are preferred to subordinate ends... for all things aim at a good end.

I clench my fists until the skin whitens and the knuckles crack. Anyone among us has seen so many die over the years—wave after wave of death sweeping in like a tide that strikes all, haphazard. The good, the bad, the virgin, and the harlot: no one is spared, all go rose-spattered with plague lesions. I see no sense, no judgment before doom strikes. Death takes us all with the black malady or the sweating sickness, or the white blindness or the winter croup, or the crops failing or bitter water in our mouths.

There is no justice to such deaths, and there is no sense.

But this fire—the flames that burned our boys—these few deaths were an act of malevolence. Someone intended this. There was a judgment made, an evil act. And in this, it is for sure and certain that there is a soul at fault. Someone can be blamed for these deaths, if not for all that came before.

I look down at the wrong-way tracks. I squint, wishing I could read more from this trail. I will find out what I can from the signs I do see. I will know the truth.

What was your good end, Christian?

The cart comes closer. Benedict throws off his hood and shouts at me for abandoning my post. He says without my guidance, the cart nearly went off the trail. At this, Hob glares at me too and curses under his breath, as if I am a wayward child. But I pay them no heed.

THERE IS A stab of pain in my side. My limbs are weak as water, for I have not been able to eat much this winter with no food in the larders or the mill. And now my feet and toes feel each lump of frozen mud. I am not that young Miriam who once climbed these hills with a babe in her arms. I am old and tired now. My legs burn with effort, but still I persevere.

Hob watches us all closely, as if he wants to be sure no one will go ahead again, and he goads the men harder to push the cart up the long hill before sundown.

Hours later, as evening shadows surround us, the hillside finally flattens, and the path opens out into a hollow encircled by boulders. Beyond a last steep embankment is the King's Highway. We will camp here for the night before gaining the highway.

I collapse into a drift and lie there nearly insensate.

Through my fog comes Liam's voice. "God's wounds, Mear, you look weary enough for Death himself to dance with. Why dontcha shove off your pack—'ave some water and a bite o' mutton. Tom there, he's already lightin' a fire to warm your bones."

In this makeshift shelter between boulders and under overhanging snow, Liam lays pine boughs and bracken over cold ground. I let the flow of his voice settle me onto the branches as he wraps me in a fur-lined cloak. Then he uncovers my numb feet, examining each inch of whitened, cold skin.

"A hard nip of frost, but they haven't gone to rot yet," Liam says. "But there's a cut on your toe too—you'll want to watch it close."

I open my eyes and look at the campsites in this ravine. There are six of us, and only five spots out of the wind. Even Cole has found a place. He puts his bedroll under the cart.

There is not a place left for me, it seems.

Liam has seen the same. "Well, I've got to tell you, Mear—there's naught left for another body out of the wind, is there? Would you have in mind to share mine own mansion?"

I stare at him. I am so weary that I cannot find the humor, and my friend Salvius never jokes like this.

Liam speaks again, his prattle lifting my spirits. "There's no roof, of course. No walls either, I'm afraid to say. And I must admit to a certain breeziness in the night, but I 'ave my standards, I'll have you know!"

He wags his finger in my face. "I'll warn you now, ol' Mear, with that wild life you lead, you can't be bringing your brewmaids and your wenches around here! An' there ain't no cows to warm the place either. But hell's bells, you've got *me*—and what a cowish girth I bear." He grips his belly and grimaces broadly.

Liam goes on in the same fashion, and by the time he finishes, I am bent over with laughter, the sounds coming out of my mouth a hacking hilarity.

I am astonished I am able to laugh at all. Then the chuckles turn into broad guffaws, and I find that my cheeks are wet, my eyes leaking wildly. Tears stream down my face, grief melding with mirth in some wild witch's brew that brings the fact of Christian's death deep into me. He is dead and gone; I am alive and able to laugh. This is the truth of it, and nothing I do will change it now.

Our camp is in the lee of a slab of rock jutting from the hillside. The outcropping looms over us, thick with snow-covered moss.

Geoff sidles into our campsite. He takes Liam's ear and whispers urgently. "Lookit this—my son had this with him." Geoff opens his clenched hand. Inside is a small carved wood animal, that great bird that nurses its young on its own flesh. A pelican—a symbol of the Christ—and it is scorched by flame.

"What is that to you?" asks Liam.

Geoff digs his foot deep into the snow. He cannot meet our eyes. "It was the first lovely thing he ever made."

"A memory," says Liam. "An heirloom of his house."

"Why would he take this to Benedict's house?" says Geoff. "Why take something so precious to our family? Was he going away from our village? Were they all leaving us?"

I have a niggling thought in the back of my mind that there is something here that ties Geoff's son to my Christian, but I cannot think what it is right now.

Christian was not leaving me, my heart says loudly, so that I cannot hear that still-small voice in me saying something true and painful.

Now Liam is telling his tale. "I saw in the cart that in my son's hand was the stick he uses to walk the sheep over to the Hartvale meadow. His walking stick."

"An' you weren't going anywhere with him."

"You know I can't leave the village." Liam's eyes slide nervously from side to side. "If the King's officers found me out here . . . I'm only on this journey now because my boy is dead, and I . . . I could not leave him."

Geoff nods. Curiosity eats at me, a poison that makes my skin crawl. *How much do I really know of Liam?* I raise my eyebrows at him, I grunt, but the two of them don't pay me mind.

"Where were the boys going?" hisses Geoff. "I don't believe for a moment that Benedict had them weaving—every time he says it, his eyes belie him."

"Do you mean to accuse Benedict of doing something with them?" Liam seems taken aback by the insistence in Geoff's face.

Geoff whispers. "Ayuh, Sophia was suppos'd to be in that house that night. An' what if Benedict was jealous of his own wife? What if he—?" Liam sighs wearily. "Foolishness. What about the other fires? And why would Benedict burn his own house? Why would Bene—?"

There is a sudden, loud laugh. Benedict has stepped into our campsite. In fact, he almost strides onto my bedroll. He claps Liam on the back.

"What's that you say—'Why would Bene—'?"

"Nothing," mutters Liam. "Just talk. It were nothing."

"Nah, tell the truth." Benedict gives that laugh again, a forced jollity. Geoff stares with the bloodlust of the accuser and raises his voice.

"You tell the truth, Bene! What journey did you plan with our boys?" Hob and Tom come closer when Geoff shouts. Benedict stares back and forth between the men, his face flushing slowly red. "The truth?" "Yes," says Geoff. "Tell us, why were the boys there, at your weaving house?"

Bene breathes out, a long hiss. "I do not know why they died."

Geoff shouts again. "Goddammit, Bene, you know why they were there—I can see you do! Why were the boys there at your house? Were they seeing your wife?"

Now the blood drains out of Bene's face, his skin white with rage.

"Wait, wait," says Liam. His hands move nervously. "That's not what we meant—"

Benedict makes fists, his fingers clenching and unclenching. "Then speak plain. What do you mean?"

Geoff does not falter. "Sophia—she saw more than one man, as you well know—and I just want to know, did she see any of the boys in her chamber, did she—"

Benedict brings his great weaver's hand up. Faster than I could have imagined, his clenched fist strikes Geoff's face, knocking him flat against the ice.

The winter air seems to freeze as Geoff falls. A stray snowflake hangs in the air. Bright blood spatters from Geoff's broken lip onto the white snow.

Benedict roars, a sound that has words in it I cannot decipher until after it is all over. "You damn'd scut-worms! Ah lost my own son—my *son*—an' you lot still accuse my wife, my own Sophia. She lost him too, you know!"

Benedict glowers in rage. We look away in shame.

"You there," Bene points at Liam. "I can turn you in, you know. There's still a reward—in gold—for poxy bastards like you."

"I know," mutters Liam. "Please . . ."

Liam scurries back from Benedict's rage. I huddle into my bedroll. But Bene has turned away from him. He glares, bloodshot and bellowing, at all of us. Only Tom holds his gaze. It would seem Tom has nothing of mortification in him, but I see a catch in the corner of Tom's eye before he locks his gaze, as if he must force himself to do this. It is as if an actor's mask drops over his whiskered face.

"Right," Tom says. "The boys had naught t' do with Sophia. She's a pure one." His tone is sincere, though the pupils of his eyes move ever so subtly back and forth.

Liam scurries back from Benedict's rage. I huddle into my bedroll.

Benedict turns from Tom. He seizes Geoff, like a cat shaking a trembling, torn rat. "Goddam you, my wife *is* pure, ah'll have you know—pure as the feckin' driven snow!"

Benedict whispers thickly as blood drips down Geoff's face. "Say it to me. Say it!"

Geoff's voice shakes. "Aye, Bene. Sophia is pure."

Benedict drops him to the snow. The anger washes out of him as rapidly as it came. He seems spent now, exhausted by his rage.

Bene is not a man familiar with emotion—he is the one who coldly calculates the odds. I have seen him in the village, running games of chance against the day of harvest—the next throw of dice, the next shot by a bow. He gives the winners their take without feeling, and takes the loser's coins without a care. But Benedict bet awry when he married Sophia. He wooed her knowing she had been a Jew, thinking her family had gold buried.

In the end, there was no gold, no dowry, nothing for him except the big weaving house that just burned to the ground and Sophia's ever-wandering eye. She seeks for something everywhere—something Benedict can't, or won't, give her.

There is an emptiness in her heart that can never be filled, a bottomless longing that causes her to hunger for affection and devour every scrap of kindness. Whatever you give her is never enough.

She has even seized on me at times—mute Mear—for conversation. For when she seizes me, I touch her hand, I look into her eyes, I watch her face, I smile when she speaks. And Benedict never does these small things.

Now Bene talks quietly, his voice hoarse. "Tha must see, these lads were not on a journey. They had naught for the open road. *My boy*—" Benedict's voice breaks.

A bird calls, distant and wounded. The woods are still as death. Quick steam huffs in and out of Geoff's open mouth.

Hob steps forward. "Enough of this shite. Look to the campsite—we must be ready for the night."

And with that, the dangerous moment seems past. We gather wood and help Tom build his fire. As I pick up spare twigs and dried bracken, I wonder how far our sounds penetrate into the black forest, and how far our shouts echo along the White Road. Anyone approaching along the road could find us here.

Supper is roasted pork we brought from the village, and warmed snow. After we have licked our fingers clean, we edge closer to the fire, heads cocked toward the whispering wind as it brushes the treetops. Night birds warble, and small creatures rustle in the snow.

Benedict digs in the straw of the cart and brings out a half cask of cider. Tom and Bene guzzle long before they share with the rest of us. The apples were squeezed in the summer and fermented all the fall. I gulp a mouthful, and the taste of it is bright and bitter on my tongue. My head goes dizzy after a single swallow.

Hob has the knife out that he used to carve our dinner meat. He passes the cider and doesn't take a sip. Instead, he painstakingly strokes a whetstone across the edge of his blade. "The road tomorrow could be dangerous. Bandits and the like."

The cider goes around the circle again, and we lean closer to hear Hob speak again. "We must stick together, that's our only hope. We will get to the monastery, seek the Abbot's protection, demand justice for our loss."

Hob's knife scrapes harshly on the stone. "We few from the village are nothing in the greater world, you understand. We could be taken for chattel, for labor, even for killing sport."

"Aye," Tom agrees, his words already blurred by drink. "Captur'd by witches."

Liam laughs aloud. "Oh, Tom, if you're fear'd of witches, you can sleep in my bed, with smelly ol' Mear." The other men guffaw, but Tom continues, the cider giving him a pompous certainty.

"They say if you creep along the right valley in the dead o' night, 'round the dark o' the moon, you'll hear them witches a-singin' an' a-chantin'."

Yet this time when he speaks, there is something in his tone that gives us pause. There are some who believe to speak of a thing is to summon it into the world, and Tom speaks with such conviction. We become so quiet that the loudest noise is the sizzle of burning tree sap.

The darkness around us presses down, as if to listen. The music of the wind rises and falls with the swirls of the snow, the creaking of the sea of branches in the darkness above us. Liam takes a long swallow of cider, and even the sound of it splashing in the cask unnerves me.

"Ah think there was more than one of them witches in our village. Ah saw them once, dancing, deep in the woods," says Geoff. He pushes the words out carefully, drink slowing his speech.

"There was one we know for sure," says Benedict. He takes the cider from Liam and spreads his hands apart, to make his point. "She was a strange woman—kept herself apart."

"Nell," says Cole. "That was her name." And as he speaks, there is a loud and distant moan, one tree moving against another. I can't tell how far away the sound is, or which direction it comes from. Sound travels strangely in the wildland.

"You hear that?" Geoff says. His eyes gleam in the light of the coals. His whisper is coarsened by fear. "What is it?"

Eventually the wind dies, and young Cole goes into the bushes to drop his pants. He returns and wipes his hands with dead leaves.

"There's someone following, on the hillside, on the open road behind," says Cole. Geoff turns from the fire and climbs up onto a stone, to see our backtrail.

"Whoever follows is not from our village!" Benedict says. "Ah think they might be—"

"There's no one behind us," Hob says shortly. "You all are pie-eyed drunks. Go to bed." Hob spits on his whetstone and keeps sharpening his knife, louder now.

Yet one by one, each of us steps away from the brightness of the flames and looks up at the hillside where the faint track winds back and forth.

"Look," says Tom. "The moon's got a fairie circle 'round it."

All of us turn our eyes higher, to see the three-quarter moon floating in a fog-flecked winter sky—glimmering around that uneven globe, an ethereal silver circle.

"More snow coming tonight, that means," says Liam. "A heavy fall of snow."

"Aye," Benedict agrees. "The new snow will cover our tracks, but it won't cover our cart. If there's someone coming, we should get ready for a fight, dontcha think?"

"Nah, there's no one there," Hob repeats calmly. "Who would be out from the village, in the woods?" Bright sparks shoot out as Hob rasps hard at his blade.

I look back at the dying fire. Cole has not moved with the rest of us to gaze up at the moon overhead, at the clouds rapidly moving in. Instead, he still scans the hillside, his mouth nervous and twitching, firelight flickering across his anxious face as he pulls aside his hood. In the faint light, I discern a faint burn on his neck, something red and unhealed, a touch of ash and pain. I see a tremble in his fingers, wide fear in his eyes.

And it comes to me that Cole knows of that night. It beats in me, in my blood.

Cole knows.

CHAPTER 5

F ROST CRACKLES ON the sheepskin as I push it away, white plumes of breath rising in the faint light. For years, I have arisen at Lauds, before dawn: in this hour, the deep darkness of the sky is touched with royal blue.

The landscape has changed in the night. A vast shroud of snow drowns every feature, the unceasing tide sweeping over the land, covering the path and the campsite.

Under the new snow, our campsites are hidden, like the holes of vermin, buried among the rocks and drifts. Above us now, the high hill is peaked with an overhang of snow that curves like a butcher's blade above our hollow.

I move toward the cart and sweep away the fresh snowflakes that lie on my son and his friends. And there, in the morning light, I see a flash of silver that catches the sunlight—the chain on my son's neck glimmering from the straw.

Drawn by that brightness, by the need to see his face, I push aside the straw. I pull aside the sackcloth that covers the boys, and I fumble at the rope tied across the cart.

Then a shiver runs up my spine. For the rope is looped with that strange triple knot tied fast across a half hitch. It is the same knot that was tied across the door of the Benedict's house. It was this knot that killed him.

The one who tied this knot might be here. He must be traveling as one of our company. *Who?*

My fingers tremble, but I slide the curving snake of that triple knot apart. I turn the bodies of our boys, blackened and charred. And here, on this one neck, is the silver chain that marks my son.

I touch the chain, and then I see a new surprise. Strung on its slender length is the ring I told Christian he must never take from our little house. I had noticed the chain, but I had not seen the ring. Christian took an heirloom of our house—he is wearing that great token of his father's love.

When I left Canterbury Abbey, I took with me everything my lover had given me, most importantly this ring. I took it from the abbey for my newborn son to have when he was grown.

At the last new moon, I told Christian of it, finally, when he had nearly reached the age of ten. I unearthed it from the small birch box in which it had been hidden all those years, and I showed it to him. The ring was his by heritage, the only token of his father I still bore.

My heart tells me the truth, but I do not want to hear it—*Christian took the ring from our croft because he would not return. He meant to leave our village forever.*

A cry comes up my throat: I choke it off unvoiced.

Now I wonder if it was right of me to stay hidden in the village all those years, wanting to protect my son from the world, sheltering under Salvius's gentle care. For all those years, I had not even taken a daylong sojourn to discover if the Earl or Edward won their clandestine struggle, or if any knew of Christian's birth.

Admittedly, my boy's life in Duns had not been much. He grew strong from work, he learned the secret lessons that I taught, but he couldn't claim what was his by birthright.

He would have gone to claim this birthright. *Oh, my son— Christian.*

Now perhaps in death, Cristian's true name has been taken from the world. But I still live, I still breath, I still know.

I unfasten Christian's chain and remove the ring. I place it ever-so-carefully on my own small chain, close to my heart. Then I refasten his own silver links around his neck, letting him keep one of his last possessions. I will give him the silver chain, even when he is buried in the ground.

Yet I grip the ring in my hand, my heart pounding. I must hold this tight. It is the last sign of my past, the last token of who I once was.

C3

OUR FIRE IS almost out now, the large heap of wood we gathered the day before nearly devoured. The men hardly stir in their sleep, the sound of their breathing deep with the residue of drink. The rotten aftertaste of cider is still in my mouth as well.

But I am sober this dawn, and cold, so I pile dead bracken and fresh wood on the fire. The bracken smokes, and we need more firewood, so I push my way through the snow toward the trees.

My thoughts turn to my companions. I have seen much through my ten years living with them, but now it seems I may not know the truth of these men. Any story is an ocean whose tide begins in a place I can't know, and my life is but a moment in that flood, my part in it only a mote in the flow.

Before I came to this village, these men and their families had a long history. They had generations to build up resentments and grudges, and stories that trickled down through the years, which allowed them to know each other in ways I will never know. For my village—generations in the building—it all disappeared when I was a child, wiped out by the plague, the last remnants of my people scattered and lost.

What do I really know of these men from the village of Duns? As I stagger through the drifts, the threads of logic weave together into suppositions, accusations.

Geoff did it. That small man with the dark and gnomish face, the uncertain expression. He was a weak boy, the butt of jokes when he was a child. Even now Geoff cannot shake the fear that he is still mocked behind his back. There were reasons for the teasing. That is an old history, full of rot and pain, and I know but half of it.

What if Geoff took his pleasure with boys, just as his syphilitic father before him? Could he have tied the house shut, set the fire, and burned them to their deaths? What if Geoff accuses Benedict to conceal his own crimes?

I come back down the hill with an armful of wood. The fire smolders hot with dry twigs. Smoke rises. Dawn strokes the horizon with an edge of steaming brightness.

I think of the several fires in our village: who lit those? And why? And then, why would the boys gather together? Perhaps to speak of their fear of Geoff? But who would be afraid of that man? He is small and frail and he and I are all too often discarded from manly work, because of our light frames.

Maybe it's Liam. He told Geoff he hides a crime. I spend my time serving Salvius's smithy and doing what I can to curry favor with Benedict, not with such a poor woodsman. Despite this, I thought I knew Liam well, with his fox-like face and his fringe of red hair, and always he seeks to ally with me.

They still call Liam "young 'un," and it is not because he is particularly young—he is older than half the men. They call him that because he came to this village a mere fifteen years ago, marrying into the village. His father and his grandfather and generations before him did not live here. And I imagine the men do not trust him, because he is still an outsider.

What would Liam do in fear of his own life?

And what of Tom's vision? Tom is an unlikely prophet, with his wide-set, staring eyes, his mad speech and his great oxen muscles. But what if, for once, Tom's eyes had seen aright?

What if there was indeed a Jew who wished revenge for the killings fifty years ago? Someone who saw his family die and came back to put a blood-curse on our village for the crimes of the past? There are still Jews concealed—what if one held a grudge?

I shake my head. I do not believe it. Tom's vision of Jews in the night is but a faint and uneven sketch: there is no truth in his fantasy of sacrifice and sorcery.

Then again, what do the men know of me? I am an old mystery to them and an outsider as well, even after all these years. If someone discovered my secrets, I would be the one accused. I am bound by silence, but that would not prevent them burning me as a witch. I have dreamed that death far too often, grinding my teeth in the fetid darkness of my little hutch.

Do they suspect? How long will it take for the men to accuse me? I wish again that Salvius was here. He has always upheld my manliness, trusted my strength in gathering wood for his smithy. Salvius is always my truest friend, my first defender. There is no falsehood in him.

Liam and Geoff, though, they worry me. I shake my head. Secrets and lies.

I trudge to the top of a hill, where the wood is dry. From the forest, we are invisible.

Yet now I can see that our camp has been revealed to anyone who travels on the open road. I have revealed it by making a smoky fire. From our campsite, a black line of smoke rises tall from the hollow, a beacon against the aurora light. I must get dry wood now, not wet, and damp the smoke.

Why were the boys together? If the murder was aimed at the village, as some rude crime aimed at all of us—or as some sacrifice to a pagan god—then someone would have had to gather the boys together. They would not have gone willingly if they knew the true purpose of their gathering.

Benedict says he had gathered them because he needed all their nimble, small fingers to move the warp and woof. He had a great set of weavings due for delivery at Lincoln.

But could he have told a tale to us? Bene the weaver is always jealous of Sophia, and always he seeks to hold her for his own. His sunburned bald head always seems worried for her. And because he has remained faithful to her—despite her many small betrayals and cheats on him—that has made me respect bald Bene despite myself.

For there is much to dislike in Benedict. He still conceals the fact of the boys' intended departure from the village. And I know for certain that they meant to travel away from us: the truth is with the boys.

The chain around my son's neck, and the ring. Liam's son's walking stick. Geoff's son, who carved a pelican, took that heirloom of their house with him.

It was a secret journey, to set out in the night—only Benedict knew the truth of it. And like our travel now, I doubt anyone had a lord's blessing. Not them. Not us.

And even now Benedict does not tell the boys' secret.

Hob, the dark-haired alderman, has some hold on Benedict, for often I see Bene's hands tremble with fear as he looks at Hob.

Could Hob have tied that triple knot? Hob has always been our leader in the village, but why now does he drive us forward with such fervor? And why would Hob have any cause to burn them up in the night?

Cole knows. If I gain his trust, if I find a way to worm my way into his heart, he might tell me more of the truth. I know he saw something that night.

I kneel on the hillside to gather dry twigs. Something catches at me, a distant sound. In this late morning, frost thickens on the wind; snow is gusting down.

Already the new-fallen drifts are hardening under a crust of ice.

Yet that fearful promise of cold is not what brought me pause. I wait, I listen. These hours are as silent and pallid as the inside of a whitewashed tomb.

Someone moves in the camp. I look down. It is Cole, pissing in the snow. Then he sees me, he finishes, and he strides slowly toward the hill on which I crouch.

I push the fresh snowflakes out of my face and peer again at the horizon, squinting against the faint dawn, my eyes tearing in the cold. There comes a faint sound, the cry of a lost winter bird. Then I see them, a shape of men on horses.

The uncertainty in me resolves into a knot of fear in my belly, a churning mass of dark apprehension. I duck quickly into the hollow, but I know it is too late. They have seen the smoke. They know there is someone in this corner of the snowbound world, someone with fire and with food.

Cole comes up into the trees, close enough to touch. I take his shoulder and push him down into a small ravine so we cannot be seen. I look at the distant figures, the moving dots of men on horses, growing visible even in the scrim of falling snowflakes.

I point and show Cole with my hands how open we are to eyes on the road, how vulnerable to bandits.

As I turn to slide back down the lee of the hill, Cole speaks: "We must tell Hob."

THE STORY OF _SINFUL FOLK_ CONTINUES in the new release of the book from CAMPANILE BOOKS in JANUARY 2014.

http://SinfulFolk.com

SINFUL FOLK by Ned Hayes, with cover and internal illustrations by _New York Times_ bestselling illustrator and author Nikki McClure.

Get _SINFUL FOLK_ today

SINFUL FOLK by Ned Hayes

Campanile Books;
JANUARY 2014;
ISBN 978-0-9852393-0-5; $12.95

North American Distribution:
Itasca Books, Minneapolis, MN

Made in the USA
Monee, IL
16 March 2020